Advance praise f[...]

'Clear the decks for this riveting tale [...] [...] seas. Tense, gripping, *The Scoop* grabs you [...] opening line until the last page and leaves you wanting more.'
Anna Smith, author of *Blood Feud* and *The Dead Won't Sleep*

'A white-knuckle, edge-of-your seat ride. Buckle up and hold on . . . Quinn sets a cracking pace.'
Ann Rickard, former Australian Travel Writer of the Year and author of six travel books

'A thrilling action and adventure novel underpinned by a heart-wrenching love story. Quinn has created a new, engaging Aussie hero in Jonno Bligh. A must read from a natural storyteller.'
Noel Whittaker AM, finance guru and author of 20 bestselling books

'An epic *Treasure Island* for the 21st Century, it reminds me of Wilbur Smith's brilliant *Eye of the Tiger*. A cracking yarn.'
Douglas Jackson, author of *Claudius* and *Defender of Rome*

THE
SCOOP

TERENCE J. QUINN

THE SCOOP

SIMON &
SCHUSTER

London · New York · Sydney · Toronto · New Delhi

A CBS COMPANY

THE SCOOP
First published in Australia in 2018 by
Simon & Schuster (Australia) Pty Limited
Suite 19A, Level 1, Building C, 450 Miller Street, Cammeray, NSW 2062

10 9 8 7 6 5 4 3 2 1

A CBS Company
Sydney New York London Toronto New Delhi
Visit our website at www.simonandschuster.com.au

A catalogue record for this
book is available from the
National Library of Australia

Cover design: Blue Cork
Cover image: Abner Kingman/Getty Images; Adobe Stock
Typeset by Midland Typesetters, Australia
Printed and bound in Australia by Griffin Press

FSC
www.fsc.org
MIX
Paper from
responsible sources
FSC® C009448

The paper this book is printed on is certified
against the Forest Stewardship Council®
Standards. Griffin Press holds FSC chain
of custody certification SGS-COC-005088.
FSC promotes environmentally responsible,
socially beneficial and economically viable
management of the world's forests.

For Pat

THE
SCOOP

PROLOGUE

Nine Island, Sumatra/December 2014

THE LUXURY cruiser was moored in the lee of a small, sheltered island that faced eastward to the Strait of Malacca. It was a large catamaran. Sleek, expensive. A charter boat, he guessed. Two women were sunbathing on the foredeck platform. They were topless and the hard sun gleamed on their oiled, naked bodies. The man with the pockmarked face and powerful binoculars smiled. '*God is great,*' he said.

BamBang Budiman was not a religious man but he was grateful for this opportunity. A few hours earlier he and his crew had tried and failed to hijack a cargo boat in the strait. That fuck-up now presented him with two problems: first, his Chinese syndicate bosses would be pissed off; those merciless men did not like failure. I'll worry about that later, he decided. The second, more pressing problem was that he had lost face with his men. They were the ones who had screwed up the attack on the freighter but they would blame him. A leader who had bad luck was not to be respected. It had not helped that, in anger and frustration, he had chopped off a crewman's arm with his parang. The man had bled to death on the deck.

Now his crew – a mix of Thai, Vietnamese and Malaysian pirates – were in a mutinous mood, frustrated by their earlier failure and angry at the brutal treatment of their comrade. They need something to keep them occupied, Budiman thought. These western women will suffice. The men will have their fun for a while. Good luck to them – the *pelacurs*, whores, were not to his taste, of course. Too white, too skinny, too old. Ha, much too old.

Ten minutes later, two skiffs streaked away from the mother vessel towards the gently swaying catamaran. Budiman and seven of his men, all armed to the teeth with guns, machetes and unbridled lust, were determined not to fail this time. When they reached the luxury craft, the pirates swarmed over the stern, danced up a couple of steps and hurried straight to the foredeck.

Two *bules* – white men – sat up on their sunbeds, shocked by the sudden commotion. Rising slowly, they stood frozen, mouths opening and closing like blowfish, palms outstretched in supplication. The first of the pirates to arrive on the starboard side shot one man in the chest with an automatic pistol while another slashed the second man several times with a parang. Both victims fell to the deck writhing and gasping, blood spurting onto the pristine white fibreglass.

A white woman was kneeling on a towel, arms over her naked breasts, her features contorted. She began to scream uncontrollably as a splash of blood, vivid red against her blanched face, oozed down her cheek and dripped onto her chest. Budiman pushed his men aside. 'Shut the bitch up,' he ordered. He stood over the two prostrate white men as they moaned and gasped.

'You very unlucky gentlemen. Wrong place, wrong time.' He shrugged and then shot them in the head, one after the other. Beaming with delight, he gestured for his men to throw the bodies overboard. Then he pointed to one of the crew and told him to go find the other western whore. Moments later, smoking a pungent clove cigarette on the rear deck, the pirate leader heard crashing noises followed by a triumphant shout and a shrill scream. He smiled again, his leathery scarred face dissolving into a mass of wrinkles as the early afternoon sun glinted on his gold tooth.

PART ONE

Generally speaking, the best people nowadays go into journalism, the second best into business, the rubbish into politics and the shits into law.
Auberon Waugh

1

I KNOW the exact moment my world turned to shit. And I know the name of the man responsible.

His name is Wes Dreyfus, a country music producer from Nashville, Tennessee. And he's the one who introduced me to Charlie. Not Charlie Sheen (although he was probably there), but cocaine.

The movie studio had thrown me a welcome party on my first night in Hollywood. I was feeling a tad shy around the galaxy of stars and household names. Wes suggested that a little coke would smooth away my social awkwardness.

'Charlie will make you feel on top of the world, Jonno. All your worries will fly away like turkey feathers in the wind,' he said.

He was right. But the moment he put that little line of white powder in front of me was the start of a downward spiral that would almost destroy me. Until then, my life had been on the up. I had been a top tabloid reporter first in Sydney, then in London. I had written a bestselling book – *Hard News* – and I was now in LA to collaborate on the screenplay.

While my professional career was going gangbusters, my personal life was less gung-ho. I was in my late thirties, had never married, had never even met a girl I could love. I put it down to a combination of the long hours I worked and my innate shyness. I hoped it wasn't for any other reason. I was a few inches north of six feet with blond unruly hair and blue-ish eyes. My best friend Cody's sister once described me as a 'spunk', so I'd always reckoned I was so-so in the looks department. Mind you, she was drunk when she said it, so perhaps it was wishful thinking on my part.

I had never once used drugs before; not so much as a wisp of weed. Back in London, I had been offered coke many times but always refused … perhaps because of the images of my alcoholic mother, comatose on the couch, that always came to mind. But now, for the first time, I was seriously tempted. I was mixing with Hollywood royalty in the epicentre of a crazy, fucked-up, clichéd world. Parties. Babes. Sex. Cocktails. Drugs. Rock 'n' roll. It was sink or swim. To my eternal regret, I sank.

Unfortunately, it was the most incredible feeling I'd ever experienced. As well as the initial euphoric rush, my diffidence quickly disappeared and I became almost as loud and brash as my American hosts. The white powder was freely available at the party in Beverly Hills – inside the palatial house, in the toilets, bedrooms and even out in the pool area. Wes pointed out film directors, studio bosses and Hollywood stars as well as 'big-ass lawyers' and businessmen. Most were high as kites.

Despite being a Grammy Award-winning producer, Wes dressed like a trucker. Even at that glossy cocktail party, he wore a dirty, scuffed baseball cap with a green John Deere logo; his oily hair curled down under it and over the back of his blue-chequered shirt collar. Jeans and two-tone lizard-skin boots completed the ensemble. He had a lazy, wicked sense of humour and he – with the help of his friend Charlie – made me feel like I was the toast of LA. Wes was a good guy really, but I'll curse him for the rest of my life. And if I could go back now to that moment, knowing where that first seductive high would lead, I'd run a mile.

I had jacked in my job as a journo in London to come to LA for the movie project. A few years before, I had broken a big news story about the sordid sex life of a Conservative government minister and his wife. Turns out the avowedly Christian couple were enthusiastic participants in sleazy suburban orgies, some of which involved drugs, underage girls and rent boys. The scandal escalated when the pair embroiled other politicians, including two cabinet members, in their tawdry adventures. That scoop ultimately led to the downfall of the UK government. It also changed my life. For better. For worse. A whole lot worse.

The movie studio party with Wes and a galaxy of screen stars set the scene for the rest of my lengthy stay in LA and the downward trajectory of my life. My partner in crime was Estevo 'Chilli' Gomez, the professional screenwriter assigned to me by the movie studio who did most of the work. Chilli was both highly skilled and highly sexed. After long days of hard work honing and polishing the film script, he would take me to Tinseltown's top nightspots for some serious R&R. The Jesuit priests at St Jude's, my old school in Sydney, would have had a fit if they could have seen me. Bless me, Father, for I have sinned. And sinned. And sinned again. In those quickfire fifteen months in Hollywood I made up for the restrained, rather solitary life I'd enjoyed for the previous fifteen years.

But the gods must have been laughing their dicks off because I finally got my comeuppance. On the night our screenplay for the film adaptation of *Hard News* won an Oscar, I had partied until dawn, sharing a cocktail of cocaine, ecstasy and margaritas with an anorexic actress who had been nominated for her work in a Quentin Tarantino bloodfest. A few hours later, lying semi-comatose on a crumpled bed in the Beverly Wilshire Hotel with one hand clasping the little gold statuette and the other cupping the starlet's bony buttock, my phone beeped on the bedside table. The message shocked me out of my stupor. A disembodied Aussie voice told me that Percy was dead.

Ah, shit. It was time to go home.

2

ANNIE GREENWOOD put down her glass, taking care not to lose a drop. 'You want me to go on a sailing trip to some island in the back of beyond? For Christmas? With people I've never met?' She laughed. 'You are kidding, right?'

Her husband Martin smiled. 'Hardly the back of beyond, my love. Langkawi is where we had our honeymoon. You loved it, remember?'

'But sailing? With me? I get seasick in a jacuzzi.'

He gave her a strange smile: 'This could be our last opportunity.'

Annie's dark eyebrows arched in confusion. 'What do you mean?'

'You're the one who wants kids. We might never get the chance to do something this crazy again.'

She pursed her lips and gave him a sceptical look.

'Oh, come on, love, say yes. It will be awesome,' Martin said with the rakish smile that Annie remembered from the first time he had asked her out. 'Gary and Dani are fun people.

Imagine it: soaking up the sun, eating exotic food, anchoring in clear blue waters next to beautiful beaches. And we can stop off in Singapore for some serious shopping.' He was on his third glass of red and his cheeks were flushed. His left leg, crossed over the other, bobbed rhythmically.

They were sitting on the balcony of their tenth-floor corner apartment in Glebe Point, looking north to Anzac Bridge and east over Darling Harbour to the CBD beyond. It was dusk and the lights of traffic on the motorway far below were starting to twinkle. A warm autumn breeze riffled Annie's shoulder-length chestnut hair. It was rare that they were both home at this time; she had assumed there was some motive for him being back so early. This sailing malarkey was clearly the reason. She took a sip of her pinot gris and pondered.

They had moved from London the year before, after Martin had drunkenly groped his CEO's secretary at the bank's Christmas party. Annie had forgiven but not forgotten. In her mid-thirties, she worked as a copywriter at an advertising agency. She was still wearing her office 'uniform' – block print silk blouse, black tailored skirt and black heels. Discreet but expensive jewellery. Her face was open and friendly: a wide, generous mouth framed white, even teeth. With diamond-cut cheekbones, a delicate nose and large green eyes, she seemed to glow with health. Only a sharp observer would spot the ghostly mesh of fine lines around her eyes that hinted at sadness.

Martin shifted in his seat and tried again. 'You're always saying we should try new things. What could be more exciting than sailing a luxury yacht in South East Asia? It will be a dream trip.'

Annie laughed. 'More like a bloody nightmare, if you ask me.' But he's right, she scolded herself. I'm not usually so negative, but the idea of being trapped in a small boat with total strangers for a couple of weeks sounds daunting. And dangerous. Yet perhaps something crazy like this could bring us back together, make or break us. She looked at her husband and sighed inwardly. He was such a lovely amusing man when I met him. When did he lose that boyish charm?

'So, Captain Pugwash, when were you thinking of embarking on this voyage of discovery?'

'I thought we could go in December. Fly to Singapore, pick up a boat there and sail up to Langkawi. We can celebrate our wedding anniversary and spend Christmas there.'

She took another sip of wine. 'Let me think about it,' she said.

3

THE MEMORY of my last conversation with Percy still haunts me to this day. I said terrible things, things that can now never be taken back.

Percy Mimms had been my mentor, Chief of Staff of the *Sunday World,* Australia's biggest, baddest tabloid. I'd first met him in Sydney when I was twenty-one, following a cadetship at my local paper in Sans Souci, just south of the city.

He was a Scottish veteran with a formidable reputation in the newspaper business. In the flesh, he was different to how I had imagined him: short, spare, with slicked-back, thinning hair; mid-fifties; extremely dapper in a dark blue suit and smart red tie. His small face had a firm jaw. He looked like Fred Astaire apart from the fact that his skin was sallow and wrinkled. A smoker's face, I thought. Intense eyes grabbed my attention: two dark pebbles reflecting a mix of menace and mischief. Another surprise – despite his effete name, his voice was pure Glasgow gravel. I introduced myself: 'Jonno Bligh, sir. Pleased to meet you.'

He squinted at me through thick, black-framed glasses. 'I turn my back for one bloody day and they go hire some beach bum from the back of beyond,' he said, his face two inches from mine. He spent the next expletive-filled minutes making it clear how completely ill-equipped I was to meet the high journalistic standards on his beloved paper. 'Look laddie, your slim chance of survival here is down to one thing – stories. A *Sunday World* hack lives or dies by the number of tales he brings in. Exclusives. Page leads. Front-page splashes. Scoops. Anything that beats the crap out of the competition.' The diatribe was meant to cow me but strangely it had the opposite effect ... I felt energised. This is it, I thought. This is the Big Time.

On my second day, the steely Scot strode over to my desk and stuck a yellow Post-it note on my forehead. There was an address scrawled on it.

'A young lad was killed last night at Kings Cross,' he said. 'A king hit. One punch and he's fucking dead. Get your useless arse over there and talk to the rellies. They'll more likely speak to a wee boy like you than one of our real reporters.'

Then he told me that if I didn't get a 'fucking top photo' of the victim, I needn't come back. Fucking. Ever. An hour later I arrived at the door of a Victorian terrace house on a quiet street in Paddo. The victim's mother took one look at me and swept me through the door before I could say who I was. It transpired she thought I was one of her son's friends. When she went off to make some tea, I called Percy. 'I'm in,' I whispered. Percy merely said: 'Don't forget—'

'—the fucking picture,' I finished.

More than an hour later, I staggered into the newsroom with a large parcel wrapped in brown paper. Percy looked up and peered at me over his specs as I put the parcel on his desk. 'And what the fuck is that?' he asked. Loudly, so everyone in the newsroom could hear, I replied: 'It's your picture, Mr Mimms.' Old Percy's thin lips tightened and his big scarred knuckles whitened. I braced myself.

'Better be good,' he rasped.

The picture of the boy had been on the living room wall in a large, ornate gilt frame and the mother had agreed to let me have it only after I told her (with a real tear in my eye) that I'd be sacked if I returned without it. Mimms unwrapped the parcel and looked at the photo. To my astonishment, he laughed out loud and clapped his hands. 'Well, well, young Jonno Bligh, we might just make a reporter out of you after all. Miracles do happen!'

Ironically, most of the little miracles that happened in my life after that were down to that man. He turned a shy cadet reporter into a top gun professional. After seven years working for him, I was fully proficient in the black arts of journalism and it was clear to both of us that I had to move on. Percy still had good contacts in the UK and so, with his blessing, I took a punt and headed for London. That led to the scoop, my book . . . and Hollywood.

I had called him the moment the Oscar nominations were posted on the *LA Times* website. Never mind that it was the middle of the night in Sydney, I was high on pride and premium coke and all I wanted to do was brag about my triumph.

Percy was unimpressed. 'Look, laddie, I'll call you back tomorrow. Hopefully you'll be a wee bit more sober.'

I wish to God now that Percy had just put the phone down right then. But he didn't and I put him down instead.

'You can bloody talk!' I said.

'What does that mean?'

I had heard a few wild tales about Percy during my time in London. Most were about his love affair with grog. The most famous story was the reason he had emigrated to Australia. One night when he had been the night editor on a national tabloid, he'd taken a call from the pompous owner, who had ordered him to put his picture on Page One. A pissed Percy told him to take a flying fuck to himself. He was fired the next day. Yet, in all the time I knew him, I had never seen him take a drink.

'Your old Fleet Street mates told me that you were a bloody alky! How you screwed up your career. Now you look down your nose at me.'

There was a brief silence at the other end followed by a sigh. 'Everybody in our trade drank in those days. Just part of the culture. Long lunches. Unlimited expenses. The stress and the pressure. Competition. Deadlines. So yes, I was an alcoholic. Still am. Do you have a problem with that?'

I did and I told him why in garbled detail. All my bitterness and resentment over my mother's love affair with the bottle must have surfaced in my addled brain and I directed it at the man I loved and respected more than any other. Eventually, Percy ended the call without saying another word.

I still feel nothing but shame and self-disgust when I think back to that episode. Why did I not call him back the next day and apologise? He would have understood. Pride is such a terrible thing.

Looking back, Percy's funeral in Sydney is a patchwork memory of hazy episodes. I am dimly aware that I screwed up the eulogy. A cocktail of coke, vodka and grief turned me into a stumbling, mumbling wreck. I think I wept. I know I failed utterly to do justice to the memory of the bittersweet bloke who had been more like a father to me than my own dad. Percy was just sixty-nine when he died.

After my pisspoor performance, I beat a hasty retreat. Percy's sister Sadie followed me outside. She'd come over from Scotland for the ceremony and to sort out his things. She pulled a small white envelope out of her handbag and handed it to me. It had my name on it.

'I found this in his papers. He wanted me to make sure you got it.' Her soft Scottish accent was a stark contrast to her older brother's chainsaw vowels.

I waited until I was safely in my room with a large vodka tonic in my fist before I opened the envelope. There was a strange-looking metal token inside and a sheet of plain copy paper. The blue ink handwriting was in Percy's familiar neat cursive style; there were few flourishes, loops or extravagant tails. The content was typically brief and to the point.

Dear Jonno,
If you're reading this, it means I'm a goner. Hopefully, I'm now in the great newsroom in the sky putting out the Daily Miracle with a few other old hacks. But I couldn't go without telling you something that I could never have said to your face.

You were the closest thing I had to a son. I remember the first time I saw you at the paper: a bit shy, but you stood up for yourself. You had real talent and I knew you would be a wee bit special. So listen, laddie — it's high time you got your shit together. You are capable of great things. And maybe think about settling down: find a fine lassie, start a family. Trust me, you really need those things in your life. I never had them and I was the poorer for it.

The enclosed gift is my greatest treasure. Maybe now it can help you too.

Take good care of yourself, son. You were a light in my life.

Your pal,

Percy

By now the words had blurred. My tears were dripping down onto the single sheet of paper, the ink beginning to spread and blot like little blue spiders. I picked up the strange token. It looked like it was made of bronze. Engraved on one side was the legend: 'To thine own self be true'. The words '15 years recovery' were writ large. On the other side: 'God grant me the serenity to accept the things I cannot change, courage to change the things I can, and wisdom to know the difference.'

Despite my pain and my shame, I shunned Percy's advice. Over the next few weeks in Sydney, I drifted into an LA-lite pattern of partying with what passes for an Aussie B-List. My agent, Drusilla Gottlieb, a red-haired Jewish firebrand, forced me to do a few more TV chat show appearances to help sell the book and DVDs of the film. I hung out at the 'in' clubs and the restaurants du jour. Invitations to media events piled up. And everywhere I went, my new friend Charlie was there too.

The hard shell of celebrity ennui that I had put on like armour in the US kept me functioning in that unreal world, aided by the coke. But underneath I felt like a fraud. I had created this external character – smooth, successful, Oscar-winning writer tinged with a down-to-earth Aussie larrikin humour. Most people who didn't know me seemed charmed.

But I wasn't fooling myself. The truth was ... I had no idea what the hell I was going to do next. I had run out of book ideas. My writing flow was truly blocked. I didn't even know where I belonged anymore – Sydney, London, LA? My future plans seem to have narrowed down to where I would score my next line of coke.

Something had to give.

4

NOT LONG after Percy's funeral I found myself sharing a pavilion with a TV weather chick called, I think, Meredith. We were at a prestigious yachting regatta on Hamilton Island. Hammo, as it's known to Aussies everywhere, is the hub of the Whitsunday Islands, on the northern tip of the Great Barrier Reef. The regatta had a shoal of other 'off-water' activities, like celebrity chefs, fashion events and parties. Meredith was quite tipsy after a champagne reception and, as we tottered to my suite, she gave me the following forecast: 'You can expect a warm front, some slight turbulence and a storm surge followed by a sunny outlook.' I had no doubt she had used that line many times before but her prediction was still spot-on.

But even she could not have forecast what followed. We went to a big party hosted by one of the main sponsors, Berenger – boat builders based in Sydney. They were using the event to showcase their new world-class creation – a fifty-two foot nautical masterpiece of design, speed and efficiency. The beautiful Berenger sloop had sleek lines, a plush owner's stateroom and a huge cockpit. It was a boatie's wet dream. And I wanted one. Now! At any cost. I suddenly remembered it was my birthday the following week, although I couldn't remember exactly which one it was. Go on, I told myself, you deserve it.

Back when I was a nipper in Sans Souci, sailing had been a passion. Still is to this day. Sans Souci means 'no worries' in French and that was just how I felt as I solo-sailed my first cat-rigged Laser one sun-kissed summer in the enclosed waters of Botany Bay. I must have been about nine years old. My best mate Cody Knox was in another dinghy as we endlessly criss-crossed each other on a sparkling sea. We have both loved the water, and boats, ever since.

The Berenger blokes played hard to get at first. Their rugged yachts are high quality, hand-built and heavily customised. They already had a waiting list for the first half-dozen and they only made two boats per year, but I persisted: 'Name your price,' I told their CEO. He wasn't impressed. Rightly so. I was behaving like a total prick, but in the end, we came to terms. I could have the demonstrator for something a little north of $2m once the regatta was over and it had been cleaned up and properly commissioned.

The boat made a colossal dent in the proceeds from both the *Hard News* book and film. I had also thrown in most of the handsome advance money on my next book ... if I ever managed to write the bloody thing. Typically aggressive, my agent Dru had harassed me several times about it since I had been back in Australia.

'Jonno darling, you now have less than six months to deliver the book, otherwise those schmucks will want their money back. You know that generous publishers are as rare as bacon sandwiches at a bar mitzvah.'

On a whim, I asked Berenger to name my shiny new possession *The Scoop Jon B.* Apart from the obvious punny references to my name and the newspaper scoop, the Beach Boys hit was the first song I remembered singing along to. I was a toddler, strapped into the family Holden, the album *Pet Sounds* playing on the car stereo. Later, Cody Knox and I used to sing it as teenagers, badly but joyously, every time we let rip on the Lasers.

They say that the two best moments in a boat owner's life are when he buys a boat and then again when he sells it. In the interval, boats cost a fortune to sail and maintain; they provide equal measures of pleasure and pain; and they provide twin opportunities of wonderful adventure and deadly risk. But at that moment, I was ecstatic. For some time I had been wondering what the future might hold: here, suddenly, was the solution. I'd live on the boat, get my shit together and write another blockbuster. It was that simple.

For the first time in a very long time I was engulfed in a feeling of euphoria that had nothing to do with pharmaceuticals. Buying a bloody great big expensive boat will do that to a man.

Needless to say, the euphoria did not last.

In a state of child-like excitement, I called my old mate Cody. These days he was a commercial boat skipper in Sydney. He'd also helmed a mega-yacht in a couple of Sydney to Hobart races.

'Captain Bligh, long time no speak!' he said. It was an old joke. When we used to sail together, he'd always played the part of Fletcher Christian, threatening to mutiny and cast me adrift.

'Mate,' I said, 'I'm sitting on my magnificent cruising boat with a beer and a map of the world. Check your phone. I've just sent you a photo. Isn't she a ripper? I'm thinking of heading off somewhere. Fancy coming?'

Less than a week later, Cody arrived in Hammo. It was good timing, he said, because he had just split from his long-term girl-friend. We spent another week in the marina at Hamilton while he worked his way around the boat during the day and we worked our way around the waterfront bars at night. *The Scoop Jon B* was like a five-star floating hotel. Cody couldn't believe his luck.

'Good on ya, mate, you weren't kidding. She's a real beaut! I bet this is as good as one of those swanky places in Beverly Hills you stay in.'

'Better,' I replied with a smug smile.

Cody was a breath of fresh air in my jaded life. We had been best mates since primary school, even though we were opposites in almost every way. While I was six-foot-three and blond, he was short and sallow; I was shy but mischievous while Cody was outgoing and a straight-edge guy who never got into trouble; I was an enthusiastic atheist and he was a passive believer. Yet somehow, despite all the differences, we had been inseparable as kids.

Now, in Hammo, sitting in the cockpit under a starlit sky as dusk crept in, we revisited our shared childhood and bragged about our more recent exploits. 'Love the name,' he said, pointing to the raised lettering of *The Scoop Jon B* on the stern. 'Remember when they used to play that song at the sailing club?'

The next day we put the Berenger through its paces around the Whitsunday Islands. The fresh wind, the glittering sea and the sheer joy of sailing a high-performance boat in such spectacular surroundings sent my spirits soaring. On a whim, I decided I wanted to go to Singapore. No particular reason other than I had always fancied going there and it would be a suitable challenge for both the boat and us.

Cody and I mapped out the journey: Hammo to Darwin, then across the Timor Sea to Kupang; through the southern coast of Sunda Islands to Bali; then it was a straight shot through the Java Sea staying inshore north-west up to the Bangka Belitung Islands before trying to catch a trade wind north to Singapore via Bintan Island.

Sounds simple enough but the distance was roughly 3500 kilometres. Without wind, *The Scoop* could motor happily for a thousand nautical miles so we were unlikely to have any fuelling problems. It would take a few months with some hard sailing ahead, but I already felt excited. I had a new purpose and the trip would give me a chance to recharge my batteries and try to get my literary mojo back.

Cody was stoked. 'Mate, I've always dreamed about a boat and a voyage like this,' he said in the Verandah Bar one night. His brown, curly hair was tied in a short ponytail under a battered baseball cap. He was dressed in his usual denim shorts and a tank top, showing strong, sinewy arms and capable hands. Tanned, his clear hazel eyes dominated a thin, open face that looked out on the world with quiet, good-natured confidence.

Cody liked the odd beer but was contemptuous of drugs. He strongly disapproved of my coke habit and made me swear that I wouldn't use while we were sailing.

'If you get completely wasted and we hit some crap weather, you could get us both killed,' he said. 'Besides, Indonesia is pretty heavy about drugs. Remember the Bali Nine?'

I nodded. I might have been overseas for several years but I knew about the young Australians who had been caught smuggling drugs. Two of them were later executed by firing squad.

'No worries, mate,' I said. 'I'll stick to beer. I want to clean up my act anyway; I need to get started on my next book.' Little did he know that I had enough Charlie in my cabin to choke a koala.

5

WE LEFT Hammo for the first major leg of our trip at the end of September. Our route hugged the east coast of Queensland, stopping at Cairns and then rounding Cape York, Australia's most northerly tip, before crossing the Gulf of Carpentaria to East Arnhem in the Northern Territory. Then it would be an easy hop to Darwin.

Heading out into the Coral Sea under a glorious sky, *The Scoop* behaved beautifully, sailing fast and close to the wind, belying her twenty-one tonnes. The sails in a sloop are generally large and heavy and need a bit of effort to hoist and trim, but we had the luxury of push-button winches, a hydraulic furling system and a self-tacking headsail. We also had the 160 horsepower turbo diesel engine to take up any slack.

Cody pressed a button and the mainsail automatically glided up the mast like a ruched cinema curtain. He trimmed the sail and we sliced forward, *The Scoop*'s bow dipping into the ocean like a playful dolphin. Soon we were running a steady twelve knots, the headsail poled out on a tight reach in eighteen knots of true wind. The ocean spray glittered in the sunlight as it danced over the chiselled grey hull.

We quickly fell back into our old sailing rhythm from the carefree days back in Sans Souci when we sailed a double-handed Feva together. We didn't need to talk much; we both quickly and instinctively learned how to keep the sloop running smoothly and efficiently as a team.

In the beginning, it was wonderful: Cody listened goggle-eyed as I fed him tales about the rich and famous I'd rubbed shoulders with, while I absorbed his sailing skills and knowledge. My childhood friend was a highly competent skipper. He stood in the cockpit day after day, looking out over the sea like a king surveying his realm.

Meanwhile, the sun, the sea and the fresh winds provided me with a natural high. That and the fact that the physical effort of keeping the boat running smoothly made me so tired that I slept like a hibernating bear each night.

We didn't see that many boats along the way. Some fishing vessels, of course, a few big motor cruisers possibly on their way back to civilisation after a visit to Broome and the Kimberley, and some other kindred sailing boats buzzing round the Tiwi Islands. Twice a Border Protection patrol vessel named *Triton*, a large, heavily armed trimaran, swept majestically past us. At ninety-eight metres and with two big, deck-mounted machine guns, the *Triton* looked businesslike. Both times they called us up on the radio and checked our details, destination and port of origin. We also heard from an 'eye-in-the-sky' Customs air patrol. It was oddly reassuring.

The voyage to Darwin was exhilarating. I realised that I hadn't enjoyed myself so much in a long time. It was fair weather sailing, a clear sky, only the occasional light breeze on the nose, a few friendly dolphins providing light entertainment.

Apart from a few joints while Cody had been asleep and a few surreptitious lines of coke at sunset, I was cleaner than I had been in years.

But Bali changed all that. It changed everything.

A few days later, we motored through the Badung Strait in a slack tide. As the sun came up, Cody carefully navigated our way into the busy Bali marina at Benoa Harbour. We were tired but boyishly happy.

After about three bloody hours wrangling with Indonesian Immigration, we scrubbed salt off our bodies in the rather smelly marina showers, changed and headed for brunch at the Yacht Club.

Cody was in an upbeat mood, looking forward to a few days rest in Bali before tackling the second leg up to Singapore. After poached eggs with spinach and a huge OJ, he headed back to *The Scoop* to do some minor repairs and arrange to have her properly cleaned. I decided to get my land legs back so took a taxi to the tourist drag at Kuta.

The sounds and smells of the crowded, chaotic streets were comforting, a sharp contrast to the sly sophistication and Hollywood glamour of LA. After a few Anker beers, I picked my way through the crush of tourists and touts selling everything from henna tattoos, Viagra and their 'virgin' sisters to pick up a taxi back to the marina.

There, I found Cody sitting in the cockpit, one leg crossed over the other, foot jerking like a puppet on a string. He looked tight-faced, pale and strained.

'What's up mate?' I asked carefully. I had a nasty feeling that I knew what was coming.

'You stupid selfish bastard, you could have got us both locked up. What were you thinking?'

'Okaaay,' I said slowly. 'What's got your knickers in a twist? Did I leave a dirty T-shirt in the galley? Or did I forget to put the trash out?' I shrugged. 'Look mate, whatever it is, I'm sorry. Promise I won't do it again. Scout's honour.' And I put two fingers to my forehead.

Cody stood up. 'I found your bloody stash!' He was having trouble getting the words out, he was so angry. 'You promised me no drugs on this trip,' he shouted.

I looked around to see if there was anyone listening but there didn't appear to be anyone on the boats on either side of *The Scoop* and the busy harbour sounds would have drowned out his voice.

'You fucking promised me!' he repeated. Now I knew it was serious. Cody hardly ever swore. 'Do you know what would have happened if the Customs people had found that stuff? They could have fucking *executed* us, mate. Or locked us up in a stinking hole for twenty years. Haven't you heard of Schapelle Corby, you dumb shit?'

'Mate,' I said defensively, 'you're overreacting. There's not that much gear and the chances of us being busted are pretty remote. Besides, I've hardly used it. In fact, I pretty much forgot I had it.' The lies came easily. I tried a conciliatory tone: 'Look, I'm really sorry, mate, I didn't think. Really stupid of me.'

The vehemence of Cody's reaction and my own feelings of guilt and shame had triggered a familiar craving. I took a deep breath and tried to sound casual. 'Where's the stuff now?' Cody pointed with a shaking finger over the side. I was stunned ... a couple of grand's worth of prime pharma down the gurgler.

He came up close to me: 'We've been mates for a long time, otherwise I'd head to the airport right now. But I said I'd get you to Singapore and I'll do it. But don't even think about getting any more of that shit. You don't put one foot off this boat before we set sail tomorrow. And when we get to Singapore, I'm getting on the first plane back to Sydney. You hear me? You're on your bloody own after that.'

6

ANNIE GRAPPLED with two Louis Vuitton suitcases and a matching handbag as she stepped off the pier onto the luxury catamaran. It looked bigger and swankier than she had expected. She noted the name emblazoned on the side – the *Lady Vesper*.

Shedding her gold sandals as she boarded, Annie was dressed in white skinny jeans and a taupe sleeveless silk blouse that laboured to mute her curves. A simple gold necklace and matching earrings rounded off her understated elegance. Martin followed close behind, laden with more luggage, sweating and swearing. 'Where's the bloody charter chap?' he moaned through heavy breaths. 'We shouldn't have to carry these sodding bags ourselves.'

She ignored him, dropped her bags and went straight up the short flight of fibreglass steps to the open flybridge. There she did a slow 360-degree twirl taking in the sights and sounds of the Sentosa Cove marina in Singapore. She clasped her hands in front of her as if in prayer. Sleek glass-tinted buildings framed even sleeker yachts moving lazily in the glittering expanse of water below. What looked to her to be a squadron of super-yachts sat majestically at the larger berths, while the smaller craft, from weekend runabouts to dangerous-looking cigarette boats and expensive charter vessels strained at their moorings as the sea caressed their keels. Stunning, she thought. Maybe Martin was right: maybe this is just what we need after all.

Annie looked over at her husband busying himself with the luggage. He wasn't a bad catch: quite tall, he dressed well, if conservatively; handsome enough, but could lose a few pounds. His hair was still lush and longish with a boyish lick over his forehead, although she thought he was rather too proud of it. He's ridiculously excited about this adventure, she thought with a smile. It's good to see a glimpse of the old Martin I fell in love with. But do I *still* love him? More to the point, do I want to have children with him?

Her pulse quickened as she remembered what he had said about having kids. Did he mean it? She felt ready; the alarm on her biological clock had gone off a few times lately. Maybe we could use this trip to start working on a baby? But the problem with that idea, she thought wryly, is that we are parked in a sexual cul-de-sac. About once every couple of months, if we're lucky. Even then it's routine, clinical — what she had once seen described in a women's magazine as 'subsistence sex'. Like scratching an itch, quick and efficient but devoid of creativity, joy or passion. Ah, well, for richer or poorer. She smiled at the sudden thought. Let's see if we can do something about that.

Annie's reverie was interrupted by shouts of greeting from the jetty below. She looked over and saw Martin hugging a younger couple, laughing and making lavish sounds of welcome.

'Annie, darling, they've arrived! Come down and say hello.'

She sighed, the moment spoiled. Behave, she scolded herself. You have to make the most of this trip. Putting her sunnies back on, she went down to meet the strangers. They weren't married, Martin had explained. But they had been together, off and on, for several months.

Danielle Johnston, or Dani as she preferred to be called, worked as PA to one of Martin's senior colleagues. Annie could see that she was a pretty, elfin-faced woman with short, spiky blonde hair gelled into resin-like rigidity. In her mid-twenties, she was wearing a simple but sexy short floral print dress and high heels that flattered her petite, toned, boyish figure. She's not exactly appropriately dressed for boating, Annie thought. And she has that awful nasal Sydney twang and annoying upward inflection that makes every comment sound like a question. Stop it, she scolded herself, the poor girl is probably perfectly nice.

The man, Gary Schwarz, was a little older: nearer my age, she thought. He was a muscular, broad-shouldered American who obviously enjoyed working out. Hollywood handsome but he knows it, Annie thought. Unlike Dani, he was casually dressed. His loose grey tank top and cargo shorts revealed bulging biceps and strong calves. Under the obligatory Yankees baseball cap, his light brown hair was cut short and several days of darker growth dappled a broad, tanned face with strong white teeth. 'Gary works for a competitor,' Martin had explained. 'Similar job to mine. We met at a conference and discovered that we share a love of sailing.'

I wonder what else they discovered a love of at the conference? The unspoken question just flitted into Annie's head.

30

Gary had the look of a predator. Shrugging, she smiled brightly and said: 'Great to meet you guys.'

Less than thirty minutes later, they all gathered on the upper deck.

Annie had found a bottle of half-decent champagne in the fridge and they toasted each other: 'Here's to a voyage of fun and exploration,' said Martin with an exaggerated wink at Dani. Annie frowned but raised the glass to her lips and enjoyed the cool fizzy bubbles on her tongue. Lunch platters had been supplied by the charter company: Asian beef salad, chilli prawns and Rojak, a delicious local dish that included beansprouts, greens, pineapple, peanuts and cucumber. There was also a large bowl of fresh fruit salad of mango, lychees and dragon fruit. They ate in the cool, spacious saloon with the shimmering images of the distant glass buildings glinting and moving in time with the boat as it swayed gently in its mooring.

7

'I FUCKING love this job.' Bambang Budiman paused to take a drag from his *kretek*, a foul-smelling clove cigarette. 'And I'm fucking good at it,' he said, pounding his barrel chest with a meaty fist. He was in the wheelhouse of his crew's mother ship, the *Pasang Merah* or *Crimson Tide*, talking to the old Malaysian helmsman, Mamat, whose wrinkled skin was the colour of nicotine. They were heading away from an island off the west coast of Sumatra. 'I know the crew think I'm a ruthless violent bastard, but you know what? Those are just my good points!' The pirate boss laughed, revealing his large gold incisor.

Bambang's criminal colleagues had quickly nicknamed him 'BangBang'. Some said it was because of his love of automatic assault rifles, while others thought it was because his head had the same shape and texture as a grenade and he would explode if anyone pissed him off. They told him he was the spitting image of General Manuel Noriega, the former Panamanian dictator convicted of drug trafficking, money laundering and racketeering. Like 'Old Pineapple Face', BangBang was broad-faced, low-browed, dark-skinned and heavily pockmarked. He wore mirrored Ray-Ban aviator sunglasses that screened sly, hooded eyes, each a curious dark yellow colour punctured by a shard of anthracite. A former crew member had once unwisely called them lizard eyes. The pirate boss had stuck a knife in that man's eye and then tossed him overboard for the sharks to feed on.

BangBang was not normally given to introspection but today he was in a curious, reflective mood. I've come a long way from the fishers' kampong where I was born, he thought. The kampong, near Cilegon city on the coast a hundred kilometres north-west of Jakarta, gazed out towards Panjang Island and beyond to the Java Sea.

'I had to grow up fast,' he told Mamat, who often thought that his boss's curious sing-song voice belied his brutal appearance. 'My old man was a bastard. A steelworker, used to beat me every day. But my uncle was worse ... when he got drunk on his fishing boat, he used to try to stick his dirty cock in my mouth. Eventually, when I was about thirteen, I got away. But not before I fixed him good.' He smacked his lips at the memory.

'How did you do that?' asked the helmsman.

'Heh. One time he was rat-arsed on palm wine, I stuck a fucking fishing hook through his dick. "Use that for fish bait, you fucker," I told him.'

BangBang was quiet for a moment, remembering his life after that, living in the notorious Jembatan Besi slum in Jakarta. Fuck, that was a dark, dense place. He remembered the tightly packed buildings, made of rough wood, dried mud and scrap metal, rising up uneasily in narrow lanes and rat-infested alleys, blocking the daylight as the top storeys teetered towards each other. He could still see the sagging lines of grey washing and smell the stench of rancid garlic, sewage and rotting refuse that added to the stale, hazy miasma shrouding the slum and its five thousand impoverished inhabitants. BangBang shivered as he recalled his time there.

He had worked his arse off for five dollars a day in a makeshift T-shirt factory, one of many sweatshops in the slum. He slept in a derelict house in Venus Alley with twenty others, including an older cousin, Yuda. There was no toilet. He supplemented his income as one of hundreds of pint-sized pickpockets that polluted the sprawling metropolis.

Ironically, the Jembatan Besi slum sat, brooding and malodorous, opposite the upmarket Seasons City shopping mall and three grand-looking apartment blocks. Every day, the young BangBang would look up at the world of wealth and opulence and brood. He once bragged to Yuda: 'You'll see, one day I'll live in that place, or one like it. Whatever it takes.'

'Yeah right.' Yuda had laughed. 'In your dreams.'

'No, you wait, I'll get there whatever it takes . . . or whoever I have to kill.'

A year later, he was an enthusiastic and energetic member of the Margonda machete gang that specialised in mugging other teenagers on motorcycles. He graduated to snatching tourists' handbags from the pillion seat of a motor scooter driven by Yuda.

'My big breakthrough came when I was eighteen,' he told Mamat now. 'I became a *preman*, working for one of the city's main crime syndicates. Then I graduated to robbing banks, drug running and working as an enforcer in the syndicate's prostitution business. It was a great life! But not as good as this.'

'So how did you end up here?' asked the helmsman.

'Shit happened,' said BangBang with a sneer. 'I did a seven-year stretch in Cipinang jail for assault and armed robbery. But when I got out, the syndicate looked after me. Put me into this pirate business.'

BangBang loved being a *bajak laut*, a modern-day pirate. There was endless sunlight, the freshest of air and, despite the cramped quarters of his boat, he didn't feel he was living on an anthill as he had back in the slum. He had patiently served his apprenticeship on the skiffs that raced after and boarded target vessels, before finally becoming a *nakhoda*, a captain. Now he and his crew of cut-throats attacked scores of vessels, from large commercial vessels to smaller pleasure boats, raping, robbing and ransacking. The Strait of Malacca is just like a shopping mall, or, in our case, a *shipping* mall, he would often joke to his men. We go there to shop for loot!

BangBang stubbed out his cigarette. He did not need to tell Mamat that he liked working for the Chinese crime syndicate or about the high he got from boarding target vessels with an assault rifle and machete in his fists. All the crew knew he loved killing people. He had a special talent for it. And that propensity for violence, allied to his strength and willingness to go all the way, helped keep the men in line as they prowled the high sea looking for prey.

Lighting another *kretek*, BangBang's mind turned to his share of the spoils from the last heist. He had hidden it along with his other accumulated loot in a secret cave on the island they had just left. And that's just the start, he told himself. With a bit of luck, I'll have that luxury apartment at Seasons City before too long. He suddenly gave a shrill laugh, startling the old helmsman, who was unused to seeing his captain in such good humour.

8

WE DIDN'T make it to Singapore. A sailing boat is no place for two people at loggerheads, even one as luxurious and spacious as *The Scoop*. Sooner or later, things were going to come to a head. It was inevitable.

We left Bali the day after we had our bust-up, easing out of the berth with a mixture of relief and angst. Relief that we hadn't got into any trouble with the authorities, and angst because the atmosphere between Cody and me was toxic. He hadn't said anything more to me, apart from occasionally barking out staccato commands relating to the sailing of the boat.

Using the remote gear, we cranked up the powered Harken winches and unfurled the mainsail and the self-tacking jib. Nudged by a friendly trade wind pushing up from the south-east, we entered the Java Sea and hugged the eastern Java coastline.

Behind the helm, Cody continued to simmer and stew. And the next day, when he thought (rightly) that I was high on something, he blew up.

'You had more stuff stashed, you bloody moron!' he shouted as he stood, arms crossed and legs braced against the pilot-house's solid teak table to offset the rocking rhythm of the boat. 'You bloody lied to me. Again.'

It was true, I did have another small cache of coke salted away in a different spot. Some reptilian part of my brain had planned for the possibility of running out.

I was mightily pissed off that Cody had chucked my main supply in the ocean and it must have shown on my face because, suddenly and ferociously, Cody spat the dummy: 'You know what? That's bloody it! I'm done. I'm getting off at the next decent-sized port.'

And with that, he laid out some charts on the table, studied them for a moment and stabbed a finger on one of them. 'Look here. I'll take you to Jakarta and then I'm buggering off.'

By his estimate, that meant just another few hundred nautical miles and two to three days sailing. I was gutted but didn't bother to try to change his mind. I was too angry and ashamed. So he was Fletcher Christian after all, I mused, deserting his captain and leaving him to unknown terrors.

We sailed almost nonstop, until a tropical storm slowly, inexorably built up over our heads, complete with massive amounts of rain, spectacular lightning and boat-shaking thunder.

Soaked to the skin despite our wet weather gear, both a tad scared and emitting waves of mutual hatred, Cody and I still managed to work the boat as a team. We took both the main and headsails down, using the handy electro-hydraulic system. The turbo diesel engine took over, its dull bass roar oddly comforting in the high-pitched crescendo of crashing wind and rain.

We helmed the boat from the spacious cockpit aft, although we could have used the more sheltered starboard helm station set forward of the main saloon. But the feeling of being out in the open, of being connected to the wild elements, kept us sharp and focused. Besides, the roar of the wind and the ocean drowned out the deafening silence between us.

The grey, Kevlar-coated hull showed remarkable stability in the conditions. In fact, *The Scoop* matched the elements with a confidence that Cody and I did not totally share. The solid, secure sloop seemed to be telling us: 'Don't worry, I can handle this.'

At one point I sat in a semi-bewildered state in the clammy gloom, surrounded by a heaving, boiling sea, buffeted by the howling gale, and besieged by swirling thoughts of what the future might now hold. I'm not usually superstitious but that malevolent maelstrom seemed portentous. Am I going to get out of this alive? And if I do, what is there for me afterwards?

The next morning we sailed into Semarang, tails between our sea legs. Cody wouldn't let me leave the boat; presumably he thought I'd try and score more dope. He was right. Instead, I lay in my cabin feeling sorry for myself and calming my jitters with some of the rapidly dwindling white powder. I alternated between feelings of guilt and resentment. Okay, I was a dick for bringing the dope but Cody had totally overreacted. After all, who was paying for all this five-star travel? He should be bloody grateful that he'd had the opportunity to sail a boat like *The Scoop*. I'll be better off without him, I thought as the coke smoothed away my anxiety. I don't need anyone interfering with my life. Look at what I have achieved on my own. An Oscar, for fuck's sake. Why should I put up with crap from anyone? The sooner he fucks off, the better. I could sail the damn thing myself.

The final leg to Jakarta was happily uneventful. Apart from the frosty face and stormy looks emanating from Cody, the heavy weather had been left behind. I enjoyed the feel of the boat and steered her for much of the way. I might not be in Cody's class as a skipper but I'd learnt a lot since we'd left Hammo.

Cody took over as we neared Jakarta. It was challenging, even for him: we were motoring into a building breeze, with the tide against us. We had to navigate through thousands of boats: tugs, tankers, ferries, fishing boats and a myriad of smaller craft. After our time at sea, it was overwhelming to be so close to a metropolis of ten million souls. The smell: brine, garlic, cooking oil and diesel. The noise: hundreds of engines, hooters, the *chop-chop* of overhead helicopters. It was both exhilarating and exhausting.

We tied up at the Pantai Mutiara marina in Jakarta's north shore and, after we'd attended to the usual arrival process, Cody silently packed up his kitbag, tidied up the pilothouse and then walked off *The Scoop* and onto the floating jetty. There he stopped and shaded his eyes as he turned to look up at me standing in the cockpit.

'Mate, I don't know what's happened to you. I used to love you like a brother. But you've become a . . . a bloody junkie or something. You're dangerous to be around. You need help. Call me when you sort yourself out.'

And, with that, he hoisted his bag onto his shoulder, gave a last gentle caress of *The Scoop*'s hull and walked away.

9

BUGGER CODY! To underscore my defiance, I immediately set about getting pissed before starting on some lines of coke. Later, I headed unsteadily to one of the bars that fringed the marina. The next thing I knew I was waking up with a sore head and a sleeping girl. The headache was familiar, the girl was not. A rather scruffy young backpacker from Wagga Wagga in New South Wales, I dimly remembered.

Ah shit. Somewhere deep in my mind, I registered that this was not a good way to start a new day. Semi-paralysis, pounding head, mouth like a wallaby's bum. My stomach reacted uneasily to the slight sway of *The Scoop*, snug in her berth.

I kicked Miss Wagga Wagga out of bed. She was a tall, rangy twenty-something wharf rat with badly-dyed neon red hair and a smattering of amateurish tattoos. Several painful-looking piercings on her face and body completed the low-rent look.

'Jonno, I've been thinking,' she said. 'Like, what if I stayed here with you?' She had a sweaty sheen to her skin as she put on her skimpy clothes – dirty Daisy Dukes and a sleeveless T showing a hint of scrawny side-boob.

I thought for a moment. The girl had shoved a fair amount of my precious coke up her studded nose the previous night. Having her on board was a luxury I couldn't afford. 'Sorry, not going to happen,' I told her. She glared at me, hoisted her cheap bag over one shoulder and left without another word. Turns out she also left without her cat. I had a vague memory of her arriving with a stray kitten tucked under one arm. That was confirmed when I stepped barefoot into a puddle of cat piss in the saloon.

My own bladder suddenly sent an urgent mayday message to my brain. I lurched to the toilet. Sometimes taking a much-needed piss can be as pleasurable as an orgasm. I looked in the dirty mirror, tried to focus. The image that gazed back was blurry, blotchy and bloated. The blue eyes were ringed in red and the rough, unshaven face had a weary look of disdain. The thought came from nowhere: what would old Percy think of you right now?

I knew exactly what he'd think. 'Jonno, what the fuck are you doing, you big selfish bastard? You need to fucking sort yourself out.' And he'd be right.

I was making myself some breakfast when the cops arrived. I got the fright of my life when they indicated they wanted to search the boat. Fuck, fuck, fuck.

'What for?' But I knew.

'For drugs,' they replied, watching me closely.

How did they know, I thought, my chest tightening. The backpacker bitch must have dobbed me in. Fuck! There were four cops, with two sniffer dogs. They spent an hour on board looking in every nook and cranny as I stood on the pier in a cold, dread sweat. Images of trials and firing squads scurried around in my brain as the dogs got busy in the bowels of *The Scoop*. The kitten must be shitting himself, I thought randomly. From the yelps and high-pitched whines it was clear the two big German shepherds were getting increasingly excited. They must have found the last of my stash. I found myself praying for the first time in twenty-five years: Please, God, don't let them find anything. I'll do anything, I'll give up the drugs, get clean. I'll donate the proceeds of my next book to charity. Please, please don't let them arrest me.

Later, when the cops had gone – empty-handed, their dogs with tails between their legs – I sat alone in the cockpit with a bottle of Tiger beer, pondering my situation. I'd checked my hiding spot and the meagre remnants of my stash had gone. Miss Wagga Wagga must have stolen it. The cops had wagged their fingers at me and made it clear I was lucky – the dogs had detected drug traces but not enough to arrest me. But I knew they'd be back – maybe they'd even plant some stuff next time, I thought feverishly. Ironically, the backpacker had done me a favour by nicking the last of the coke.

The steaming humidity was softened only by a slight breeze. There was a perpetual background *ting-ting-ting* of steel halyards knocking against masts. The Blue Nile's 'The Days of our Lives' played mournfully in the background as the kitten emerged from its hiding place and started pawing a bit of loose rope on the decking.

The breeze brought with it wafts of brine and diesel and the ever-present, unidentifiable pungent odour of Asia. Scores of people were visible, some lounging in their boats, some working on repairs or simply chatting on the many long piers that punctuated the glittering green water. Wrapped up in my own misery, I had no desire to talk to any of them.

Opening the bottle with shaky hands, the beer foamed out, spraying my cargo shorts and Billabong T-shirt. I hardly noticed as I took stock of my situation: here you are on the downslope to forty, never been married, have never even come close to meeting a woman you could love. You have few real friends and are largely estranged from your family. What a pathetic loser, I thought.

I had two other pressing problems: first, the money was fast running out and second, I had to produce a new book within a few months or I would have to pay back the advance. There were heaps of messages on my phone from Drusilla, my agent. Initially cajoling, the messages had grown progressively shriller until they became out and out abusive: 'Jonno, get fucking back to me, pronto. Immediately, now, this minute. The publishers are screaming blue murder. Unless they see some physical evidence of a new book, they want their money back. I don't know what the fuck you're up to but you need to call me ASAP. If you don't, I'll kill you. Worse, I'll cut your useless balls off.'

All this was depressing. But what really shattered me, what really cut me to my very soul, was Cody's contemptuous 'junkie' comment. It kept replaying in my head. The worst thing was he was right . . . I had been selfish and put us both at risk.

I'd always reassured myself that I could give up cocaine anytime I chose. But now, deep down, I knew the truth: the dope had got its hooks into me big time. I had to do something about it. I picked up the kitten and looked into its bright eyes:

'Mate, I've got to change my life around. Tell me, how the bloody hell do I do that?' I smiled wryly; I was talking to a bloody cat. Then once again, I thought about Percy and his fighting spirit. I had once asked him where the scars on his knuckles came from. 'How easy do you think it was going to school in the Gorbals with a name like Percy?' he replied.

That image of him tipped me over the edge. He had such high hopes for me. He would have been appalled at how far I had fallen. I wrapped my arms around myself and cried. I cried more than I'd ever cried in my life. Waves of self-pity and self-loathing swamped my brain. Finally, eyes red, nose running, I managed to get my shit together. My heart gradually stopped racing. My body ceased heaving. But then my reptile brain said slyly, 'you need a hit'. But there was no gear left. I would either have to go into Jakarta and score some more stuff or . . . what?

'What the bloody hell am I going to do?' I asked the kitten again.

10

AS SHE showered and got ready to go out to sample the delights of Singapore city, Annie examined her feelings of unease. The conversation with Gary and Dani that afternoon had been pleasant enough but there had been some odd undertones. It was clear that there was some tension between the younger couple. It was equally clear that Martin was flirting with his pixie-haired colleague. Annie noticed the looks they gave each other and the way their hands lingered on each other's shoulders or arms as they sat around the table.

She had smiled, however, when Martin, who was paying the lion's share of the charter costs, had put on an ostentatious captain's hat complete with gold braid on the peak. Less amusing was the fact that he had then got rather pissed; after several glasses of fizz, he had progressed to some New Zealand sauvignon blanc and then a big Aussie red. Gary had been more circumspect, thankfully. Someone needed to take responsibility for the boat. To her relief, Gary had declared himself the trip's 'designated driver'. He explained that he had had a lot

45

of sailing experience, much more than Martin. He came from Portland, a US seaport in Maine, where his father ran a charter boat business; Gary used to crew for him on runs up to Halifax in Nova Scotia.

Dani was harder to read, Annie thought as she towelled herself. It seemed that the younger woman was trying a little too hard to please. But it could be that she's just tired after the flight from Sydney, she decided, giving her the benefit of the doubt.

The two couples had decided to spend a few days moored in Singapore to give the girls a chance to check out the great shopping in the city while the guys familiarised themselves with the big boat.

Annie found herself warming slightly to Dani when they went shopping at the famous Bugis Street Markets. Her excitement about the amazing array of clothes and accessories on offer was infectious. 'The only problem,' she warned Annie, 'is that all these great bargains could be Chinese knock-offs and we'd never know.' Who cares, Annie thought.

Nevertheless, she caught the shopping bug and, by lunchtime, was weighed down by a battery of brightly coloured bags bearing many of the top fashion brand names. As they stopped briefly at a street café for mouth-watering oyster *mee sua* (vermicelli) and *pisang goreng* (banana fritters), Annie told Dani she may have to buy another suitcase to take all her new clothes home with her.

'I know what you mean. I only brought one small carry-on case with a few clothes with me, 'cos I thought I'd be spending the whole time in a bikini. Gary thought I was mad,' Dani said.

'How long have you guys been together?'

'Oh, dunno, must be, what – nine months now? To be honest, like, it's been a bit hot and cold. Gary's all right but sometimes he can be a bit . . .' She paused.

'A bit what?'

'Well he's, like, up himself a little? Maybe 'cos he's American. He can just be a pain in the arse. Not like Marty, he's a cutie.'

Annie thought this was an odd thing to say about someone else's husband. Besides, *no one* called him Marty! She sipped her light beer. 'How did you meet?'

Dani took a gulp of her Mai Tai. 'Um, I was in the pub with Marty and a few other bank colleagues when he introduced me to Gary. Seems a long time ago now. They were talking, like, about doing this trip. It sounded really exciting.

'It's the main reason I've stuck it out with Gary all this time, to be honest. I didn't want to miss out.'

'Too much information!' Annie laughed.

'What about you and Marty, how long have you been married?'

Annie closed her eyes and sighed. 'Nearly eight years. Seems a lot, lot longer somehow.'

'Why? Aren't you happy? Only, I know he spends a lot of time away from home. And of course he doesn't really want kids, does he?'

'He told you that?' Annie was shocked but didn't want to make a big deal of it to Dani. I'll bloody kill him, she thought. How dare he say that to a virtual stranger. 'Well, you know, marriages have their ups and downs. We rub along okay, I suppose.'

'Have you ever, like, cheated on him?' Dani said with a mischievous smile.

Annie was more than a little irritated by the way the conversation was going. She looked sharply at the other woman. 'I don't think that's any of your business,' she snapped. 'It's time we went back to the boat.'

Dani rolled her eyes. 'Okay. Whatever.'

That evening, all four of them went back to Bugis Street, where they found the cobblestoned shopping area had transformed into a colourful scene of bustling crowds, loud street food vendors and nightspots. Over dinner, Annie watched Martin and Dani closely. But they did nothing, said nothing to arouse any further suspicion.

Over the following two days they went sailing to Jurong Island and some of the other smaller islands in the Singapore Strait. Annie was relieved to find that Gary skippered the boat with easy confidence. She was also relieved that she hadn't felt seasick.

Finally they were ready to set off for Langkawi in Malaysia. Gary had plotted a course through the Strait of Malacca and they should arrive there in time for Christmas. The Malaysian island had been the destination for their honeymoon almost eight years before, although Annie sometimes felt it was a lifetime ago.

'A toast,' Martin said, standing up with glass aloft the night before their departure: 'To calm seas, warm winds and wild times!'

The four of them happily clinked glasses, completely oblivious to just how wild it was to become.

11

'HI, I'M Jonno and I'm an addict.'

The kitten sat up and looked at me in alarm. I had said it aloud, in a wry, mock American accent, although I now knew it in my heart to be true. Cody had been on the money. Charlie had entered my system like a Trojan horse and it was now attacking my body and my brain from within.

So far I had only snorted it. The problem is you develop a tolerance for coke fairly quickly. You need more and more to experience the same rush, the sublime high that beats all else – including sex and booze. In my heart I knew it was just a matter of time before I started smoking or injecting it and perhaps other, even more heinous substances. I knew that if I started injecting that shit, I'd be lost forever.

On the earlier legs of the voyage, I'd eased back. But since Cody's abrupt departure, the terrible craving had returned. If I stayed here, it was odds-on that I would descend even deeper into the drug abyss.

What to do? I was sitting quietly in the cockpit with the kitten snoozing in my lap. I had decided to call him Wagga.

'Mate,' I told him, 'as I see it, we've got three options: one, we can try to sell *The Scoop* here and head back to Sydney; two, we could stay here, live on the boat and try to make ends meet; or three, we sail off somewhere – anywhere – and try to kick the coke. What do you think?'

Wagga just yawned. He had a grey–black stripy coat, a cute face and whiskers as long as his thin tail. 'Much bloody good you are,' I said, tipping him onto the deck. In the end, two things affected my final decision. I was becoming increasingly paranoid that the Jakarta drugs squad would come back and plant some evidence. The thought of being executed or, worse, locked up for twenty years in some nightmarish Indonesian prison was too much to bear. But it was Percy's letter that really clinched it. For the millionth time, I unfolded it, taking care not to add to the creases and wrinkles that cut lines through the blotchy ink on the paper. With the fingers of my other hand, I rubbed the AA bronze token that had meant so much to him.

Maybe I had just hit rock bottom because I suddenly realised what a whiny, selfish, self-pitying shitbag I had become. It wasn't who I was, or at least who I'd been. I figured I had been a decent bloke once, a man Percy had admired and even loved, as his letter proved. *'You were a light in my life.'*

I owed it to his memory to sort myself out. I screwed up my eyes. 'I. Am. Going. To. Beat. This. Bastard. Thing,' I said through gritted teeth.

And that was how the decision was made.

The next morning *The Scoop*, freed from its mooring ropes, seemed to spring forward with a new eagerness. Perhaps it was just my imagination, or the result of my heavy-handed grip on the throttle. I had never single-handedly sailed a boat the size of *The Scoop* before and, as we left the throbbing Pantai Mutiara marina, I was excited but apprehensive about the challenging sea voyage ahead. The fact that I also faced a rather choppy voyage of self-discovery did not escape me.

I gingerly picked my way through the teeming traffic as we slipped out into Jakarta Bay, narrowly missing a commercial catamaran with a bevy of backpackers on board. I wasn't confident enough yet to use the sails so we motored along the northeast Java coast, inshore of the islands of Kapal and Rambut. My immediate intention was to reach the Sunda Strait, a narrow strip of water that divides Java and Sumatra, then head west into the vastness of the Indian Ocean. After that, who bloody knew?

Sailing north to Singapore had been an option but I felt that navigating through the Malaccan Strait would be challenging for a nervous solo sailor at the best of times but bloody dangerous when he was going cold turkey. I had used the dregs of my credit card to refuel and provision *The Scoop*, even remembering to buy some cat food for little Wagga, who seemed perfectly happy to scamper around the boat. To my surprise, I enjoyed having him around. I had also cleaned up the cockpit and saloon and stowed away the bits and pieces that had accumulated on the foredeck since Cody's exit about a week before. I put all of this activity down to the optimistic mood I was in, literally and metaphorically clearing the decks for the next chapter in my life.

A day into my new voyage I felt like shit. I had been well aware that cold turkey would be no picnic. While I had no nasty rash or scabs, I was throwing up a lot and my body felt like it had been hit by a flying refrigerator.

The main problem was mental; the most crippling effect was my feelings of paranoia. On the water, sitting rigid in my lonely cockpit, splattered by the wind-driven spray, my mind raced with thoughts of how various people were out to destroy me. They were all at it: the nuns and priests from St Jude's, the book critics, my agent Drusilla, German Shepherd dogs and, of course, that turncoat Cody. Any moment, I expected an Indonesian patrol boat would scream up alongside *The Scoop* and arrest me for drug smuggling.

I was shaking, my hands struggling to hold on to the helm. My energy levels were in the toilet and I just wanted to crawl into a bed and sleep for a week. Obviously, the demands of skippering a boat made that impossible. So, kneading my red-rimmed eyes with aching knuckles, I pumped up the sound system to give me the illusion of company. Nothing like a bit of AC/DC to give my body something to shake about.

After a couple of days, I would have given my Oscar for a baggy of coke. The craving was debilitating. My nostrils flared at the thought of it. I could actually feel the stinging sensation on my gums where I used to rub in the last smear of coke. I'd even frantically searched the places I had stashed it while Cody was around in case there were any little specks of white powder still remaining. Maybe, I thought, those police pooches missed something.

At some point, I realised that I had managed to guide the boat round into the Sunda Strait. You know when you are driving a car and suddenly you arrive safely at your destination and you can't remember how the hell you got there? Well, that's how it felt. Both the boat and my brain were on autopilot.

As I approached Pulau Sangiang, the island that sits in the middle of the Sunda Strait, I had a decision to make. If I went left, that would mean heading south, perhaps down the west coast of Java. That would be sensible if I were heading back to Oz. Or, if I went to the right of the island, I could keep heading due west out into the Indian Ocean where the next landfall would be the Maldives, thousands of kilometres away. Alternatively I could turn north up the coast of Sumatra. Either of the latter two options would take me further from home.

I chose north. The Maldives was a stretch and, although I was feeling a bit Garbo-esque at that point, it was a helluva long way to go on your own. But I didn't want to go home either. Looking at the charts, I saw that Sumatra had plenty of islands dotted along its west coast. They would provide shelter, perhaps a refuge where I could ride out the nightmare of cold turkey.

12

THE SAIL from Singapore had been a million miles from the relaxing, carefree pleasure cruise Annie had been promised by Martin.

Her dismay was due in equal measure to both Martin's bad behaviour and the boisterous sea. The *Lady Vesper* had exited Sentosa Cove and headed west across the narrow neck of the southern tip of the Malaccan Strait to the coast of Sumatra. Gary said there were more islands on the west side of the channel to provide shelter if the going got rough.

And it did get rough. For a start, the weather had been poor: dull, overcast with occasional high winds. The sea was very choppy – caused by a mix of wind and the heavy volume of traffic churning through the brown, murky water. They were sailing just north of the equator and the heavy, stagnant air seemed to hang over them like a wet tweed wool coat.

'Like wading through pea soup,' Annie said. She felt queasy, more so because Dani was already throwing up. The stench of vomit made her gag. 'It's ridiculous,' she continued as they passed a container ship. 'There's so much traffic on the water. I thought they were supposed to stick to shipping lanes.'

'It's the world's most important trade route,' Martin said, as if he were addressing a group of banking execs. 'Five hundred ships use this channel daily and small vessels like ours have no right of way, so we just have to take our chances.'

Gary did exactly that, trying to find gaps between the cease-less procession of ships heading north or south, before shooting through a hole like a scalded cat as another big container ship threatened to turn their boat into matchwood.

'It's just like Piccadilly Circus,' Annie smiled, hoping to lessen her companions' rising stress levels. The sea was churning like the inside of a washing machine; a strong headwind was blowing while a shoal of local fishing boats made the *Lady Vesper's* way ahead seem like an obstacle course. Martin continued to drink and Dani continued to puke. Only Gary remained outwardly upbeat. 'This is a millpond compared to the Gulf of Maine,' he said, but Annie could tell he was lying. His normally tan face looked increasingly pale and drawn, his white lips tight as he concentrated at the helm. And as the *Lady Vesper* continued north up the east coast of Sumatra, he got increasingly stressed out, snapping commands at the other three and blowing up when they didn't respond fast or well enough. Annie simply bit her lip but Martin reacted badly.

'Look, matey, I'm bloody well paying for all this and you fucking well better not speak to me like that,' he warned Gary one afternoon. The row continued later that evening, after they had gratefully slunk into safe harbour at Dumai to refuel and stock up on provisions. Gary accused Martin of being a useless, lazy sailor. 'You suck, buddy. I'm doing all the heavy lifting here. If it wasn't for me, you'd all be fish bait.'

Martin, who was already completely pissed, shouted something unintelligible and swung a fist; he missed and fell over. The two women helped him to bed.

When Annie went back up to the flybridge, Gary was alone. 'I don't know how you stay with that asshole,' he said. His eyes suddenly glinted: 'Me, I'd treat you better, ma'am. A whole lot better, if you take my meaning.' He flashed his white teeth.

Flattered despite herself, Annie replied with a smile: 'Thank you, but I'll just have to put up with "the asshole", as you put it, for now.'

'Okay, lady, but I'm here if you ever feel like a change, you know what I'm saying?'

Annie knew *exactly* what he was saying. She retreated to bed.

The next morning Martin complained of an almighty hangover. He gulped down a whole jug of Bloody Mary by himself while a tight-lipped Gary steered the *Lady Vesper* out of the marina and back onto the strait. They had originally intended to stop off at Belawan, a major port about four hundred kilometres to the north-east, but the plans changed after Annie got talking to a Kiwi couple berthed next to them at Dumai. The Kiwis invited them on board their big cruiser for drinks, where both husband and wife regaled them with stories about piracy in the Malaccan Strait. They warned that Belawan was a hub for the modern-day Bluebeards.

At the mention of pirates, Martin, by now several sheets to the wind, started hopping about on one leg, put his hand over one eye and said in a comic pirate voice: 'Aargh, Jim lad, shiver me timbers, we be going to Treasure Island!'

'You can laugh,' the husband said, 'but just a few weeks ago, six armed pirates boarded a chemical tanker at the port's outer anchorage and stole a load of stuff. Apparently they simply climbed up the ship's anchor chain. No one saw them. They took a crew member hostage before escaping. No one was hurt but there have been plenty of other casualties in the area.'

Why not sail a bit further north to an island called Pulau Sembilan, Nine Island, the Kiwis suggested. There was plenty of shelter there and clean, calm water for good anchorage. They could then refuel at Banda Aceh and from there it was a straight shot north and east to Langkawi.

'Sounds good to me. This trip's been pretty hairy so far, it would be nice to, like, have a bit of a break,' said Dani.

The next few days followed the same pattern as before: they sailed north, buffeted by a medley of rain, gusty trade winds and faster, more aggressive vessels. Throughout, Annie kept a sharp lookout for potential danger. The talk of pirates had spooked her. And she knew that the others felt the same.

She was tidying up the saloon when, halfway to Nine Island, they were hit by a sudden, violent squall. Up to then the sky had been overcast with light winds on the nose and relatively calm seas. But now, out of nowhere it seemed, a swirling, snarling gust of wind came roaring up behind them and enveloped them in a maelstrom of warm, stinging rain, rolling waves and boiling air. She sat down and braced herself against the saloon table as everything turned monochromatic: the smudgy sky turned black and grey and the angry, lace-topped waves broke grey and white over the Vesper's twin hulls.

Dani moaned. 'Bloody hell, not again! I can't take much more of this shit.' She promptly lurched down to the galley and puked in the sink. Up top, Gary, drenched to the skin, battled to keep the rolling and pitching catamaran stable. The shrieking wind rattled and rocked the flybridge's hardtop bimini as the bows dipped and the stern came up. Beside him, Martin held on grimly to the sides of his seat, knuckles as white as his face.

13

BANGBANG WAS angrier than a rodeo bull. The plan had been simple, business as usual, but his crew had fucked it up.

He gulped down the smoke from a Gudang Garam clove cigarette and sucked on his gold tooth. He was furious but also, if he were honest with himself, a little bit afraid. The feeling was strange, alien to him; he wasn't normally afraid of anyone or anything. But he knew his syndicate bosses would be mightily pissed off; chances are they could make me a sacrificial lamb to 'encourage' other crew bosses to do better, he thought. The Chinese man who headed the syndicate – BangBang had never met him but he had heard whispers of a 'Mr Fong' – was rumoured to be a Triad 'boss of bosses'. At worst, BangBang knew he could expect little mercy. At best, it could jeopardise his ambitions of moving into the big league.

He had also lost face with his crew. They expected him to plan and organise attacks with precision and perfection. Failures like this could lead to their arrest or even death. In the pirate business, there were no HR protocols. A disgruntled crew could simply throw their captain overboard on a dark night if he didn't deliver suitable spoils.

BangBang spat out the bitter aftertaste from the clove *kretek* and thumped his tattooed knuckles on a gunwale. The target vessel was a mid-sized Malaysian cargo ship carrying palm oil from refineries in Port Klang, just south of Kuala Lumpur, to Mumbai. The syndicate had provided all the relevant details: times, route, cargo, crew. BangBang's job was straightforward: intercept the ship, hit hard and 'lighten its load'.

His ship, the *Crimson Tide*, was a twenty-eight metre wooden Thai fishing trawler they had hijacked the previous year and renamed after one of BangBang's favourite films. It looked like a floating disaster: the hull a dirty, rust-stained orange–brown colour with the bulwark topped in white and festooned in black rubber tyres acting as fenders. A filthy canvas shade speckled by bird shit stretched across amidships. The large, two-storey wooden wheelhouse slouched forward as if it was going to fall over. A medium-sized crane squatted on the foredeck. But the old, ramshackle appearance was deceptive. A wolf in sheep's clothing, BangBang always thought. He had created more storage space for stolen cargo and he'd installed sophis-ticated technical equipment, including radar, sonar and GPS. A new Scania turbocharged diesel engine, still shiny, provided solid power. He was particularly proud of the ship's arsenal of automatic weapons and rocket-propelled grenades. Two wooden skiffs trailed behind, tied firmly to steel cleats on the transom. On longer voyages, they were stowed away on top of the wheelhouse. Down below there was a dark, dank storage space that smelled of old fish and diesel. Some of the crew slept there, others on the main deck.

BangBang and his crew of twelve had anchored close to the island of Pulau Nasi, slightly north-west of Banda Aceh on the northern tip of Sumatra. An hour before dusk, they ventured out across the top of the Malacca Strait, ready to intercept the cargo ship as it entered the channel from the Andaman Sea. As planned, they reconnoitred the freighter four or five miles away, steaming south.

BangBang ordered eight of his men into the two motor skiffs to circle round behind the vessel and hit it astern to take advantage of a radar blind spot. Standard operating procedure. But the attack went awry for one simple, stupid reason: the cargo boat's freeboard was higher than expected and the pirates' makeshift rope ladders and grapples were not long enough to reach the top of it.

The syndicate had failed to provide BangBang with the necessary info, but he knew they would still blame him. His men attempted to board several times but eventually gave up and veered off, frustrated and furious. When the two skiffs returned empty-handed to the *Crimson Tide*, BangBang went berserk.

'*Keparat bajingan bangsat!*' he screamed. 'Bloody bastard assholes!

'Do I have to do everything my fucking self?'

Deep down, he knew it probably wasn't their fault but he lashed out at one of the nearer pirates with his machete anyway. There was a wet, meaty *thwack* sound and the man went down on his knees, screaming and clutching the wound, bright red blood spraying everywhere as his severed arm flopped on the deck.

The rest of his crew, some covered in a fine red mist, moved away from him. They were exchanging dark looks and muttering to each other, clearly pissed off with their leader's unjust barbarity. The atmosphere was charged with a heavy, metallic mix of blood and malice.

Just then, the *Crimson Tide* slowed and the helmsman, Mamat, shouted from the wheelhouse, 'Boss, you come quick!'

14

THE SCOOP had cleared the south-west tip of Sumatra and we were well advanced into the Indian Ocean when the shit-storm hit like a sledgehammer. Before then the boat had been creaming through gentle waves as we headed aimlessly on a general north-westerly course. My vague intention had been to tack first north and then east before dropping anchor before dusk in the lee of one of the hundreds of islands dotted along the Sumatran coast.

In my moribund state, I had failed to notice the dark-ening skies and the freshening wind even when it started whipping the sails and flapping the hatches. A second later the boat started pitching and rolling madly in a broiling sea. Wagga suddenly shot off from below my feet and I heard a massive roar coming from the port side. Hunched over the helm, I wearily turned my head to the left. And there, about 500 metres astern, was a vertical wall of grey water bearing down on me. To my dull eyes, it looked as high as the Sydney Harbour Bridge.

At the same time, gale force winds hit the mast like a ten-ton truck hitting a telephone pole. The mainsail soon lay ripping and rattling at a dangerous forty-five degree angle to the steep, white-tipped waves. The tall black mast threatened to dip in the boiling water as the port side hull rolled over dangerously to starboard and my world seemed to turn upside down.

The only reason I wasn't jolted overboard was simply because, when the cyclone hit, I was hugging the wheel desperately like a long-lost love, my hands clasped tightly around it to stop them shaking. I had had no time to shorten the sails, close the hatches or secure the loose items that can clutter up the decks. For Christ's sake, I wasn't even wearing my safety harness or life jacket. It's a bloody miracle I wasn't immediately killed.

Almost as quickly as *The Scoop* had gone into its seeming death roll, the boat suddenly shuddered and righted itself. The brush with death must have galvanised my survival instincts because I frantically stabbed on the winch button to shorten the mainsail and, after a few moments of violent rocking and rolling, *The Scoop* began running north-easterly on a broad reach. I pressed another button with a shaking finger and the electric diesel engine powered up. The boat seemed to leap forward, the wave of water still following behind us, ready to pounce.

I had neither the inclination nor the energy to point *The Scoop* into the wind and establish some sort of control. It would have taken superhuman effort for a sustained amount of time. So I hoped merely to use the boat's sail and engine power to keep ahead of the weather. I was vaguely aware that we were being pushed and prodded in a north-easterly direction. Dimly,

I thought, that's where the land was. Weren't there some islands in the way? Reefs probably. Could be dangerous. But I was happy to go with the flow now that the boat was relatively stable and I was no longer being used as a punching bag by the elements. The state-of-the-art autopilot would keep us on reasonable track, I hoped.

My ordeal was far from over, however. I could now see the sky, a dirty grey and ivory smear, low-slung cirrus clouds scudding across it. *The Scoop*'s bucking bow crashed through giant Toblerone-shaped waves. White-slashed gouts of sea boiled over the decks; the wind whipped the rigging, cracking and fizzing like Chinese fireworks. The cockpit had a self-draining deck but the sea still foamed around my feet.

The Scoop negotiated the high peaks and troughs of the manic sea, as surefooted as a mountain goat. Not for the first time, I was grateful for my choice of boat. I don't know how long I hunched there, wet through, welded to the sleek metal wheel, shit scared and exhausted. Then suddenly the engine and all the electrics fizzled out.

Fuck, no power! That meant the autopilot, the SatNav and other vital instruments were gone; I wouldn't even be able to furl the sails automatically. God knows where we'll end up now, I thought. The stalking storm caught up to us and the wind and rain quickly resumed their onslaught. The noise was incredible. It was like being next to a 747 taxiing for take-off. Six-metre waves crashed and cascaded over us. My eyes were red and stinging from the salt water. It was hard to breathe. All around, there was commotion – shrieking, banging, clanging and crashing. It was as if someone had thrown a stun grenade into the cockpit. Meanwhile *The Scoop* was being swept helplessly along the churning ocean like a paper cup on a windswept lake and the sixty-knot wind was like a giant hand splayed on my back.

Later, probably several hours later – because it was now as dark as a dungeon – I stopped functioning altogether. My body, battered by the elements and aching from wrestling the wheel in the violent seas, was shutting down; my brain, overloaded by the need to make instant decisions and anxiety about the perilous circumstances, was about to blow a fuse. I simply could not take any more.

In the wet, howling darkness, I lashed the wheel with aching fingers, winched down the remaining sail and dragged my sorry arse down through the two timber-framed doors that connected the cockpit to the saloon and resignedly closed them behind me against the tumult outside. Let the elements fight it out, I thought.

It was a shock to suddenly find myself no longer assailed by the banshee wind and shrapnel rain. The terrible cacophony dulled to a low roar. I had to brace myself as I walked down a step to the galley, picking my way gingerly in the darkness through broken plates and scattered cutlery lying in about three centimetres of scummy water; the pitching and tossing movement was just as pronounced in the comfortable confines of the plush saloon. My face was scratchy, my stubble crusted in salt. I was thirsty from inhaling salt water but too tired to do anything about it. I wearily took off my soaked clothes, grabbed some leather cushions and wedged them into the narrow space on the galley floor. If a higher power wanted me to die, then so be it. I was done. Finished. I lay down on my makeshift bed and was instantly asleep.

I dreamt I was back in Sans Souci. Cody, me and a few of the lads were out in Kogarah Bay on Hobies. It was a lovely day. We were scooting around like dragonflies on a garden pond. It was idyllic, the hot, hard sun glinting off the calm water. But, suddenly I saw a massive wave, as big as a mountain, looming menacingly over us. It was eerie, there was no sound and everything seemed to be in slow motion. I saw someone on the beach waving and shouting a warning through a cupped hand but I couldn't hear the words. It looked like Percy in red Speedos.

The towering wave broke and we were deluged, the Hobies swamped, shattered, the lads flung like rag dolls under its murderous assault. Eventually, I surfaced, gasping, choking. Bobbing up and down in the aftermath swell, I saw that the rest of the boys had made it to the beach. The Hobies were lying broken, poking up in the sand like driftwood. Then a second wave broke over my head and I was dragged down.

The last thing I saw before I went under was Cody. He was standing at the water's edge looking at me, one hand on his hip, the other shielding his eyes from the sun. Then he turned around and walked away.

15

THE KIWIS were spot-on, Annie decided. Nine Island was perfect. After the heavy squall they had endured earlier, she felt almost heady with relief as they approached the small, uninhabited island. It was jammed between two headlands in a massive cleft in the north-east Sumatran coastline. The quiet, sheltered west side of the island faced away from the throbbing traffic of the Malacca Strait and fronted the wide, sweeping bay and the mainland. Two narrow channels, one north and one south of the island, allowed access to a massive bay called Teluk Aru. Standing at the bow of the *Lady Vesper* with binoculars, Annie could see a number of other, smaller islands in the bay area and an oil terminal on the southern headland.

Gary navigated the *Lady Vesper* around the island's coastline searching for a suitable anchorage. They found it on the northwest corner. A nice beach fringed by tall Sumatran pine trees, with clear green water lapping the white sand. They dropped anchor about forty metres out and the two women swam to the shore to explore while the men put the boat to rights.

Later, sitting in the saloon over a quartet of gin and tonics, the collective relief was palpable. 'Oh my God, I don't ever want to go through that again,' Dani said in a small voice. 'I thought I was going to, like, die. You told me it was going to be a nice, easy passage,' she said to Gary.

He shrugged. 'Shit, darlin', that was nothing. A few more hours from here and we'll be out of the main strait. It should be plain sailing from then on.'

They all clinked glasses. 'Here's to plain sailing,' said Martin, chugging down his drink.

None of them had any energy. They sat in air-conditioned comfort for a few more hours, talking and drinking. Dani put on a Bruno Mars CD that helped lighten the atmosphere. Apart from some nibbles, they hadn't eaten and Annie started to feel a little tipsy as Martin kept filling everyone's glasses from a seemingly bottomless bottle. Even Gary started to seem a little drunk.

The conversation grew increasingly raunchy. It started with a competitive discussion between the two men about whether American or British film stars were the sexiest; it then got sidetracked into a general, rather drunken debate about whether supermarkets selling sex toys meant the end of civilisation. Annie was unsettled by the sight of Martin and Dani almost draped over each other on the leather-covered bench seat.

Suddenly and rather unsteadily, Dani stood up and pulled Martin's arm. 'Come 'n' dance with me. I feel like partyin',' she slurred. They wrapped their arms around each other and started moving clumsily around the tight deck space. After a moment, Gary looked over at Annie and said, in a fake upper-crust British accent, 'Please may I have the pleasure of this dance, madam?'

Although a bit reluctant, Annie replied: 'Thank you kind sir.' And they began to dance slowly, awkwardly, she trying to keep a little distance between them while he tried to press his muscular body against hers. Shortly after, Martin, by now completely shitfaced, suggested they play cards. 'Poker,' he declared. 'Strip poker!'

Annie decided it was time for her to go to bed.

The next day dawned warm and bright, a slight breeze ruffling the stern ensign. The sea looked inviting. Annie was up and about early. She felt fine but the other three looked queasy and a little sheepish. None of them would meet her eye. I do *not* want to know what happened after I went to bed, she thought.

It was Dani who suggested having Buck's Fizz to complement the large breakfast Annie had prepared. 'We need the hair of the dog,' she declared. As Annie started to protest that it was not such a good idea, Martin interrupted with enthusiasm, 'Good thinking! That'll perk us up nicely.'

Martin carried on drinking throughout the morning while Dani prepared lunch and Gary and Annie went snorkelling. For a change, they had a picnic on the foredeck. Dani had laid a large tablecloth down on the open, lounging platform and they lay on their sides like Roman senators, eating, drinking and chatting.

'Now this is the life,' Martin said, slurring slightly. 'We survived the worst. It's going to get better from here on in. A lot better.'

Dani raised her glass and said 'Hear, hear'. She was topless and she spilled some Prosecco over her naked breasts.

'Oooh, I'm all wet!' She laughed suggestively.

'Said the actress to the bishop.' Martin guffawed at his own joke.

The conversation then deteriorated as it had the previous evening. This time Annie felt revolted. She got to her feet and took charge of the clearing up. When she returned to the foredeck, the others were sunbathing on mats and Martin was massaging oil on Dani's already tanned back. When the younger woman turned over, Annie could see from her small, gleaming breasts that Martin had already taken good care of her front side.

The bastard! So when Gary offered her another glass of bubbles, against her better judgement, she accepted. Then he challenged her to take her bikini top off. 'Hey, it's hot and we're all friends here.'

Martin weighed in: 'Yeah, don't be a spoilsport, love. Get yer tits out for the lads,' he said in a coarse cockney accent.

Annie considered for a moment. She wasn't a prude by any means. She'd never had any problems sunbathing topless in southern Europe. Plus a nasty little voice in her head said: 'And you've got a better body than she has!'

So she took her top off to the cheers of the others and lay back on the mat with a deep sigh. She declined Gary's offer to rub sun cream on her and soon she drifted off, sluggish from the warm sunlight, the wine and the gentle rhythm of the boat.

Annie woke up to a nightmare. She felt disoriented, mouth dry, head throbbing. Too much fizzy wine at lunchtime. Where am I? Oh, the boat. I was sunbathing on the foredeck. Must have dozed off. The sun, high in the sky, was strong;

harsh white light stabbed her eyelids. She couldn't fully open them. Something was tapping her cheek. Cold and wet and hard. What the hell? She managed to half open one eye and squinted against the sun. A dark figure was swaying above her. Then, out of the corner of one eye, she flashed on a shocking, surreal image: Dani leaning over Martin and giving him a blow job. Annie shook her head. I must still be dreaming, she thought. She propped herself on one elbow and immediately saw what had been patting her cheek. A cold bottle of beer, the outside bubbled with condensation. Thick fingers were wrapped around the neck. And the fingers were attached to a half-naked, leering Gary who loomed darkly over her, blocking out the sun, tongue protruding from wet lips, his eyes dancing.

'What the bloody hell is going on?' she said angrily and swatted the bottle away before sitting up, her arm still shielding her face from the sun. She looked across at Martin again. He was lying on a sun mat, eyes tightly closed, as Dani knelt on a towel beside him.

Gary laughed obscenely. He was obviously drunk. 'He looks like he's died and gone to heaven, doesn't he? And now, lady, it's my turn. Fair's fair. Martin said you would be okay with it.'

Annie stood up with some difficulty. She felt dizzy, nauseous. Her headache was hammering her skull. She realised she was still topless. Gathering what dignity she could muster, she covered her naked breasts with a towel. 'This is totally screwed up!' she said and then stormed down the steps to the lower deck. She steamed through the saloon and locked herself in the main cabin's bathroom. She sat on the closed toilet seat, head in her hands, elbows on her thighs.

How could I be so bloody stupid, she thought. I should have seen this coming a mile off!

Moments later, she was stunned to hear what sounded like gunfire, then loud grunts and shouts and the *thud-thud* of people running on the deck above her. There were more shots and then, finally, a long horrible scream.

16

I WOKE up with a headache and Wagga sitting on my face. His scratchy tongue was rasping my cheek. You're still alive, then, I told myself . . . a bloody miracle after that incredible shitstorm. The air was hot and thick. I was bollock naked, my sweaty skin stuck to a leather cushion. It made a farting noise as I sat up, startling Wagga. He jumped off and looked at me reproachfully. I looked down at my body; I felt curiously detached from it, as if I was looking down on myself from a great height. I was still intact, a few cuts and bruises but nothing serious. I felt dehydrated, my tongue thick in my mouth along with the throbbing in my head; I needed to drink something.

It was light. All seemed calm. It was the lull *after* the storm. The boat was no longer pitching and tossing like a drunken sailor. The cyclonic jet roar of wind and water the previous day had died to a gentle slip-slap of water against *The Scoop*'s hull. It felt comforting.

I checked the time: 7.37 am. I must have slept for ten hours or so. Yawning, I bent over to switch on the kettle. In the

74

absence of some coke (yes, the craving was still there) I was dying for a cup of java; it was funny to think Java itself was just down the road a bit. Nothing happened. Then I remembered the power had gone. Fuck. Shit. I got a can of Coke instead (*not the real thing*, I thought wryly). It was warm; the fridge was also caput. When I stepped up into the saloon, I felt like a man emerging, blinking through a prison door to freedom. I was stunned to see land in the far distance through the big tinted windows, despite them being splattered by dried droplets and bits of debris. The sea was a glacial green with just a soft swell.

Still naked, I tiptoed across the debris-strewn floor that still carried traces of water. I thrust open the glazed door and stepped out into the open. I grabbed a pair of binoculars from one of the storage lockers and trained them over the starboard bow toward the shoreline. About five kilometres away, I reckoned. Looked like an island. Patches of white sand, greenery, a small mountain (more of a large hillock really) poking above tall trees.

Looks promising, I thought. Just then, I detected a tickling around my bare ankles and a squeaking noise; it was Wagga come to tell me he was hungry. I felt a rush of pleasure that the wee fella had also survived. I picked him up and held the little ball of warm fur to my cheek as he started purring. 'Okay, mate, let's go and get some brekkie.'

Some dried kibble and water for the cat, bread, tinned sardines and OJ for myself. I was unusually hungry. In recent days I hadn't eaten much, due to a mix of nausea and apathy. The bread was a bit stale but I opened another can of sardines, gave Wagga a taste and wolfed down the rest.

My headache had subsided and I actually felt a sense of mild euphoria that I had survived my violent date with the storm (I found out later that it was the tail end of Cyclone Patricia). The whole horrible thing was a bit of a blur. I mainly remembered hugging that helm for dear life, my hands seemingly superglued together. When I was about six or seven years old, my father had taken me on a ghost train at a visiting carnival. The whole terrifying experience had remained vivid in my memory: the inky dark, the rollercoaster ride, spidery things brushing against my skin, spooky moans and groans, the screams of the terrified kids and unknown terrors lurking in the gloom. Yesterday was like déjà vu all over again, albeit with a different soundtrack. I sighed. Thank God it was over. I didn't want to go through anything like that again.

Wagga sat at my feet, eyes shut, contentedly licking his paws. I scratched one of his stripy ears and he looked up at me adoringly. At least I've got one friend, I thought. I began to tick off the priorities in my head: first, put some clothes on; second, see if you can sort the power; third, clean up the boat; fourth, try to find out where the hell we are. Oh, and fifth, check out the island, if that's what it is.

I accessed the engine room through a hatch in the saloon floor. In the torchlight, it looked startlingly clean, apart from the thin layer of water on the floor. Everything was tightly fitted into a relatively small space: the diesel engine, generator, batteries, fuel and water tanks, bilge pumps and an array of filters, valves and hosepipes. Plus a rather complicated-looking touchpad control panel.

I scratched my head. Frankly, I didn't know where the hell to start. Apart from the lingering mix of rain and seawater on the floor, there was nothing obviously wrong. I had always been hopeless at DIY and happily described myself as 'technologically dyslexic'. My approach to any technical or mechanical problem was to hit the broken device with a hammer or another blunt instrument and hope for the best. So, I thought, let's just wait until everything dries out, and maybe the electrics and computer systems will fire up again. I went back upstairs. It was time to get *The Scoop* looking shipshape again.

The deck wash pump was also buggered so I had to fill buckets of salt water from the bow pulpit and sluice them over the foredeck and cockpit areas. I actually quite enjoyed the hard labour. Afterwards I upturned a couple of buckets over my battered body. Then I sorted all the loose items remaining on deck and the bits of flotsam and jetsam below, some of it salvageable. I figured that later I would make an inventory of everything that had been lost during the storm but for now I was eager to get an idea of where we had washed up.

First, I had another long look at the land ahead. The brilliant, sun-sharpened tropical palette of colours came into focus: vibrant greens and blues and whites crystallising into clear objects, such as vegetation, sea, sky and clouds.

Feeling more human than I had in days, I had another tepid soft drink before digging out some charts and laying them on the teak cockpit table. A pleasant breeze ruffled the edges of the charts. Leaning over, my finger traced the route I'd taken from Jakarta up and then through the Sunda Strait and westward into the great ocean. I tried to remember how many hours we'd sailed before the edge of the cyclone hit and changed our direction. There was no land immediately west or north of that position. I knew we had been nudged (more like ramrodded) onto a north-east track. My finger slid in that direction.

It arrived at an archipelago off the west coast of Sumatra called the Mentawai Islands. This must be it, I reckoned.

I had heard that the Mentawai archipelago was a popular surfing destination but so far I had seen no sign of life, not even one of the ubiquitous fishing smacks. But, come to think of it, the surf season was probably over. Only the die-hards or the death-wishers stayed on to brave the north-east monsoon. The other possibility was that the storm had pushed me even further north; certainly, the surge and the wind had been strong enough. There was another archipelago hundreds of kilometres further up the north-west Sumatran coast, centred on Nias Island. Lots of smaller islands abounded too, including the Batu chain and the Hinako Islands. Indonesia had thousands of bloody islands and half of them weren't even named and even fewer still were inhabited.

I looked at Wagga, who was now sitting squarely on the chart. 'Well mate, where the bloody hell are we?'

17

BANGBANG STOOD in the main cockpit of the *Lady Vesper*, smoking a foul cigarette and mulling over the assault. He spat overboard. Neither of the two white dogs had put up much of a fight. Nor had their whores. There wasn't a huge amount of valuables on board – a bit of cash, a couple of laptops, a few decent baubles, including a large diamond ring. And, of course, they had stripped the boat of electronics and other sellable items. But the real prize was the white pussy. BangBang smiled. The women were not to his taste – too old, too *big* – but the men were happy with their new playthings. That was all that mattered.

Earlier, he could not believe his luck when Mamat had handed him the binoculars and he had seen the catamaran about a kilometre ahead, the two women lying half-naked on the deck. Grabbing them had been a breeze. He knew that if he let the crew have their way, they would start on the women right there and now. But that would be too dangerous. They were in an exposed position. Vessels were passing on either side of the island on their way to and from the bay. No, better to go to our island hideaway, he decided. There the men can have a couple of days R&R. Rape and relaxation, he thought with a smile. He would enjoy listening to their pleasure while he made plans for the next job.

When they pulled it off successfully – and he would person-ally make fucking sure they did – he hoped his bosses would hold back from having him maimed or killed for the previous fuck-up. They might even reward me with a much bigger project, he mused, one that will use my particular talents to the full. It would also add a healthy chunk to my stash. BangBang knew that money, and lots of it, was the key to seizing control of his future career. That lay back in Jakarta, he had already decided. A shrewd, ruthless operator like me with enough money and the right connections can carve out a major slice of the drugs and prostitution industries. All it takes is balls plus the capacity to maim or kill anyone who gets in my way. No problem with that! He grinned with pleasure.

Lighting another Gudang Garam, his thoughts returned to the present: so, what shall I do with the women afterwards? Sell them? Perhaps the younger one. The older is pretty for an *ang mo*, a westerner, but too old for the sex trade. No, better just to get rid of them, too much fucking trouble if one of the patrols finds them on board. I wouldn't be able to bribe my way out of that one, he thought wryly. Fuck it, it will be easier to kill the round-eyed sluts once the men have finished with them.

He flipped his cigarette overboard and told a couple of crew members to take the *Lady Vesper* further out and scuttle it before any other curious vessels turned up. With any luck the authorities would just assume the stupid tourists had sunk in a storm.

18

THE ANCHOR splashed down into the sea like a space cone returning to earth. About twenty-five metres of chain clanked down after it before the steel plough embedded itself on the ocean floor. The electric anchor winch was out of action, so I had to manipulate the big thirty-seven kilogram anchor by hand, cutting my pinkie in the process.

It was even harder to get the small tender down into the water but at last it was done and I got ready to start the Yamaha fifteen-horsepower motor. Cody and I had last used the rubber dinghy at the Hammo marina. I knew he would have left it in good order, cleaned and fuelled. Nevertheless, I crossed my fingers that it would go all right. Pressing the little red ignition button, the Yamaha coughed discreetly a couple of times but failed to fire. I tried again and it started with a mini roar and a puff of smoke. Hallelujah! I felt excited, energised for the first time since Cody left. The realisation hit me that I had not once thought about Charlie since waking up.

Taking a final squiz at *The Scoop* to make sure it wasn't drifting, I fastened my lifejacket and pointed the dinghy at the smallish island about a kilometre to the south-east. Its dominant feature was the mini mountain I had seen earlier that rose up rather apologetically in the central part of the landmass. The peak looked about four hundred metres high and its west face was stubbled with green and brown vegetation.

The sea was clear and clean, the swell slapping against the narrow V-shaped bow, a slight wind misting my face and chest with a fine, salty spray off the wave tops. I could see large birds that looked like sea eagles circling the trees and swooping down to the surface of the jade sea.

As I drew closer, I could see mangrove swamps dead ahead; it looked unappealing so I decided to go round the south tip of the island and see if there were any better anchorage prospects on the east coast. There the sea was even calmer. Initially the shoreline was speckled with small sandy coves, more swamp and a few rocky outcrops. Tall cliffs of volcanic rock stretched down to shallow fringing reefs. Still no sign of human habitation. I was slightly apprehensive on this score: there were, I had read, still people in this part of the world who combined a Stone Age lifestyle with a warlike antipathy to visitors. I'd really like to avoid ending up in a cannibal's cooking pot, I thought with a wry smile.

Then, about a kilometre further on, I came across quite a large bay framed by two high headlands at the south and north ends. There was a small barrier reef protecting the shore. The whole vista looked almost Disney-like with an even crescent shape, white sand and palm trees swaying in the light breeze.

With the outboard motor on idle, the dinghy bobbing in a gentle swell, I stopped to weigh it up: on the one hand, this looked the perfect spot for me to spend a few days rest.

However, on the other hand, the reef would make it impossible to take *The Scoop* in close to shore. Reluctantly, I pointed the dinghy north again. A few minutes later, rounding the bay's northern headland, I thought I spotted a gap in the rocky cliffs.

Edging towards it, on low throttle, I thought at first it was just a large cave entrance but the closer I got, the more I realised that the sea had carved out a wider gap over the centuries. Vegetation on both sides helped obscure the narrow, curving passage and I carefully manoeuvred the dinghy through it for about another thirty metres until I reached a vertical wall of jagged rock that jutted out from the left side of the cliff-face. On the right of it, there was a narrow channel of water leading to what, I could not see. I doglegged around it and the channel suddenly widened out, revealing an extraordinary sight. I gasped.

Fuck.

Me.

Gently.

I could not believe my tired eyes.

By the time I got back to *The Scoop* in the early afternoon, it was hot and humid again. A sudden torrential downpour courtesy of the monsoon did nothing to help. My tank top was wet through and my clammy skin glistened from a mix of sweat and rain. But my spirits weren't dampened; I was still tingling with amazement and elation over what I'd found on the other side of the island. I tied the little dinghy to the stern of the sloop and sat down in the shelter of the saloon to think things through. How do I steer *The Scoop* round the mystery island without power or electronics? The answer was obvious: tacking. When Cody and I used to sail in racing competitions, we often had to work our way around a slalom course in and out of multiple buoys. Our tacking skills were highly honed as a result. Once I got to that hidden entrance I would face another, bigger steering challenge but I would worry about that when I came to it.

I grunted as I hauled up the anchor, enjoying the manual labour again. Rigging the sail came naturally to me and I enjoyed the hands-on feel of the sheets and winches, despite the warm rain. It felt good to be out in the elements, doing something I'd always loved. Before long, *The Scoop* was zipping downwind, the sea a bit choppier now. The sloop's bow sliced through the puny waves and tiny, glistening spumes of water frothed over the bows like loose diamonds.

The rain started to slacken but the breeze had freshened from the north-east. We began to run downwind; then I eased out the mainsail to effect a broad reach before steering at right angles to the wind on a port tack. That allowed us to skate around the southern tip of the island; then a close reach took us into the wind and north up the east coastline. The long, lazy zigzagging as I veered from port to starboard tack and back was invigorating.

Soon I could see the edge of the large pristine bay I'd noticed on my earlier recce. It still looked inviting, but the waves breaking over the reef showed again that *The Scoop* would not clear it. Besides, I'd found a better option. Although there was a different problem with this one – the dogleg. Easy enough for the tender to negotiate, it would be a whole different story for the fifty-two foot sloop.

Sure enough, it was not long before the partially concealed

entrance came into view. But by then it was late afternoon; dusk would not be far behind ... too late to get the sloop through the narrow channel that day. It was disappointing but better to hunker down for the night and be fresh for the challenge tomorrow. To the right of the northern headland there was a long rocky curve of shoreline that would provide sheltered anchorage for the night.

Wagga and I settled down to spend the evening in candlelight. In other circumstances it might have been a romantic setting, the sloop gently swaying in the slight ocean swell, a warm breeze wafting through the saloon from the stern and the occasional tinny protest from the anchor chain as the current gently moved the boat one way and then another. But I was starting to feel like shit again. The craving had come back. My earlier adrenaline had given way to angst and, feeling tight and brittle, I went to bed.

Lying in the dark, I felt loneliness snuggle in beside me and take me in her arms. It made me think of Frieda. As a young reporter on the *Sunday World*, I'd had a brief affair with an older woman who worked nights in our cuttings library.

Frieda was forty-one and divorced. She looked severe in her high-necked blouses, scraped-back hair and tailored skirts. Large-framed, tortoiseshell glasses hung down her chest on a gold chain. Some reporters were a bit scared of her but I came to see that she was just reserved, a little insecure and very lonely. Just like me, when I come to think about it. Despite the age difference, I was attracted to her and one night asked her to go for a drink after work.

Our date started awkwardly, both of us aware of the sexual undertones but lacking the confidence to move things forward speedily. Nevertheless, after a bottle of pinot noir and a few clumsy overtures, we eventually managed to navigate the necessary niceties. In bed, Frieda was a different animal. Her inhibitions came loose along with her long, auburn hair. Everything about her seemed to soften: the sharp planes of her face, her skin, her surprising curves, even the stern demeanour. Our shared shyness slowly melted away and she became assured when telling me her needs. I remember her mouth pursing into a tight wrinkle when she climaxed, eyes closed tightly, her curved eyebrows arching as if in surprise.

Nowadays it would probably be labelled 'friends with benefits'. Every once in a while, Frieda and I hooked up, had sex and assuaged our lust and loneliness. It wasn't love, it was just lust made tender by mutual affection. We both knew that, for different reasons, it wasn't going to become any more than that. She once said to me: 'Loneliness is when, if you died in the night, no one would really know or care.'

Maybe it was paranoia, but that night, as I lay there alone on *The Scoop*, I doubted if anyone would care if *I* died.

I dreamt of sex: soft, hazy images of Frieda. I woke up with another headache and a hard-on. Both were unwelcome. It had been a sweaty, exhausting slumber. I squinted out of the tinted stateroom window from my damp, rumpled bed. The sky was overcast and the hazy horizon was the colour of cigarette ash. As the sloop turned lazily on its mooring, the panorama changed and I was now looking at the dark and forbidding rockface. The vibrancy of the previous day had vanished and I felt a shiver despite the humidity.

Getting out of bed was a struggle. I felt as if I had the flu. But then I remembered what a treat was in store that day and my spirits began to lift. Wagga appeared from nowhere and jumped on the bed. He immediately started attacking a corner of the pillowslip. I felt a sudden pang of affection for the little guy – *he* would care if I died. I picked him up. 'Come on, mate, let's eat.'

Over a cold croissant that had already thawed out from the dead freezer, I thought about how I could get *The Scoop* safely through the narrow passage between the two headlands without power, particularly at the dogleg where it choked into an even tighter squeeze. Then I had an idea: the tender had an engine ... could I use that to navigate my way through? It would take some careful planning and execution, I thought. But it could be done. Not for the first time, I wished Cody were still with me. He'd know exactly how to handle it.

By late morning the early wind had subsided and the swell had reduced sufficiently to have a go. I was excited but apprehensive. Carpe diem, as my old Jesuit tormentors at St Jude's used to say – seize the day. Going downwind a couple of hundred metres, I dropped anchor as close as possible to the cleft in the cliffs. I dangled fenders from the guardrails on either side to protect the boat from the rocky cliff walls and then lashed the wheel in place to keep the rudder straight. Finally, I untied the rope tethering the tender to a stern cleat and walked it around the starboard side to the bow and retied it to the stanchion. The dinghy bobbed and weaved slightly on a generous line.

Now comes the tricky part, I thought nervously. Taking three deep breaths (Percy used to tell me to do that whenever I got upset at the subs rewriting my copy), I pulled up the anchor as fast as possible. Next I tightened the tether to the dinghy until it was bobbing just underneath the bow. I then had to climb over the bow pulpit and drop down into the little boat.

Despite my quick actions, the sloop had already started to drift a bit by the time I started the tender's motor. I quickly engaged it and pushed forward slowly, carefully tightening the line to the bigger vessel. There was a tug and the dinghy stopped dead as the line tautened, the heavier boat acting like a dead man's brake on a train; I increased the throttle slowly and steadily and, after a moment, we began to move forward, the little tender bravely pulling the sloop's twenty-one tonnes like a muscle man towing a truck with his teeth. I knew it was vital to keep the rope taut between the two vessels. The slight drift meant that the entrance was no longer dead ahead and I had to steer in a wide arc to line us up again before heading straight into the narrow channel. The rubber dinghy sat up proudly in the water as *The Scoop* twisted and resisted, dragging its heels as if mortified by the indignity of it all.

The Berenger was close to five metres in the beam, spacious and handsome for living purposes but a pain in the butt to pilot through a tight space. I watched as the dogleg came towards us. The huge out-hanging shard of rock had helped make the entrance even more difficult to spot from the ocean side because it prevented a clear view of what lay beyond. But it only left less than a metre either side of *The Scoop* as we eased through and my lovely boat suffered a series of heavy bangs, bumps and grinds along the way, despite the fenders. Fingers

88

crossed nothing's seriously damaged, I thought. Finally, as we curved around the dogleg, I got my second sight of the spectacular vista from the day before. And again, the breath stalled in my throat.

All morning I had been worried that I might have exaggerated the beauty of the scene in my head. Those doubts now disappeared. There in front of me lay a small, beautifully formed horseshoe-shaped lagoon about the size of a football pitch.

It was framed by red–grey cliffs – high on the left, lower on the right – banking away like the tiered seats at a Roman amphitheatre. A dense fringe of swaying trees bordered the white, sandy beach. Suddenly the sun came out and the clear water rippled towards me, glinting and sparkling in the fresh light. A large rock, shaped like a miniature version of the island's feature mountain, rose from the centre of the lagoon. A baby biosphere, I thought.

Yet, I dared not stop or slow down in case the heavier sloop tailgated the dinghy. So I kept the line taut and we performed a majestic half-circle curve from port side to starboard, slowing gradually on the final arc of the turn. The stern of *The Scoop* was left pointing at the shore, about thirty metres out. Both vessels came to a gentle halt without colliding; there didn't seem to be any current and the boats bobbed together on the surface, like two synchronised swimmers maintaining their choreographed distance.

During the previous day's recce, I had discovered that the beach shelved quickly and deeply into the sea; that meant the sloop's 2.2 metre draft could be accommodated comfortably. I dropped the forward anchor manually and let plenty of chain out before attaching a heavy line to the port stern stanchion and swam to the shore with the other end tied around my waist. I tied it securely to one of the trees then repeated the exercise with a line from the starboard stanchion. Next I adjusted the bow anchor so that *The Scoop* was moored firmly about eight metres from the beach. Finally, just to be sure, I donned a mask and swam underneath the sloop, double-checking that the big, cast-iron fin and bulbous six tonne lead keel were well clear of the sandy bottom in the shallows.

Then, tired but elated, I flopped down on the beach with my legs and arms spread out and closed my eyes. I had done it! The thought made my body wriggle with pleasure in the warm white sand. Somehow, it felt as if I had come home.

PART TWO

*Between two worlds life hovers like a star, twixt night
and morn, upon the horizon's verge.*
Lord Byron

19

THE HOLD in the pirate ship was as dark and fetid as a medieval dungeon. The hot stink of diesel clashed with the stink of fish scales to create a thick fug that Annie could almost taste. The ceaseless clatter of the engine made her head spin. The old boat rolled and pitched against buffeting waves. She felt drained and disoriented. She wanted to throw up.

Her brain was like a pinball machine with thoughts crashing around, colliding, smashing in different directions. Fast, furious, frantic. What had just happened? Where was she? She was dimly aware of Dani squatting near her in the darkness, shaking violently, her breathing a mix of gasps and sobs, the air whistling through her chattering teeth. But where was Martin? And that bastard Gary? Were they up top? Were they hurt? Who were these people who had plucked them from the boat? What's going to happen to us? She had a horrible flashback of her husband and Dani entwined on the deck.

Gradually, her tumbling thoughts became more ordered. Okay, we are in some sort of floating fleapit; we seem to be alone down here; the bastards who attacked us must be all up top; obviously these vile men are pirates, and we are in great danger. My wrists are tied. I'm semi-naked. Shit. Basically, we've been captured, abducted, kidnapped probably. Hostages? Her mind started to race again: were they to be ransomed? Would they hurt her? *Rape* her? Sell her into sexual slavery? Who would even know where she was? Her parents in the UK were vaguely aware that she was off sailing somewhere in Asia, but they didn't know the details. She had just told people in her office she was heading to Langkawi. Absolutely nobody would be looking for her for a while. Panic started to take hold of her again.

Jesus Christ, get a fricking grip! Annie told herself fiercely. She looked around in the dim light: there was a bucket sitting next to her, sliding back and forward slowly with the boat's rocking motion. God, from the smell, that must be the toilet.

Her mind went back to the other toilet – what was it, just an hour ago? Two hours ago? Bloody hell, is that all? She couldn't tell for sure, her Cartier Tank watch – a thirtieth birthday present from Martin – had been ripped off her wrist earlier, along with her wedding and engagement rings. She had been slumped on the toilet reliving the horrible scenes on the deck: Martin and Dani having sex, and then Gary's proposition. Then she had heard the strange sounds from above. The next thing she knew there was a huge bang on the toilet door, followed by the tip of a machete bursting through the middle of the thin wood. She jumped up in great alarm, screaming in terror while instinctively clutching her towel to her bare breasts.

The blade of the parang had struck again and the door splintered. A brown hand reached through and undid the catch.

The door swung inward and there stood a sinewy, Asian man dressed in stained shorts, singlet and a red bandana. He bared yellow and black teeth at Annie as she reared back against the toilet wall, her face convulsed in terror. The man reached in and grabbed her arms, pulling her through the ruined doorway and dragging her into the saloon. There stood a squat, barrel-chested man with a pitted face. He looked her over, his yellowed eyes like a serpent's. He was wearing dark cargo pants, garish Adidas trainers and a short-sleeved, maroon chequered shirt over a stained singlet. A greasy baseball cap that was too small for his huge head carried an incongruous New York Yankees emblem.

There were sounds of activity above. A number of men, Annie registered. She could see shadows and shapes in the sunlight through the windows.

Annie had blustered: 'Wh-wh-who are you? Wh-what are you doing here? Where's my husband?' It sounded so clichéd! It was as if she was someone else, floating above while watching the scene unfold below.

The stocky man had said nothing, but continued to appraise her. Annie shrunk from his intense gaze; his whole presence oozed a casual but intimidating malevolence. Then her captor smiled cruelly, a gold tooth glinting in the sunlight filtering through the saloon window. He gestured brusquely for the other man to bring Annie forward. She struggled and shouted, 'You bastards! Don't touch me.'

The man with the gold tooth reached forward and wrenched the towel away from her, watching as she tried to cover her breasts with her hands. His eyelids were peculiarly large and thick, she noticed; when he blinked, it was like curtains coming down on a Broadway performance. Then he slapped her face hard and said: 'Lady, you come with us' and put the towel over her head. The second man started hustling her forward again. She cried out as hot, rapid tears of terror began streaming down her face, soaking into the large striped beach towel.

'Martin?' she screamed. She screamed his name again. There was no reply.

Annie was vaguely aware of other sounds – shouting, laughter? Then she was outside, the change of light and temperature dimly permeating the thick towel. She slipped on something. Looking down, she saw glistening smears of blood on the teak deck. Moments later, she felt hands lifting her into a smaller boat, her feet half slipping on a rough, wet floor as she was forced to sit down. She noticed streaks of blood on her feet. A woman screamed. Dani, she thought dully. She could hardly breathe, gut-wrenching panic paralysing her body, her brain.

Shortly afterwards there were more loud words spoken in a foreign language, and she sensed others getting into the boat. They smelled of sweat and cigarettes and rancid cooking oil. They were talking excitedly. She felt hands on her body, pawing her naked breasts and thighs. Revolted, she shrugged them off violently to the mocking sound of more laughing. Trembling, Annie had never felt more afraid in her life.

20

I MAY be an avowed atheist but I swear to God that my initial exploration of the horseshoe lagoon came closer to making me a true believer than all the years of religious brainwashing I'd suffered at the hands of priests and nuns at St Jude's. The school's Rector, Father Benjamin Lafferty – AKA 'Big Ben' because, the legend said, he would often strike six, or twelve while caning naughty boys – had once pointed out to me that St Jude was the patron saint of lost causes. 'In your case, Jonathan,' he had once told me, 'the blessed Jude would have conceded defeat.'

The sand was pristine, without a single sign of human visitors. Behind the palm-fringed beach I discovered a dense, lush tropical rainforest, punctuated by small streams of water filtering down from the small mountain.

Hundreds of different species of birds, including gaily coloured parrots, swooped and capered in the high canopies of these timber giants. I could hear but not yet see monkeys, their excited chatter somehow comforting in this alien place.

I doubted there'd be orangutans but there could be gibbons and probably leaf monkeys, perhaps even a simpai Mentawai, a black and yellow species unique to the area. A glorious spicy, heavily seductive aroma that spoke of wet soil and rotting flowers rose up from the dark, pulpy undergrowth.

After the heat and stickiness of the rainforest, I was grateful for the refreshing embrace of my own private swimming pool. Masked and flippered, I swam to the rock in the middle of the lagoon. In the water I spotted grouper, trevalla, barracuda, stingrays, and a shoal of small wrasses; clinging to the rock were sea fans and sponges, sea cucumbers and large clams. A lugubrious-looking turtle swam by nonchalantly.

I must have floated around the rock for hours, excited but sated by the kaleidoscopic sights and sounds and smells that I'd experienced since arriving at the island just a few hours ago. It was like a secret Shangri La, cut off from the world. My feelings of energy and euphoria lasted until the sun went down in a stunning gold–red blaze of intensity. Back on the boat, I felt exhilarated by the afternoon's adventure and relieved to have found a safe haven. Alas, the euphoria didn't last. In the dark velvet embrace of night, my crippling paranoia returned. Dark thoughts intruded. What will become of me? Is the boat buggered? Will I ever get back to civilisation? What if I fall ill? Perhaps there are dangerous creatures out there: spiders, snakes, malaria-carrying mosquitoes. I went to bed early, fearful and fretting. I felt exhausted but couldn't relax, I was hungry but didn't feel like eating and I felt intensely angry but did not know why. Before long I was drowning in familiar saw-toothed waves of self-pity. Damn that blasted Charlie. He's a mind fucker.

★

My Jekyll and Hyde mood swings were gone by the next morning. Sitting at the polished teak table in the cockpit having a raw Pop-Tart for breakfast, I felt calm, almost serene. No headache, just a slight fuzziness. I'd slept for God-knows-how-many hours. The sun was already quite high in the sky and the placid lagoon looked so perfect it was as if it had been created by a Hollywood animation team. A sparkling jade green, the colour of sunlight washing through an old-fashioned medicine bottle, and the big charcoal grey stone casting a slight shadow on the unruffled water.

Wagga was basking on top of a seat, his eyes screwed up, licking his unmentionables. What he made of all of this I had no idea but he seemed happy enough. My own dark hysteria seemed to have faded and I dared believe that I might be beginning to heal. It had been about a week since I'd last had any dope. Looking around the lovely lagoon I thought: what better place to detox? The stillness and serenity was soothing, uplifting.

'The fact is, mate,' I said to Wagga, 'I can't go back to my old life. All those money problems, book demands and ... drugs. I can't cope with all that again.

'So, I'm thinking, why not just stay here? On this island? You and me. For a little while at least. Whaddya think?'

Wagga ignored me and continued licking his privates.

I reckoned I had enough food and water, between what I had on board and what the island could provide, to survive. I would not have to slum it like Robinson Crusoe. I even had my own little Cat Friday. Above all, my old false friend Charlie was, mercifully, conspicuous by his absence. Another benefit: no Twitter or Facebook or emails. Bliss!

Sure, I would be without human companionship but that didn't worry me. I had always been a bit of a loner. Having grown up an only child with an alcoholic mother and a semi-detached father, I was used to it. Anyway, I thought, in my present state of mind, having no one else around was a positive thing. Okay, I'd suffer a little discomfort if I could not get the power back up and running – no hot showers or cold air from the aircon, for example. But I could also live with that.

I can easily stay put here – for weeks, possibly even months, safe and snug in my secret refuge, I thought with growing excitement. And with a bit of luck I may even be able to start writing again. A new rush of euphoria suddenly kicked in. That's it! I'm bloody staying here, I decided. I stood up, arms in the air and shouted 'Rehab Island, you beauty!' The name just came to me. The noise startled Wagga, who sprang up and bolted into the saloon. I laughed my head off. I did not know it in that joyous moment but it would not be long before I was laughing on the other side of my face.

21

I DESPERATELY need to find out from Dani what happened to Martin and Gary, Annie thought as she sat and sweated in the hot gloom of the ship's hold. But first I need a pee. The fear and panic she had experienced had put a ton of pressure on her bladder. She stood up awkwardly, gingerly stretched one leg out and drew the bucket towards her with a bare foot. She used her bound hands to shimmy down one side of her bikini bottom, then the other, then carefully got her feet clear and squatted above the pail. Blessed relief, she thought, letting go. But then the boat lurched violently and she lost her balance, the bucket clanking over and spilling its contents over her feet and lower legs.

'Ah shit! Shit, shit, shit!' Annie stood up again, located her bikini bottom with her toes. It was wet. She used the towel as best she could to dry the fabric and then wiped her legs. Getting the small strip of cloth back up her legs was a real challenge thanks to the dim light and the bucking motion of the boat. But the last thing she wanted was to be fully naked when their abductors finally came for them.

Dani had gone quiet, her sobs and shuddering gasps reduced to a mild shaking and deep breathing. Annie moved very close to her until she could see her properly. The girl looked catatonic. Her eyes were staring straight ahead and she didn't register Annie's presence. Annie's mind flashed briefly on the scene of Dani pleasuring Martin on the foredeck of the *Lady Vesper*. Grimacing, she squatted down right in front of Dani, her face inches from the younger woman's. She gently shook her and whispered loudly to combat the engine noise: 'Dani, Dani, talk to me. Come on, you're okay. We'll be fine, I promise you. I need you to tell me what happened.'

Just as she was about to slap the younger woman in a bid to shock her into consciousness, suddenly the words, jumbled and confused, poured out of her like a torrent. The information was chilling. Bit by bit, Annie was able to piece the story together.

After she had stormed down below, the others heard the sudden roar of high-speed boats from behind them. Startled, the two men jumped up to look at what was happening. There was a rapid burst of gunfire. Dani had watched in horror as Martin clutched at a bright red wetness that had suddenly appeared on his naked torso. And then, a moment later, she saw a glint as a long, double-edged knife curved down on Gary. The attackers had then thrown both bodies overboard. 'It was all a bit of a blur. I had been drinking. They were so fast. I-I-I can't remember much,' Dani said, tears glinting in the darkness.

'Maybe they could have swum to the shore,' Annie said numbly. But Dani shook her head. 'I'm so sorry,' she whispered. 'But there is no way either Marty or Gary could have survived. It was too brutal . . .' At that point Dani broke down.

Annie was devastated. Her head dropped, tears came. Despite their recent unhappiness, she had been fond of her husband. 'Oh Martin,' she wailed out loud. He had not deserved such a terrible end. She silently said a prayer, asking God to have mercy on her husband's soul. Gary's too, she prayed.

Annie Spencer had had a conservative Christian upbringing as part of a solid, middle-class English family that worshipped together every Sunday at their local Anglican church in Stroud, Gloucestershire. Her faith had remained intact all this time, despite Martin's disinterest. A fragment from her favourite hymn that the Spencers had all sung together came to mind and she began to whisper the words:

I fear no foe, with Thee at hand to bless;
Ills have no weight, and tears no bitterness.
Where is death's sting? Where, grave, thy victory?
I triumph still, if Thou abide with me.

It seemed to help and gradually she pulled herself together. She looked around at the hold she and Dani were trapped in. Their situation appeared hopeless: they had no weapons, no clothes, no money to bribe the pirates with. And, thought Annie forlornly, no hope. Suddenly nauseous, she quickly righted the bucket with both hands and vomited into it like an erupting volcano until her throat hurt and there was nothing left but a corrosive fear in her stomach. Then, wiping her lips with a dry corner of the towel, she prayed again: 'Oh my dear Lord, what is to become of us?'

Focus, she told herself sternly. You can grieve later. Right now you and Dani are in deep shit. These guys – these pirates, for fuck's sake – are not pissing around. They have already demonstrated a ruthless savagery and a total disregard for the law. She thought back to a previous episode in her life – the only time she'd ever felt real fear. She'd been about thirteen or fourteen years old. She was taking her dog Paddy for a walk in the neighbourhood park. They came across a young, heavily tattooed man with a pit bull terrier. The pit bull was not on a lead and it ran over aggressively to confront Paddy.

Annie's little Jack Russell was as brave as a lion and squared up to the slavering brute. Soon they were snapping and snarling at each other before the larger dog gripped Paddy's skinny haunch in its powerful jaws. For a moment, everything went quiet. Annie was standing, horror struck, rooted to the spot as she saw Paddy's liquid brown eyes look up at her almost as if to say 'Sorry I didn't do better'.

Something snapped inside Annie. Nothing was going to hurt Paddy. Screaming something, she could never remember what, she took three quick steps forward and started whacking the pit bull's rump as hard as she could with Paddy's lead. The big dog loosened its grip on Paddy and snapped at Annie, its bared fangs wet with white-flecked saliva tinged pink with Paddy's blood.

The savage beast bit Annie twice before the young thug managed to drag his dog away. With tears of pain and relief running down her young face, Annie was taken to a nearby hospital for a combination of jabs and stitches to her right arm. Later, at the vet, Paddy endured a similar routine. He would live to fight another day. Annie was badly shaken, surprised but fiercely proud that she had somehow found the courage to face up to danger and rescue her dog. She decided that her natural instincts had simply overcome her normal reason and caution.

I need those same qualities to save myself now, she thought. Just then, the engine noise began to subside and the boat slowed. They must be about to arrive at their destination. Wherever that might be, Annie thought fearfully. She started to half-speak, half-hum the same hymn:

> *Shine through the gloom and point me to the skies.*
> *Heaven's morning breaks, and earth's vain shadows flee;*
> *In life, in death, O Lord, abide with me.*

She glanced over at Dani. The younger woman had returned to her catatonic state. Annie almost envied her. Closing her eyes, she braced herself for the terrible ordeal that she knew awaited.

A few minutes later, they came for her.

22

THE FIRST day of the rest of my new life started with an inventory of *The Scoop*'s provisions. The galley cupboards yielded a ton of usable stuff including a couple of big sacks of rice, containers of pasta, lots of tinned food (sardines, tomatoes, tuna, baked beans and soup), a few litres of cooking oil, a range of herbs, condiments and spices and a box containing packets of curry sauce. Of course, there was also tea and coffee. And plenty of water − the boat's twin tanks held more than seven hundred litres of fresh water. I'd only made a small inroad into that so far. In addition, there was an abundance of coconuts on shore. I didn't need to be Bear Grylls to survive in this place; with the fruits of the forest and the sea as well, I would not starve by any means. Wagga would not starve either − not many sardine or tuna tins left but there were plenty more fish in the sea, I thought cheerfully. Finally, there were a couple of cases of wine and beer, as well as soft drinks. They'd do for heydays and holidays.

I checked the storage lockers for supplies and found two dozen boxes of matches, some torches, lanterns, candles and umpteen batteries to add to my treasure trove. Happily, I also came upon a large cardboard box that held a pile of new books I'd bought in Hammo to read on the trip. The box was still sealed with brown tape. Under a hatchway in the cockpit deck I found what appeared to be about half a kilometre of fishing line. But my biggest find was a ream of bright, white copy paper. I guess I already knew it was there but hadn't really focused on it before. If I wanted to write, I had no excuses.

The only missing ingredient was music; the radio didn't work and I couldn't charge any of my three I's – pod, pad or phone. That sucked. But all in all, not a bad haul. I celebrated with a swim, followed by a splendid lunch of cold soup and sardines with sun-warmed baked beans. A warm beer chased it all down. I decided to have a nap before attempting what I knew was going to be an onerous and frustrating task – trying to get the generator going.

Later in the afternoon, down on my knees in the engine room, I swore several times. The instruction manual could have been written in Sanskrit for all I knew. Pity my old man's not here to translate, I thought, he'd know how to fix it. He was always tinkering with stuff in the shed. The irony is he can't fix the things that matter most – his marriage and his relationship with me. My dad doesn't much like boats – he gets seasick standing on a pier – but without a doubt he'd be able to get both the main engines and the generator working on *The Scoop*. I'd have settled for the latter. The genset provides the power for hot water, lights, the oven and all the other important electrical appliances and instruments.

Even the bloody toaster. But I just couldn't work out what was wrong.

'Fuck it,' I said to Wagga and went for another swim instead.

That set the pattern for my first few weeks on Rehab Island. I had everything I needed. There was no requirement to build a roof over my head, or scrabble for food or fashion clothes out of reeds or animal skins. I had no need to go anywhere, see anyone, do anything.

So I mostly chilled. I went to bed early – before 9 pm most nights – and woke with the sunrise around 6 am. I built a barbecue on the beach, up against the rocky base of the headland. I used flat stones as bricks and a grill from the galley oven. Pretty rudimentary, and it smoked a bit, but it worked well enough. I cooked fresh fish I caught in the lagoon. I'd paddle the kayak to the far corner where there was a little rocky overhang and where the fish seemed to shelter from the sun. Crabs and lobster were also plentiful. There was no shortage of wood for the barbie – the tropical pine trees growing up the side of the mountain had particularly flammable resin and provided excellent kindling – but I had to dry some of it out after the constant heavy showers.

Most days, I swam and snorkelled on the reef in the bay next door. I had only ever seen tropical fish in a small aquarium at the doctor's surgery years ago. They were small but cute as they flitted around the glass rectangle with its green plastic vegetation and little treasure chest half buried in the fake sand on the bottom. But the reef was like an explosion in a paint factory with hundreds of staggeringly beautiful fish of every hue and stripe swimming past me incuriously. The beach there – 'Big Bay' I christened it – was a lovely expanse of white sand only blighted by the black remnants of fires lit sometime in the past, most of them towards the far end.

A couple of times, sweating and panting, I made my way up the mountain. It wasn't Kilimanjaro; it only took a few hours, but it was a heavy-duty workout for a man in my condition. From the top I could see distant, nebulous shapes that were probably other islands and, to the east, a bigger landmass that I assumed was the western coastline of Sumatra.

Despite not doing a lot, the bits and bobs of exercise – paddling, swimming, trekking – were having a positive effect. That and the healthy diet of seafood and fruit were already making my long-abused body leaner and fitter. I felt good. Healthy in body and mind. I was sleeping better than I had in a long time. And there is something particularly rewarding about catching your own food. I'd never been a great fisherman but now I enjoyed the daily challenge of finding seafood to supplement the tins and packets of food I had in the pantry. I alternated between concocting tasty stews with coconut, rice or pasta and throwing a few prawns on the barbie. I could even enjoy a chocolate dessert courtesy of the beans of a cocoa pod.

Nightfall was often accompanied by more torrential rain and I was glad to be cosy in *The Scoop*, reading by candlelight with Wagga snug on my lap. My mind was becoming clearer as Charlie's grip loosened and, to my delight, I found myself starting to think more and more about my next book. After months of frustrating blockage, the dam had started to crack and ideas were beginning to flow.

Since arriving, I hadn't seen any humans on the island or, indeed, out to sea. Not even a distant boat on the horizon. But I was fine with that. I might be alone but I didn't feel lonely. Besides, I had Wagga for company. And Percy. Most days I conversed with my old mentor. There was plenty to discuss: the island's incredible flora and fauna, the 360-degree views from the top of the cute little volcanic crag, even the relentless monsoon downpours most afternoons. Then there were the snakes, scorpions and stinging insects. Not to mention loathsome leeches. 'I hate those suckers,' I joked to Percy. I once spotted a big, pale green snake with black bands coiled around a tree branch. It smiled at me with grisly fangs but the really scary thing was the red tip on its tail. I just knew that meant danger. There were rats, of course, and creepy-crawlies every-where, including ants three centimetres long.

Percy and I also discussed my withdrawal symptoms; he had helped get me through a couple of bleak moments early on when I wanted to do something stupid, like chuck myself off the mountain or tie myself to the anchor on the sea floor.

Me: 'I want to kill myself.'

Percy: 'Don't be so fucking silly.'

Me: 'No, I've let you down, you can't have any respect for a junkie.'

Percy: 'You forget, I've been there too, son. You haven't done anything as fucking stupid as I did.'

Me: 'Are you kidding? What if I'd got Cody arrested for drug smuggling?'

Percy: 'The pious bastard deserved to be locked up.'

Maybe I *was* crazy. But imagining a gruff, ghostly Percy by my side helped me to heal. He never asked me 'How does that make you feel?' He never made soothing noises or talked about my childhood. He never sugar-coated things; he just gave it to me straight: 'You're a fucking twat but you'll be okay.'

23

I WAS halfway up the little mountain when I saw it, a dim, dark shape looming large in the hazy distance. I didn't have my binoculars in my backpack so I couldn't make out exactly what it was – a fishing boat or a sizeable pleasure craft? – but there was a distinctly iffy look about it. I stared at the shape for a long time as it gradually increased in size and definition. My spirits sank as I realised that it was heading straight for Rehab Island. The thought of meeting anyone – having to actually talk to them – was unwelcome. It was too soon; the solitude had been a treat, the ideal salve for my dodgy state of mind. Besides, something told me that whoever was on board that sinister-looking vessel was not going to provide me with friendly social interaction. I'd just decided to hightail it back to *The Scoop* when the heavens opened and the vessel disappeared from view in the misty rain.

What had been a challenging hike up the mountain now became a dangerous scramble going down. Navigating the dense foliage, the thorny vegetation, hanging vines and sharp bamboo, I tried to keep sight of the water on my right to maintain my bearings. The teeming rain had reduced the visibility to a couple of metres. I slithered and slid my way down the mountainside, the image of the dark shape on the water speeding my descent. It had given me a bad feeling.

It was nearly 5 pm when I finally limped through the palm trees on to the shore of my lagoon. *The Scoop* moved gently on the darkening water. The sky was overcast and the mozzies were on the prowl. The little bastards always treat my body like a Happy Meal from Maccas. I was dehydrated, completely knackered and, boy, was I hurting: my body was covered in cuts, bruises and scratches. Insect bites itched horribly and my torso had apparently become a tasty new food source for several black leeches. Disgusted, I burned them off with salt, my blood oozing out of the loathsome creatures as they wriggled on the cockpit floor. My next job was to clean my wrecked feet and anoint them with antiseptic cream. While I worked, Wagga amused himself by pawing one or two of the leeches before rubbing himself against my ankles, indicating his desire for a more palatable dinner. I petted him for a few moments before diving overboard to cleanse my dirty, lacerated carcass in the clean embrace of the lagoon.

It was approaching dusk as I made my way along the sand towards the forty-metre cliff that formed a barrier between my lagoon and Big Bay. The grey light was fading. The climb up was reasonably easy, even with my torn feet and aching limbs. There were plenty of footholds and shallow shelves and less vegetation than the rainforest so I made rapid progress, wading through the scrub to the ridge at the top, startling a few nesting owls along the way.

Despite a continuing deep sense of unease, I was feeling a bit better after a bite to eat and lots of water. Sitting with my legs around a thin tree trunk, the sharp stink of bug spray twitching my nostrils, I trained my binoculars, adjusting the zoom until a vessel came clearly into focus against the twilight gloom beyond the reef. Looks like a large fishing trawler, I thought. No worries then, it's probably just a bunch of local fishermen looking for safe anchorage overnight. They'll be gone in the morning.

I could see some activity towards the stern; tightening the focus again I could see indistinct figures dropping down into two small boats. Then two large bundles were lowered down to outstretched hands. Moments later, the small boats zoomed towards the reef, leaving angry wakes behind that rocked the fishing boat. Gradually, my ears picked up the muted roar of their engines. I tensed. Were they coming to the lagoon or Big Bay? Probably the latter, I guessed. That could explain the signs of old fires I had seen on the sand there.

My sense of foreboding heightened. The light was disappearing fast by now but I could just make out the dark shapes of the fast boats as they neared Big Bay and the wide, white ripples they left in their wake. There were maybe three or four people in each boat but I couldn't distinguish their features or clothing. About fifty metres from the shore, both boats slowed and then ran up on the beach.

There was some shouting and some of the men clambered out onto the beach. Then both bundles were lifted up and thrown roughly onto the sand. Something about this scene was making me more and more alarmed and I struggled to keep the binoculars steady, my grazed hands shaking. One of the men stooped down and pulled one of the bundles upright. He took off a covering. What I saw in the gathering gloom chilled me to the bone. It was a woman, her pale face contorted by fright or a silent scream.

24

THE BEACH towel was back over her head and shoulders as she was bundled off the bigger boat. It was still damp and smelt of stale urine. Annie's other senses were on full alert. After about fifteen minutes, she heard the engine on the small, fast craft she had been dumped into slacken and then cut. The boat carried on forward silently under its own momentum; then there was a soft crunch. Sand? Her legs turned to jelly again and her lips moved silently: 'In life, in death, O Lord, abide with me.'

Rough hands took hold of her again and pulled her to her feet. Two men took her ankles and arms and dumped her over the side of the boat, half her body in the water, half on warm sand. She gasped in shock and pain. Someone ripped the towel off her head and she could see. The light was fading but she looked around. Men with sun-darkened faces and burning eyes stared back. *Shit.* She glanced at Dani, naked and kneeling on the sand, face contorted, her eyes wild. The young woman was gibbering in white-faced terror, a stream of spit-flecked staccato that made no sense to Annie.

She could not find the will to make any sign of comfort to the young woman; she was too consumed by fear herself. You can get through this, she told herself, but without much conviction. The gold-toothed man came and stood in front of her. Before she could demand that he set them free, he grabbed her chin with one powerful hand and squeezed her jaws hard, making her eyes water.

'Sexy lady, you and other womens now to make my men happy. They want fuck *memek*,' he said, pointing to her groin. Then his hands dropped to below his waist, palms facing each other, and he thrust his hips back and forwards a couple of times in a crude parody of a sex act. His teeth bared in a terrible smile, his eyes disappearing into slits as he mimicked grunting. The other men guffawed and gestured lewdly. Annie began to feel faint as her worst horror was confirmed. She started to collapse and the pirate brute grabbed her elbow to steady her. He patted her bottom and signalled his men to take her.

They cut off her bikini bottom with a parang, the last shred of her dignity going with it. She was pulled back to the sea edge and thrown down into the shallow surf. She closed her eyes tightly as hands roamed her body, rubbing and kneading her skin and her most intimate parts in some bizarre attempt to cleanse her. She was violently ill, the vomit floating on the surface of the water as the gentle waves pushed it forward to the sand and then drew back. The brown, hard-looking men just laughed and made obscene gestures, their greedy eyes devouring her breasts and naked buttocks.

25

THE DREADFUL screams haunted me into the night. I sat on top of the ridge, completely paralysed, my hands around the tree trunk, knuckles white. Angry as hell but impotent. Thankfully I could not really see what was going on, though I could guess well enough. The men had set up a camp on the far end of the beach. I could make out shapes and shadows moving around haphazardly, thanks to the flames from a huge fire and the pale light from the ivory moon glinting on the water. There was some shouting and laughter. The smell of barbecued meat drifted towards me on the evening breeze. I suspected alcohol was fuelling the obscene 'party'.

Even from a distance, it was a scene from hell, the flickering flames providing a grotesque strobe backdrop. At times I tried to cover my ears; the distant, anguished cries pierced me to my core. It sounded as if the women were being raped and tortured. I must do something, I kept thinking. But what? What could I possibly do on my own against that number of men? The only weapon I had was a spear gun but what good would that be against so many men? Who *were* these bastards? Fishermen? White slavers? Pirates? My mind raced with possible plots and plans to rescue the women. But I knew it was a waste of time; nothing could save them now. I just sat there feeling cowardly and frustrated.

At one point, deep in the night, I found myself muttering incoherently: 'Bastards, bastards, bastards' over and over, my fists hitting the tree. For the first time in days, I missed Charlie. At that moment, I would have taken it in a heartbeat. Anything to dull the unrelenting horror. But finally, apart from the sorrowful song of the surf, there was a merciful silence. The dying embers of the bonfire glowed dully in the darkness and, exhausted, I fell into a ghastly, fitful sleep, my head full of nightmarish visions.

26

COMING ASHORE at dusk with the two women, BangBang brought a large briefcase from the *Crimson Tide*. Locked securely and handcuffed to his wrist, it contained his spoils from recent attacks. The pirate did not have a bank account or a safety deposit box. He did not own stocks and shares or property of any kind. Hard cash was the only thing he trusted, or the nearest thing to it ... like drugs or diamonds. And this uninhabited, unnamed island acted as his private bank.

BangBang decided it was too dark for him to locate his secret cache in the jungle. He would go at first light the next day. For now he was content to relax on the beach and eat the chunks of goat his men had roasted on a spit over the fire, the dripping fat causing the flames to spark and crackle. He didn't normally allow the crew to drink alcohol but had decided to relax the rule this evening. The men needed compensation for the aborted heist and the maiming of their fellow crewman. Despite many of them being Muslims, they liked to drink alcohol. And, of course, they liked pussy. It was a masterstroke to kidnap the two *bule* bitches, he thought to himself with a smile. They would raise more than the men's morale. He chuckled. With a bit of luck, his crew would be happy as pigs in shit tomorrow and they'd forget about the crewmate who had died from blood loss after he had chopped his arm off. Then we can all concentrate on the big job ahead, he thought; I'll give them the good news in the morning.

He didn't drink alcohol himself – not because of religious beliefs, he had none – he simply didn't like losing control. He'd got drunk a few times when younger and he'd nearly killed somebody in a psychotic rage. So tonight, he watched some of the men play football in the dying light while others started on the women. Even naked and tied up, the women didn't excite him sexually but the spectacle of their humiliation and degradation amused him greatly.

Sucking on a clove cigarette, his thoughts turned to the communication he'd received a short time ago from his Chinese masters – a big heist in five days time. The syndicate had, as usual, managed to place one of their men on the crew of an oil tanker in Oman. This spy was now relaying critical information back to his bosses about the ship, its route and the captain and crew. If he screwed this job up, his chances of survival would be even worse than those of these two western women. The cigarette suddenly tasted bad and he spat it out.

27

IT WAS not shame she felt. After all, she had no control over what was being done to her. It was *their* shame. Their depravity. She felt humiliation, yes; pain, yes; rage, definitely; hate, absolutely. But shame did not enter her head. In fact, somewhere in her delirious state, her spirit resolved that she would *not* let this affect her permanently; she would not let it define the rest of her life. If indeed she was to have one. The chances are that I'll end up like Martin and Gary, she thought dully. Murdered and left to rot. Hot tears flowed as she realised: I'll never have children. Never fall in love again. Never be the person I always wanted to be.

The pirates had thrown her roughly onto an old, stained square of crinkled tarpaulin smelling of petrol and dog piss. Her hands, already tied, were looped around a stake driven into the sand behind her head. Dani's arms were also looped around the same stake but her body was spread-eagled in the opposite direction.

Soon after the initial shock and horror of the relentless violation of her body, Annie ceased feeling the pain and anguish, her mind mercifully shifting to a different plane; the stinking, sweating, grunting animals swarming over her did not reach the core of her spirit. They hit, bit and spit on her, scratched and ripped; pinched and punched. They abused her body but not her soul. Her faith continued to comfort her: *Dear God in heaven, help me get through this ordeal with my life and my spirit intact.*

Hot bitter tears squeezed out of her tightly closed eyes; she felt like a rag doll being torn apart by a pack of rabid dingoes, drooling, dribbling, snapping and snarling. She was dimly aware of Dani keening like a wounded animal; Annie knew that the younger woman was the main target for the brutes. Later she would feel immense guilt that, at the time, she had thanked God for that small mercy.

Occasionally, as she drifted in and out of consciousness, she wondered dully what the pirates would do with them once their lust had gone. One part of her didn't care. But another part cared very much indeed. She wanted a life. She wanted to *give* life. Children. A home. Love. God help me, I *will* survive.

The nightmare continued until she completely blacked out. Her tortured mind mercifully shrunk down to a tiny, dark recess that no one but her could reach.

28

BANGBANG ROSE stiffly from his beach mat. Brushing grains of sand off his clothes, he stretched, muscles creaking in the pale, growing light. He looked out of his crude tent. The sea was calm but he knew the tide would come in soon. All around, he saw bodies lying inert on the beach, exhausted from the night's debauchery. The two white bitches had served their purpose, he thought with satisfaction. The fire, once red–hot and roaring, was now timid, little trails of smoke still rising from the grey–black stain on the white sand. He rubbed his eyes then lit a Gudang Garam – the first of a hundred he'd smoke that day. He coughed harshly and spat out a gob of phlegm. Clutching his battered briefcase, he began to make his way to the far corner of the beach where the volcanic rock rose up and the sand kissed the fringe of palm trees.

Despite the fact that he'd walked this way many times there was no clear trail. BangBang had been careful to minimise any physical signs that might lead someone else to his secret stash. He always took a different route and did his best not to damage any of the vegetation, although it was impossible to be a hundred per cent perfect. He comforted himself with the thought that if any crew member were stupid enough to try, he would meet a sudden and savage death.

His destination was just over five hundred metres from the beach but it took him twenty minutes to reach the familiar rockpool, the dark blue water coloured by the minerals leeching out of the volcanic rock. The pool was framed by a steep, moss-covered rock face on one side and dense vines and rotting vegetation on the other, making access difficult. He looked back, not for the first time, to check he was not being followed, then carefully picked his way through the foliage to the far end where there was a small clearing by the side of the pool, covered in bark and animal dung. Although the sun was still not fully up and the towering canopy cast the whole area in its sombre shadow, he was sweating like a pig and wheezing from the effort. He dropped his half-smoked cigarette to the ground and stubbed it out with his foot.

Finally he came to a half-hidden gully running alongside the rock face; pulling back some foliage, he saw the small, dark entrance. A large stone barred the way and BangBang had to squeeze his bulk through. The cramped space immediately widened out into a huge cavern. He took a torch from the briefcase and the beam illuminated dramatic shark-toothed lavacicles, similar to stalactites, on the ceiling. There was rubble and other debris on the floor. A sudden commotion disturbed the gloomy silence – a colony of bats startled by the intrusion. They were the source of the overpowering stench that permeated the cavern. BangBang smiled: the first time he'd found this lava cave, those stinking creatures had surprised him, now he was used to them; relied on them in fact. Those noisy fuckers are better than a bank's security alarm, he mused. I even have my 'safety deposit boxes' – three heavy-duty, moulded plastic suitcases. They were watertight, dustproof and remarkably robust with two padlocked hasps. Each was similar in size to a carry-on bag and virtually indestructible. And I'm here to make another deposit. He chuckled at his little joke.

From a stone ledge just above head height, he pulled down the three suitcases. Each one was undisturbed apart from where the bats' foul-smelling guano had fallen on them. BangBang carefully opened each one and examined its contents delicately. There was jewellery, mini bars of gold and small packets of cut diamonds in one; another held five bricks of heroin, each weighing a kilo and wrapped in freezer bags covered in brown duct tape; the third case contained mainly banknotes in a number of key currencies, and his pride and joy: four US-issued bearer bonds worth a combined total of $200,000. BangBang smiled happily and kissed the small sheaf of certificates. Next, he opened the briefcase chained to his arm and put the various valuables stolen from the *Lady Vesper* into the relevant cases; finally he took out some documents and put them in with the bond certificates.

BangBang was not a nervous man by nature – far from it – but these particular documents made him anxious. They were detailed plans from the syndicate for two shipping raids that were scheduled in the next few weeks. They were worth a hundred times more than the other contents of the cases put together. His Triad masters would have him killed if the plans were compromised. He couldn't keep them on the *Crimson Tide* in case a patrol boat stopped them. And his men were not to be trusted. The cave was the perfect place to keep them safe.

BangBang locked the cases, put them back on the shelf above and went outside. Pausing to light another cigarette, he headed back to the beach.

29

THE BIRDS woke me at dawn; normally a delight, the raucous, rapturous chorus was a shock that morning. It seemed a sacrilege in the light of what I'd witnessed a few hours earlier. Similarly, the cheerful morning sun seemed a betrayal of the dark terror of the night that had just ended.

I was still sitting upright, arms round the tree, my bum completely numb. My face was chafed from sleeping against the rough bark and my knuckles raw from hitting the trunk during the night in impotent frustration. As I rubbed my cheek gently, I caught a movement on the beach. Snatching up the binoculars, I trained them on the far end of the bay. A slightly surreal sight greeted my red-rimmed eyes: a stocky brown man was strolling towards the right-hand corner of the bay with a bulging briefcase in his hand, for all the world as if he were an insurance broker heading to the office. His right shoulder was sloping down so the case must have been heavy. The man was slightly bow-legged and had a distinctive roll as he walked before disappearing into the trees. What the hell? Where was he going? For a pee? But why would he take a briefcase?

The rest of the encampment was dead to the world; and, for all I knew, the women were also dead. I could not begin to imagine what that unending brutal assault must have been like for them. Nothing was moving, apart from some wispy smoke from the fire. The whole setting looked eerie. Moving the glasses, I could just make out the two women, both lying in the fetal position, arms outstretched backwards to a stake in the sand near the remains of the campfire. A few brightly coloured tents formed a rough horseshoe. The lenses suddenly blurred; I felt light-headed. Dehydration, I self-diagnosed. Nothing appeared to be happening down on the beach so I decided to nip back to the boat to get some water.

When I climbed back up to my hiding place at the top of the ridge a short time later, I saw a hive of activity. The two skiffs were being loaded up with the tents. The stocky man was back and shouting orders. He still had the briefcase under one arm, although it didn't look quite so heavy now. I couldn't see either of the women. My binoculars swept backwards and forwards around the beach but there were only a bunch of slovenly men moving listlessly. Where could their victims be? Just then, I picked out two round objects on the sand right at the waterline a couple of metres apart. For a moment, I thought they were rocks or something washed up on the shore. But, when I zoomed in, I saw that they were the women's heads, faces turned towards the sea. 'I don't fucking believe it,' I said. The cruel bastards had buried them up to their necks in the sand. And the tide was coming in! Surely they weren't leaving them there to die? No one could be that mind-blowingly evil.

My question was answered moments later when the stocky man walked casually over to the women, bent over and obviously said something to one of them, then savagely kicked the other one's head as if it were a football. Jesus fucking Christ! I thought I heard a scream but it might just have been one of the nesting birds. My head dropped, the bile rising in my throat. Taking three deep breaths, the way Percy had once taught me, I looked back to the scene. The skiffs were puttering away from the beach, the leader on board the rear one. He's no insurance broker, I thought savagely, he's a murdering bloody psychopath. He had deliberately positioned the women so they would be forced to watch the boats leave. What must those two wretched human beings down there be thinking as they realised they had been left to die?

My rage and shame finally boiled over. I started scrambling down the ridge towards Big Bay, being careful to stay hidden by the scrub – the scumbags might still be keeping an eye out. I slipped and slid down the incline to the jungle and started making my way as fast as I could behind the tree line, staying parallel with the shoreline. When I drew level with where the women were buried, I crawled through the palm trees and wriggled commando-style down to the waterline with my elbows and knees, my belly flat on the sand. The two small boats had reached the larger vessel beyond the reef about a kilometre away.

From behind, the women's heads looked like blocks of driftwood washed up on the beach, covered in sand and debris. The tide had already reached up to their necks, pulling at the tips of their hair. *Hurry!* I propelled myself forward into the water in front of them, desperately afraid of what I would find and praying that the bastards on the boat were not looking back at the beach.

Their faces were both grotesque. One of them, a blonde, had an earlobe chewed off and one eye was out of its socket; she was the one that the gang leader had booted in the face. Her head was pulped, lolling to one side, her tongue slightly protruding. Horrified, I figured she was already dead.

The other one was in marginally better shape although it was hard to make out her features, her face a rictus of terror and pain. She had two black eyes, her lips were mashed and crusted in dried blood. Her dark hair was clotted with sand and twigs. Wet tears had cut clean spider lines through the grime on her face. But at least she looked alive. One eye blinked slowly, painfully. The other was closed in a sticky mess. Her bruised lips moved slightly but I couldn't make out any words. The sea was now up to her chin.

'Don't worry, I'm here to help you,' I said feebly. Christ, I sound like a fucking jailhouse lawyer, I thought. The single eye blinked again.

I began scratching the sand away from her buried shoulders with my bare hands but it immediately filled in again. I tried scooping it out with a diving mask from the bag I'd brought from the boat. That didn't work either. I was becoming frantic; the tide was rising inexorably, centimetre by centimetre; it would reach her mouth and nose soon. She would drown in a matter of minutes. Think! What the bloody hell can I do?

30

I HAD almost given up hope when I had an idea. I took my snorkel out of the bag and attached it to the mask and put both on the dark-haired woman, gently massaging the mouthpiece past her damaged lips. The sea was now nibbling at her mouth. I crouched down in the surf in front of her and put both my thumbs up in front of the mask. There was no response from the battered visage behind it but what did I expect? I looked over at the other woman: her head had drooped forward slightly and both her mouth and nose were now under water. God help her, I thought, because I cannot.

The head of the woman in front of me also began to droop forward and, in desperation, I sat behind her with my legs on either side of her head, my thighs propping her neck and chin upright. The tide continued to rise. Eventually it covered her head completely and swished warmly over my stomach; soon the top of the snorkel was only poking about two centimetres out of the water and I was terrified that it wouldn't be enough. I had no Plan B – if the snorkel idea failed then she would drown. 'Hang on, don't give up. We can do this,' I told her many times. Having been an impotent witness to her shocking treatment during the night, I was determined not to let her down this time. The hours ticked by. Occasionally I would lean forward and touch her neck to feel her pulse and ensure she was still alive. I hoped she was unconscious otherwise she would be out of her mind with fear. One good thing: the fishing trawler had disappeared from sight.

Finally the water stopped rising. Then, slowly, inexorably it began to edge back. By now, my legs were cramped and numb. I was tired, itchy and hot from the midday sun. My thoughts constantly turned to the men who'd done this and what I'd like to do to them in return. How could any human being treat another person like a piece of meat, to chew on and then discard the bones? I figured the pirate leader had decided to kill the two women to ensure their crimes went undiscovered. But why do it in such a barbaric way? When I eventually return to civilisation, I vowed to myself, I will do my utmost to have that monster found and brought to justice.

Even with the tide gone, it took some time to free the woman from the clammy grip of the wet sand. Once clear, I laid her gently on the beach, covered in a towel, before returning to the lagoon for the dinghy. I was careful to face her away from the ghastly sight of her friend, whose head was now unrecognisable after its battering and subsequent immersion in the sea. She didn't even look human anymore.

Less than thirty minutes later, when I brought the tender back round to Big Bay, I found the woman in some distress. Muttering and moaning, she had somehow shaken off the towel – her otherwise naked body was still caked in sand. I put my ear close to her face but couldn't make out what she was saying: something sounding like 'martini'. It was a struggle to get her into the tender, the wind had picked up and a slight swell caused the small boat to twist and turn. Then, to make things worse, it started to bucket down.

Once back at *The Scoop*, I half carried, half pulled her up onto the swimming platform at the stern. I sat down beside her for a moment, exhausted but relieved that she was still alive. And, yes, proud that I had saved her. I looked at her with pity: the rain had washed most of the sand off her and the parts of her body not covered by the towel were a mess of ugly bruises and abrasions. I almost cried at the sight. Then I carried her through the saloon and laid her on the bed in my stateroom.

Later, sitting on the side of the bed in my cabin, I held her head up slightly and tried to dribble some water down her throat, but most of it ran down her chin and onto her bruised body. I tried talking to her but got no response; she was completely out of it. At that point I'd have given my right arm to have a lie-down myself but I had unfinished business. Grisly business. The other woman was still buried in the sand and I didn't want her body being targeted by animals or birds. She had suffered enough. So, after a little food for myself and Wagga, I climbed back into the tender in the driving rain and returned with a heavy heart to Big Bay.

31

I'D NEVER seen a dead body before, far less touched one. Once, as a teenager, I went to an auntie's funeral and she was lying there serene in an open coffin, everyone going up in single file and kissing her cold corpse. Not me, I'd have rather died myself than do that. The only other funeral I had been to was Percy's, but fortunately he was in a closed casket.

The rain was still steady when I returned to Big Bay. On the way there I'd thought about what I was going to do with the woman's body. The options included burying her at sea or in the jungle, or cremating her: I could build a big fire and turn her into ashes. The idea of putting her in the ocean was the most practical solution but I worried that the woman I had saved might want to say farewell to the dead woman – she might have been a good friend or even a family member. So, in the end, I dug a hole just behind the palm trees on the edge of the jungle, underneath a casuarina tree. The ground was quite soft and wet and it was easy enough to dig a shallow grave.

Digging the dead body out of the sand was a lot harder. I was bone tired and the rain didn't help. I tried not to look at the woman's face while I was getting her out. I was too spooked to carry her small, broken body, so instead I used a towel as a litter, dragging the towel by two corners up the beach to the burial site. There I carefully put the body in the hole and covered it in earth and rotting vegetation. I put a large rock on one end as a marker. No cross, I'd make one later if her friend wanted it. Then I stood there. The rain was beginning to ease off and I wondered if I should say something. It seemed a bit crass but then again, given her ordeal, I felt she deserved some sort of send-off. So I said a prayer, the words coming back to me with ease; no real surprise, I'd been being made to mouth it a million times at St Jude's.

Hail Mary, full of Grace, Our Lord is with thee. Blessed art thou among women and blessed is the fruit of thy womb, Jesus. Holy Mary, Mother of God, pray for us sinners, now and at the hour of our death. Amen.

I felt a bit silly standing there saying those familiar words out loud but it seemed appropriate – even if I didn't believe a jot of it.

Soaked to the skin, smeared in mud and pebble-dashed with sand, I felt weary but glad my grim mission had been accomplished. After a quick dip in the lagoon back near *The Scoop*, I towelled myself dry and went to check on the mystery woman. I found Wagga curled up asleep on the bed beside her.

There was no sign of life apart from her shallow breathing. I wondered if she might be in a coma and I wished I knew how to tell one state from another.

The woman's face was still bruised and puffy, her eyes closed in horizontal slits. The bruises on her body seemed even more grotesque against the white sheets: a mass of dark grey and yellow bruises, cuts and abrasions. Her hair was still a tangle of knots and frizz. From what I could see, her injuries were mostly superficial; there did not appear to be anything needing urgent medical attention. No doubt she could use some penicillin or tetanus jabs but *The Scoop*'s first-aid kit did not quite run to that.

Despite the fact she looked as if she'd been in a car crash, the woman still possessed a fragile dignity. I guessed she was probably an attractive woman underneath the bruising. Yesterday I'd been too busy saving her life to consider her properly. Now I was keen to discover more about her. Of course, whether her mind or spirit ever recovered was a different matter. I sensed a difficult road ahead, perhaps for both of us. Not least when it came time to tell her that the other woman had not made it.

Sighing, I scooped Wagga up and went through to the saloon to reward my endeavours with a welcome, albeit warm, beer. Later I stood on the foredeck gazing across the lagoon in the fading daylight with a fishing rod in one hand, the beer in the other. My mind pored over the sequence of incredible events of the last twenty-four hours: the first sighting of the ship in the distance, the shock of seeing the men arrive on the beach with their two prisoners, and the bestial savagery that had ensued. And then my rescue bid and the horrible process of digging up and then burying the other victim. To be honest, I felt a little proud of myself for the first time in a long time ... Perhaps I had a gone a little way towards redeeming myself after all the drug-fuelled selfish and stupid behaviour since arriving in LA.

My gaze took in the familiar beauty and tranquillity of the island; it looked the same but something had changed. And not for the better. Somehow the idyll had been tarnished; it was the old turd in the swimming pool syndrome ... this place, for all its beauty and serenity, could never be the same again.

Yet, despite my gloom, I felt my pulse quicken a little when my mind returned to the woman lying in my cabin. Who was she? How did she end up here? What had happened to her and the other woman? I felt a slight shiver of excitement at the prospect of finding out the answers to those questions.

32

THE NEXT morning she was conscious. I had slept restlessly in the cabin I still thought of as Cody's. The woman was hot and a little feverish when I went in to see her and I gave her some more water. Her eyes were still dark and damaged but I could see a little glint in one as she looked up at me. Her face was too swollen to register any real expression but I imagined she must be scared and perplexed: 'What happened to me? Who is this big blond bloke and where the bloody hell am I?' I sat down on the edge of the bed. She cringed under the sheet and I jumped back up, hands outstretched, palms outward.

'Sorry, I didn't mean to upset you.' I smiled reassuringly. 'My name is Jonno Bligh and you are on my boat. You are safe. The other, um, men have gone.'

She whispered something; I couldn't make it out. Bending down beside her to listen more closely, I was just able to make out her stuttering words:

'W–where is D–Dani?'

Shit. I presumed she meant the other woman. I didn't want to answer that yet. To distract her I asked if she wanted some water. She nodded slightly; I went to the galley and got a glass of water and a straw. I helped her sit up a little so she could drink slowly. The effort clearly pained her and she lay back down.

'Look, I've got very bad news. I'm afraid your friend didn't make it. She passed away. I'm very sorry.' I blurted this out like a complete prick; surely I could have made it sound a little less harsh? Tears squeezed out of her slitted eyes and I went to the bathroom for some tissues.

'I don't think she suffered. She was unconscious at the end.'

Her tears continued for a while, her shoulders moving slightly under the sheet.

'Where am I?'

I told her about the storm that had hit *The Scoop Jon B* and that was why I did not know exactly where we were. I skipped over the bit about cold turkey. She nodded slightly.

'And the p–p–pirates?'

Pirates? Yes, that made sense.

'They left yesterday; they probably think you are both dead. I don't think they'll be coming back.'

That was a lie. The evidence was to the contrary – the remnants of previous fires, the guy with the briefcase – they probably came to the island on a regular basis. But I wanted to reassure her, not scare her further.

She went quiet for a few minutes and I thought she'd gone back to sleep. I noticed that the sheets were covered in sand and other small bits of debris. Then she croaked:

'M–more water please.'

I asked for her name. Her cracked lips moved painfully as she whispered 'Annie'. I asked her if she could eat something and she nodded. There was some barbecued fish left over from the previous night and I mashed it up with some cold rice and a little water. I spooned a couple of tiny amounts into her mouth but she brought it all back up again. I cleaned her up and suggested she try and get more sleep. Another slight nod, then her eyes closed.

It was disconcerting but oddly energising to have another person back on the boat. I spent the morning tidying up. Wagga thought it was a game, following me everywhere, pouncing on items I was about to pick up and generally getting in the way. I smiled at his antics, scratched his chin. Chances were that he was also happy to have another person on board.

Annie was out of it for most of that day; I looked in on her once or twice to put a damp cloth on her forehead and dribble some water into her mouth. Without aircon, the room was stifling and the soiled sheets were damp from her sweat. Later, I had to carry her into the bathroom. I fetched a clean shirt of mine to put over her. It must have been pretty galling for her to rely on a man after what had been done to her by others of my gender. But she didn't seem to notice. This time she was able to eat a little and drink properly through the straw while I changed the sheets. The food seemed to revive her a little and there was even the ghost of a broken smile when Wagga jumped on the bed and tried to get under the sheet.

That evening, for the first time, I worked on an idea for my next book, scoping out the plot and putting notes down on characters. The process was fluid, the creative dam having fully burst at last. It felt so good to be writing again; to be free of Charlie's destructive grip. Lying in bed later, I returned to Annie's revelation. Pirates! I knew, of course, that modern pirates existed, I'd read many news agency wire stories about their evil exploits. But I thought they were mainly based in Somalia. Even though it was obviously a terrifying ordeal, part of me couldn't wait to hear how she and the other woman had been kidnapped and brought to Rehab Island. Drifting off to sleep, I felt a sense of foreboding that we weren't finished with those pirates. But my last waking thought was of the woman next door. Something about her, something beyond her ordeal, really intrigued me.

Washing my face the next morning I realised that I hadn't shaved for, what? – seven, eight weeks? My thick blond hair was bleached to a white–gold colour and sprawled over my ears and down the back of my neck; my knotty beard was just a few shades darker. The deeply tanned face in the mirror looked like a Viking warrior. Jeez. I smiled; I bet I'd scared the shit out of her when she first saw me. On the upside, I looked healthier than I had in a long time. The whites of my eyes were clearer and I had lost a little weight. I decided to shave . . . for some reason it seemed important that I make a good impression on her.

She was half sitting up against some pillows when I went in with some tea. I had got the barbecue going early and boiled some water for shaving and also to make her a cup of tea. If she noticed my beard had gone, she didn't comment on it. But I swear Wagga did a double take when he saw me.

'Good morning, how are you feeling?' I asked with my best bedside manner. But when I put my hand forward to give her the mug of tea, I noticed that she flinched again.

'Bit better, thanks.' The stutter was gone but her lips still hardly moved. She still spoke through her teeth. She looked slightly better, although still hideous. The dark bruising had paled to a pastel palette of greys and mauves and yellows. She held the mug in two slightly shaky hands and was extremely tentative when putting it to her bruised lips.

'No milk, I'm afraid, but I put a little lemon in it, hope it's okay.'

Her demeanour was still expressionless. I figured the facial muscles were probably damaged and moving them would be painful.

'Thank you so much . . . Jonno,' she whispered.

I blushed. How ridiculous. I felt like a schoolboy being told by the French mistress that I'd conjugated a few verbs *avec beaucoup de style*. Strangely, I didn't know if she was thanking me for the tea or for saving her life.

'It was nothing. I only wish—' I was about to say I wished I'd been able to do something earlier, to save her from the brutal assault. But that would have opened up a can of worms that needed to stay shut for a while.

'I only wish I could have saved your friend,' I said instead.

A single tear ran down her cheek. 'She wasn't really my friend but I regret . . .' She paused. '. . . she had to suffer like that.'

As she held the mug of tea, I noticed a faint white line on her wedding finger. I had a sudden terrifying thought: maybe there had been other people apart from Dani. When I asked her, her eyes closed and she gave a slight nod. Then she handed back the mug and eased back down on the bed again.

'I'm sorry, I'm very tired; I need to be alone now,' she said in a quivering whisper, her chin beginning to tremble, more tears leaking from her eyes.

33

OVER THE next few days, Annie felt her body steadily repair itself. Her face had lost most of its puffiness and her eyes had opened up. She still did not know if she had any internal problems or even – try not to think about it, she told herself – some *disease*. The thought made her sick. All she could see was that the visible cuts were healing and the bruises fading to smudgy shadows. But her spirit lagged far, far behind. She felt flattened, defeated, her brain numb. The pirates had not just taken her body, they had stolen her pride and self-confidence. A wave of bitterness and dread washed over her. For the rest of my life I will never be able to forget what those disgusting animals did to me. Revolting images flicked through her mind along with dreadful sounds: screams, grunts, laughter ... even the crackling of the wood in the campfire. She vomited into the washbasin, her hot cheeks wet from bitter tears.

When she looked up into the mirror moments later, she was startled by the image that squinted back. It was both familiar and foreign. The face was thin and gaunt, the eyes red-rimmed and haunted, and the cracked lips turned down at the corners as if in disappointment. A greyish pallor still tinged the skin in between the fading bruises. I look like an old, haggard crone, she thought. Well, what do you expect, after what you have been through ... Scarlett Johansson? That thought brought a weak smile.

She looked at herself in the mirror again. That's right — at least you are alive; Martin and the others are not. They suffered a lot more than you. You should thank God that you still have the luxury of feeling sorry for yourself. If it had not been for Jonno ...

Annie's mind turned to the mysterious Australian who had rescued her: he saved my life but I'm not sure what to make of him, she thought. A man of contrasts. He is so big and solid, yet seems gentle and a little shy. A hint of sadness about the eyes. Reminds me of Pascal, she thought with a pang.

Pascal Marchand had been her first love. He was the son of a well-known French chef. She had met him in her very first week at Bristol University. Before that she had been the proverbial pig-tailed 'goody-two-shoes' at her CoE convent school. She had worked hard and never got into trouble; deputy head girl, captain of the netball team and popular with her classmates. Pascal had had seemed such an exotic creature: dirty blond dreadlocks, brown sympathetic eyes and sharp, handsome features that somehow always looked tanned, even in Bristol's harsh winters. He introduced Annie to marijuana, Daft Punk, and his old Japanese motorbike. The shy schoolgirl was now bewitched, bewildered and, a week later, bedded for the first time.

They had been together for seven years when he died, after

moving to London together after uni. He had worked part-time as a motorcycle courier while he tried to write a novel and Annie worked in a boutique advertising agency. Since then, Annie always thought of it as 'that bloody bastard motorbike'. Pascal had been on a rush job delivering documents to a law firm in the West End when he skidded on a patch of ice, fell off and slithered 30 metres along the road before being struck by a black cab. Senseless. Stupid. Shattering.

Jonno has the same sensitive, sympathetic eyes as Pascal, she thought. I have vague pictures in my head of when he held me in the water. How compassionate he was. Now my saviour keeps his distance from me, which is a good thing. I don't know if I will ever be able to trust *any* man again . . . even him. And what is he doing here anyway? What did he see, hear that night? Does he know what actually happened? What the pirates did to me? Another sudden wave of nausea hit her. Those, those fucking bastards! She heard herself shout that out. Especially the boss man. He may not have touched me but he was still the worst. Then she felt panic set in – what if they come back! Oh my God, I need to get out of here. Get back to somewhere safe. Tell people what happened to Dani and Gary and my poor husband. Get the bastards who did it. The image in the mirror morphed into the grinning man with the gold tooth.

Then she was sick again.

34

I WATCHED in wonder as Annie's innate loveliness emerged bit by bit like a beautiful butterfly from a drab carapace. And like a butterfly, her beauty was fragile: her cheeks looked hollowed out and dark shadows still underlined dull, troubled eyes. Now that there were no longer sticky slits I saw that they were large and green.

To my chagrin, I detected a slight attitude towards me – not exactly hostile but there was a definite coolness there. We had not talked much; so far she hadn't told me anything about herself and how she had come to be abducted, and I did not want to press her despite my intense curiosity. Besides, she wasn't there most of the time. She would walk past me on the boat seemingly in a trance, her face a deathly white mask, climb down into the water and then disappear to the far corner of the lagoon beach for hours on end.

At first I was resentful: 'For Christ's sake, I'm just the guy who saved you from certain death, why are you pissed off at me?' But then I realised that perhaps there was indeed a fate worse than death and she had just experienced it. So I decided to let her be, giving her time and space to be on her own, to work things out in her own way. It broke my heart to hear her sobs and moans in the night but there was nothing I could do other than ensure she had food and water and a shoulder to cry on if ever she asked for it. Wagga also seemed to be doing his best to comfort her, sleeping on her bed at night and jumping on her lap whenever she was around.

Once out of her sickbed, I watched Annie go off on her own, walking unsteadily and lowering herself gently in the calm water. On the second day, she asked me to take her to Dani's gravesite.

We took the tender and when we landed on the beach, she walked over to the spot where the two of them had been buried in the sand; her head dropped to her chest and tears dampened the dress shirt she'd borrowed from me, along with one of my silk ties for a belt. I stood quietly a few feet behind to give her room to grieve. Then she turned towards me, her smudged eyes glistening. She had an air of ineffable sadness about her.

'Jonno, I haven't properly thanked you for what you did. Not just for saving my life but also for the compassion you showed. Not just then, but since.' Her voice, still a bit throaty, was soft, a bit posh. But then, like many Australians, I still think all English accents are posh.

'You know, that day on the beach is a hellish blur but I do remember the sheer helpless terror I felt when I saw the sea rising towards me. But then, when you held me, it was an unbelievable comfort, the first time I'd felt like a human being since those ... men,' her voice broke at this point, '... captured me.

I will remember that extraordinary act of kindness as long as I live. Thank you.'

Her voice was still low and slightly hoarse and this gave her words an added intensity. I was stunned, I didn't know what to say; to be honest I felt like just taking her in my arms and squeezing her tears dry but I knew that would freak her out, so in the end I just nodded. After an awkward moment or two, I gestured towards the palm trees and led her slowly up the pristine beach to Dani's makeshift grave.

I didn't know if she was religious but I knew she would do a better job of paying her respects to the dead woman than I had. I watched her gingerly kneel down beside the heap of earth and then I left Annie to say goodbye to her friend in her own way.

35

AS I WALKED away from Annie, I realised I was heading in the same direction the stocky man with the briefcase had taken ... towards the jungle. That piqued my curiosity: where had he gone and what was he up to? I reached the spot where he had walked through the tree line and started walking inland.

The intensive sights and sounds and smells of the rainforest were a shock after the clean sand and seascape I had just left behind. It was a different world entirely as I picked my way through the dense undergrowth, watched by thousands of hidden eyes – birds, reptiles and sundry other wildlife. The humidity clutched at my chest and the sweat streamed off my bug-bitten body.

I may not be Tonto but anyone knowing what they were looking for could have made out the occasional trace of the pirate's progress: a broken branch here, a twisted plant there and the odd dent in the rich, earthy forest floor that had not been washed away by the monsoon rains. But the clincher was a soggy cigarette butt that I found near a natural rock pool after I'd trudged through the rainforest for about fifteen minutes. I picked it up and sniffed it – there was the hint of a spicy aroma.

Memories of an Enid Blyton *Famous Five* book from my younger days came to mind – pirates and hidden treasure, who could resist? Then, when I found the entrance to a cave just past the rock pool, I was beside myself. My imagination raced ahead: what would I find? Would it be like Aladdin's cave, full of gold plates, jewelled crowns and artefacts? My enthusiasm was dampened slightly when I peered in because it was very dark and I could hear some movement and high-pitched sounds. What the bloody hell was going on in there? I couldn't see a damn thing and didn't want to risk injuring myself. Frustrated as hell, I made my way back to the beach, resolving to return with a torch as soon as possible.

Annie was quite composed when I got back; she had made a flimsy cross out of a couple of pieces of bamboo and placed it on Dani's grave. 'I don't know if she was a Christian, but I don't believe she would have minded either way,' she said. We stood there in silence for another few moments before returning to the tender that I had pulled up onto the sand.

That night, after dinner, Annie opened up a little for the first time . . . helped, I think, by the large glass of warm white wine she was gulping down.

'I'm sorry, Jonno, but this whole nightmare has been doing my head in. I'm still in total shock. I've got to talk to someone about it or I'll go crazy. And, as you are the only one available, I am afraid it has to be you.'

So, sitting up straight, chin high, her gaze focused on some distant spot through the saloon window, she told me in a low-key tone all about the pirates' attack on her boat, the murder of her husband and another man, followed by her capture. She didn't want to elaborate about what had happened on the beach and I certainly didn't want to interrogate her about it. In fact, I stayed completely silent throughout what was a virtual monologue, letting her get it off her chest, occasionally nodding sympathetically to show I was listening.

Annie didn't look at me once as she spoke, both hands gripping her wineglass so tightly I thought she would break the stem. She shed no tears and her voice was steady, almost a monotone, except when she came to the bit about her husband being killed. Her speech became slower and there were a lot of pauses. Once or twice she gave a slight choke. Eventually she came to a halt. She looked at me for the first time and said in a brittle voice: 'So that's about it. Not a pretty story, I think you'll agree. One minute we were on holiday, having fun, the next my husband and our friends were brutally murdered and I'm in the middle of a . . . of a Stephen King horror story.'

And with that, she apologised and said she had to go lie down. I sat there for a long time, nursing my tepid beer, processing what I had just learnt and wondering what might become of Annie. How could this lovely woman ever find her way from the hell she was in – grieving for her husband and friends and grieving for the pain and humiliation she had suffered at the hands of the pirates.

Then, I am ashamed to say, I started thinking about the fact that she had been married. I had noticed previously that there had been no wedding ring on her finger. I now realised that the pirates would have taken it. Was it a happy union, I wondered. That rather crass question was still knocking about in my head when I went to bed.

36

IN THE morning I got up early to avoid seeing her because, frankly, I did not know what to say or what to do after hearing her story. Besides, I had a mission of sorts. After feeding Wagga, I set off eagerly to go back and check out the lava cave. During the night I had dreamt uneasily both of pirates and dark sinister shapes against a red, flickering light that I couldn't make out, but I knew were somehow evil. A woman was screaming in the background. I woke up with a dry mouth and damp sheets again.

I found the rock pool again easily enough and carefully navigated the cave entrance brandishing not one but two torches. I had also brought some candles. When it comes to solving problems, belt and braces, my father had taught me. Once through the narrow hole, the space widened out gradually, first to a cylindrical tunnel shape but then to an area almost as tall as a cathedral. There was a ferocious stench and my thongs squelched on sticky patches on the tunnel floor. I knew it was batshit because hundreds of the buggers were flying around above like demented bees; obviously the light was pissing them off.

Apart from rock-like formations, and an impressive display of what looked like stalactites, the cave was empty. I was crushed; I had expected more. A lot more. Surely this was the pirate boss's hidey-hole? Surely this was where he'd stashed his treasure? I looked around again, training the torches on the ground to see if there were any fresh marks from digging. Nothing. But then, I saw another cigarette butt. Eureka! I went over, flashed the torch around the floor and up and down, the action stirring up the bats even more. Seeing a faint footprint on the ground next to the wall, I looked up: less than a metre above my head a natural stone ledge stood out.

Standing on tiptoe, I reached up and felt with my hand over the top of the ledge. At first there was nothing but dust and dried batshit but then my fingers touched something more solid, something that seemed to be a box or a small chest. My excitement soared. Holding one of the torches in my mouth, I reached up with both hands and brought down what looked like a small suitcase or toolbox. It resembled the protective cases photographers use to carry their equipment around.

I put it on the ground and knelt down; it was padlocked and I couldn't get it open. Fuck, fuck, fuck! How bloody frustrating. I stood up, went back to the ledge, felt again. Two more boxes. I lifted them down. Both also locked. One was much heavier than the others. My first instinct was to find some sort of tool to force the locks open and find out what was inside. I've got to know what's in there, I thought, my mind feverish with a mixture of excitement and greed. But, after a moment of demented delirium, normal thinking prevailed: if you open them, I thought, there's no going back. You'll have to break the locks and he'll know they've been tampered with. Alternatively, you can simply put them back and no one will know you've touched them. The good angel whispered in one ear: 'If he finds out that you've been screwing around with his stuff, he'll find you and kill you.' But then the bad angel sidled up close and said: 'You'll regret it your whole life if you don't find out what's inside those boxes. Go on . . . just take a little look. You know you want to! You can always put them back. He might know someone's had a look but as long as nothing's taken, he'll let it go.'

Of course, I told myself, you could just grab the cases, pack up *The Scoop* and simply hightail it away from here. The pirates will never know who took their loot. The thought was seriously tempting. But, despite the danger, I was strangely reluctant to leave. Rehab still felt like home and, besides, I did not think Annie was strong enough yet to handle a sea voyage, particularly if conditions were rough. Maybe in a day or so, I mused.

So, in the end, the good angel won and I put the cases back on the ledge. When I got back to *The Scoop*, I didn't reveal my discovery to Annie; I still hadn't made up my mind what to do about them and so decided not to burden her with it. Also, I was afraid that any mention of the stocky man might also trigger more mental anguish for her; that was the last thing I wanted so I kept my mouth shut.

37

THAT NIGHT Annie dropped two bombshells. The first came over dinner – a barbecue on the beach. Against the background noise of gentle rolling surf, we were serenaded by the usual nocturnal noises of frogs and cicadas, as well as birds and monkeys. I had built up a big fire to provide some light, and also to keep the damn mozzies away. Earlier I had caught a fairly large fish near the reef, some sort of trevally, I thought, and Annie had boiled some rice and flavoured it with some mushrooms she had found. For dessert we had some fresh figs. We were sitting on towels on the sand, the only light coming from the starry sky and the glowing barbecue embers.

'Jonno, this morning, when you were gone, I had a bit of a panic attack. I felt paranoid that the pirates would return any minute. It was horrible.' She shuddered and took a big gulp of warm wine. 'I really, really need you to get me away from here as soon as possible. Can you do that? I mean, this boat can still sail, can't it?'

Ah, shit. It was hardly a surprise but it was not what I wanted to hear. I had hoped for more time on the island to ensure that I had fully got over the drug withdrawal process. I did not yet feel ready to go back to civilisation. And, to be honest, I was enjoying the opportunity to get to know Annie. I turned to look at her and immediately realised how selfish all that was: even in the shadowy darkness I could tell her face was strained and her eyes haunted by unimaginable horror.

'Yes, of course. I understand totally. We can leave any time. Soon as you are ready, I guess. Obviously *The Scoop* has no power but she is seaworthy.' I looked over at the ship on the water. 'She'll need a little bit of preparation but I can get started on that tomorrow morning if you like. Depending on the tide, we could be ready to go by early afternoon.'

She nodded eagerly. 'That would be good, Jonno. I haven't felt well enough before now, but I really must report what's happened … Martin's death and, of course, the others. I have to tell the authorities. Let the families know, including mine, that I am safe. All that stuff. I feel so guilty that it's taken me this long to, you know, think about that.' Her eyes glistened. 'And I really don't know what I would do if the pirates came back. I think I'd go out of my mind.'

'That won't happen,' I said reassuringly. But I knew fine well that the pirate leader would not stash those suitcases full of stuff – whatever it was – in that cave if they did not come back regularly. Annie was dead right … we probably should leave as soon as possible. But, first, I really wanted to get back to the cave.

When we returned to the boat, I felt it was my turn to talk. I hadn't told Annie much about myself earlier as she had needed space. Now I gave her an edited version of my life; I told her I was simply a 'mere humble spinner of words' and outlined my journalistic career in Sydney and London. Being British, she knew the *Daily Tribune*, of course. I avoided any mention of the book, the film and all the Hollywood nonsense. I don't know why I didn't tell her everything; perhaps I didn't want to sound like a braggart, or perhaps it still felt a bit raw. To my credit, I did tell her about my problems with cocaine and the reason I had 'checked in' to Rehab Island. She smiled wryly at the name.

'I was wondering what to call it. Rehab Island suits the place very well. After all, this is a sort of rehab for me too. From what you've just told me, it sounds like we're both damaged goods.'

Damaged goods, I thought, that describes me perfectly. But somehow I couldn't think of Annie that way. Unlike me, she was not to blame for any part of what had happened to her. In fact, she was showing incredible courage and character. She looked more rested and composed, and once again I was drawn to her. But then she dropped her second bombshell.

'Jonno, I've been wondering. Where were you when the pirates were ... well, when they were attacking Dani and me? I mean, did you see what was happening? Wasn't there anything you could have done?' Her voice faltered at this point and she took another gulp of wine.

My head dropped. I had hoped that she would never raise the subject. What, could I say? That I was scared? That I had felt rage and frustration and impotence? But then I looked her straight in the eye and told her the truth.

'Annie, I am so sorry. I was up there,' I pointed up towards the shadowy cliff now highlighted by the milky moon. 'And

I guess I saw and heard enough to know what was happening. But I had absolutely no idea what to do. There were so many of them and they had weapons and it was dark and well . . . what *could* I do?' How feeble that sounded. But it was the truth. 'You have no idea how that made me feel. Still makes me feel. I will spend the rest of my life wondering if there was some way to rescue you. I guess it's why I was so determined to stop you from drowning the next morning.'

Annie was silent for several moments, her eyes still locked on mine. Then she nodded. 'That's what I reckoned.' And with that she said goodnight.

38

I WAS sitting in the cockpit, having breakfast and still feeling ashamed about our conversation the night before. I was also wondering how I could get the boat ready to leave that day . . . *and* get back to the cave. The morning sun had already turned the air sultry and I was naked apart from a pair of boardies as I tackled a healthy breakfast of fruit salad – bananas, mango and dragon fruit with grated coconut. When we get back I'll have a huge fry-up, I promised myself.

Just then Annie appeared from the saloon and brandished something right in my face. It was a paperback copy of *Hard News*. She was holding it open at the flyleaf, which was graced by a photograph of yours truly; not a bad one in fact . . . I'm looking directly at the camera, fist holding my chin up in a serious but, I think, rather sexy pose. Uh oh, I thought, she must have found it in one of the cupboards. Bugger.

'This *is* you, I take it?' she said. 'Jonno Bligh, bestselling author? The same person who told me he was just a humble hack?'

Despite the book being centimetres from my nose, I tried smiling modestly. She whacked the book down on the cockpit table with a sharp crack, causing Wagga to jump almost a metre in the air, his fur sticking out as if he'd been electrocuted.

'I feel such a fool. An Oscar, for God's sake! When were you going to tell me you were famous?' She was standing, hands on hips, her brows furrowed. 'Well? You did lie to me, didn't you?'

'Look, Annie, take it easy, I can expl—'

'Take it easy? Take it easy! I told you everything about me. Now I find you're a . . . a big hotshot celebrity and you didn't think to tell me?' Two red spots fired her pale cheeks.

'Wait, let me explain . . .'

But she was gone, her back disappearing through the saloon door. Jesus Christ, what was that all about? I thought. A bit of an overreaction, surely? But I knew I should have told her the truth. Her behaviour was understandable given what she had been through. I went to her cabin door, knocked gently. 'Annie, I'm sorry, I didn't mean to—'

'Piss off, Jonno. I don't want to talk to you right now.'

I sat on the floor outside and told her everything anyway. I mean *everything*: the tawdry life I'd led in Tinseltown, my dysfunctional family, Percy's death and his letter to me, the row with Cody, the whole nine yards. Even how Wagga ended up on board. Man, it was like baring my soul to Dr Phil. I was just getting to the part about Percy urging me to find a good woman, and that I thought I'd found her, which would have been a huge mistake, when the door opened.

'Jonno, you are an idiot. After everything that happened to me, I thought you were a man I could trust. But you lied to me.'

I was still squatting on the floor, looking up at Annie framed in the doorway, her face flushed and serious. My heart turned over. I stood up awkwardly and almost bumped into her; she put a hand on my chest to steady me.

'Sorry,' I said. 'I didn't mean to upset you. It was stupid, I just didn't think. Forgive me? Please?'

She stood there for a moment and then put her hand on my shoulder. 'Well, right now, everything I believed in seems to have been ripped to shreds. It's like the ground has opened up under my feet. I just want to be able to rely on something. On *somebody*.'

'You can rely on me,' I said, my eyes stupidly welling up, my throat constricting. 'You can *totally* rely on me,' I repeated hoarsely. 'Annie, I promise you I'll never let you down again.' And I put my hand on my heart.

It must have been the right thing to say because she started crying herself and then she put her arms around me, her face salty against my bare chest.

39

'SORRY. DIDN'T mean to be so dramatic. I'm just feeling a bit emotional right now. Horrible mood swings, you know,' Annie said a little later. I noticed, not for the first time, that she talked like an Italian orchestra conductor, her long-fingered hands waggling and waving, clenching and chopping. It was always a virtuoso performance. We were sitting in the cockpit of *The Scoop*, taking advantage of an early afternoon breeze.

'So you're famous,' she said. 'Does that mean you're incredibly rich too? What about this lovely boat? Is it chartered as you said?'

'Actually I own it. Sorry. Another silly fib. Mind you, the name should have given you a clue.'

'Of course!' She gave her forehead a soft tap. 'Shows you how screwed up I am – *The Scoop Jon B.* Would have been an almighty coincidence if you had managed to find a boat to charter that already had your name on it.'

'Quite. And I am far from rich. The fact is *The Scoop* is about the only thing I do own and I'll probably have to sell her unless I can sort out a new book.'

'And how's that working out?'

'What, the book?'

'Yes. Have you started writing it?'

I explained about my inability to write a word during my struggles with Charlie. But in the few weeks I'd been on Rehab Island, the juices had been miraculously released and I was starting to feel cautiously optimistic that I'd be able to deliver a fat, bankable piece of work.

'Is that why you write, to make money?' she asked.

'No, but I've got rather attached to *The Scoop* and if I don't want to pay back the advance I got, I'll need to come up with another bestseller.'

'Tell me about *Hard News*. I hope to read it when we get back. And I'll definitely watch the film.'

So I told her how it all came about – the story that destroyed a government, that turned into a bestseller and an Oscar-winning film, the story that changed my life . . . The Scoop. Of course, Percy was the catalyst.

I sat back in the sunshine, thinking that it was great to be back on good terms when Annie leaned over and put one hand on my arm: 'Look Jonno, I want to apologise if I made you feel guilty earlier . . . you know, about not doing anything to help me on the beach that night? It would have been suicidal for you to try. We both know I wouldn't even be alive now if it wasn't for you. Can you forgive me?'

'Nothing to forgive. I just wish I was some sort of movie superhero who could have stopped those bastards ruining your life.'

'Jonno, let me tell you something. When I was captured and put in that dark place in the pirate ship, I swore to myself that, whatever happened, I would not become one of those people who spend their waking hours bitter and twisted, never able to move on. I *refuse* to be a victim for the rest of my life.

'So don't pity me or think of me as some pathetic creature who is permanently sorry for herself; I couldn't stand that.'

This woman is amazing, I thought. After all she's been through, her spirit is still so strong. And in the weeks that followed I was to find that she did indeed have incredible reserves of courage and a will to survive.

That lump was back in my throat again; but I was saved from responding when Annie abruptly changed the subject.

'Okay, when are we leaving today?'

In the spirit of my pledge never to lie to her again, I decided to tell her about the pirate cache I'd found in the lava cave. Taking a deep breath, I said: 'Annie, I need to tell you something important.' Her face darkened when I related the story about the squat, stocky man leaving the beach with a briefcase under his arm. I told her that I had retraced his steps and found the cave and, when I described the hidden entrance, the bats and what I'd found there, her eyes grew larger and her mouth formed a perfect 'O'.

'Oh, my God, Jonno, what was in the cases? Where are they?'

I explained that I had left them in the cave unopened. There might not be anything of value in them. Deep down, I knew that was unlikely. There was something special about those cases. Why else would the pirate guy take so much trouble to hide them in such an odd, out-of-the-way place? And why have the briefcase chained to his wrist? There was no doubt in my mind that there was valuable stuff hidden in that cave.

'Annie, you should think about this: if we open them, there will be no going back; if those guys come back to the island they'll know someone tampered with them and they'll come after us.'

Annie looked instantly fearful. I could have kicked myself. You stupid prick, I thought, why did you say that?

'I'd rather die than have those animals touch me again.'

'And I'd rather die than have them hurt you again,' I murmured.

'What did you say?' she said.

'Nothing,' I lied, breaking my earlier promise before even a day had gone by.

'Look Annie, maybe we should just pack up and get going right now.'

To my surprise, Anne shook her head. 'No! First thing tomorrow morning. If there is valuable stuff in those cases, I want to take it from him. Make him suffer. My God, I'd like to see his ugly face when he discovers it's gone!'

It would not be long before we both came to regret that decision.

40

'DO YOU realise tomorrow is Christmas Eve?' Annie asked as I steered the tender towards Big Bay. She seemed to have improved both physically and mentally; the outward scars of her ordeal were fading and her inner spirit was beginning to re-emerge.

'Well, let's hope Santa has left us our presents in the cave,' I said with a smile. It didn't feel Christmassy. It was hot and humid and the sun was ablaze above us. I hadn't really been keeping track of the days. It had been – what? Three weeks since I'd arrived at Rehab Island? Four weeks? The place had lived up to the nickname. I felt better than I had in years. I was sleeping like a burped baby: no bad dreams, no paranoid thoughts at 4 am, no sweaty sheets. Sure, the craving for Charlie was still there, in the basement of my brain, but a new craving had super-seded it, one that was beginning to dominate my thoughts and dreams, one that provided a very different brand of euphoria. She was wearing another of my dress shirts, the sleeves cut off, a piece of cord around her middle. Shoes had been a problem.

Mine were far too big for her but I'd found a pair of Cody's old thongs and we'd cut around the rubber heels, contouring them to fit Annie's small feet. To protect her from the hot sun, she wore a cap, sunscreen and a spare pair of my sunnies.

We paused briefly to allow her to pay her respects again at Dani's grave; she stood, eyes closed for a few minutes, her lips moving silently. One thin tear ran down her cheek as she turned to me,

'Did I tell you that that poor girl took the brunt of it? The pirates, I mean. She was younger and prettier. Well, at least Martin thought so. Anyway, she suffered more than me. Those bastards started with her and by the time they got around to me they ... well, anyway, she didn't deserve any of it. Those bastards ...'

By now her sobs were coming thick and fast, punctuating her speech and making it difficult for me to make out what she was saying. Her face became wet and ugly with pain and sorrow and her body shuddered as she struggled to get the words out. I put my arm around her shoulder but she shrugged it off angrily and walked away. A few minutes later, when she had recovered her composure, we set off through the rainforest.

I found the rock pool again easily and we quickly made our way to the lava cave entrance. There, Annie hesitated; she told me apologetically that she was a little scared of dark, enclosed places; her experience in the pirate ship's hold hadn't helped. But she took a deep breath and followed me in. I had forgotten to tell her about the bats though and the sudden flurry of activity and screeching startled her; she gasped and clung to my arm, her hand claw-like. 'Don't worry,' I said, 'they might poop on you but they won't harm you.'

She held the torches while I stood on tiptoe and reclaimed the cases, one at a time. We squatted down and looked at them on the ground, the torchlight giving them a sinister look. 'Can you open them now?' Annie asked.

'No, look at those padlocks. I'll need something strong to prise them open.'

Transporting them back to *The Scoop* was easier said than done. Annie was able to carry the lightest case quite easily but one of the other two was very heavy and I struggled to lift it with one hand. That meant a second trip back to what Annie wryly nicknamed 'the bat cave' before we finally got all three cases on the tender and made our way back to the lagoon.

As we broached the entrance to the narrow channel, I noticed that the sun had gone and the temperature had dropped. I felt a few drops of rain on my head. I looked up and grimaced – ominous charcoal-coloured clouds were banking in from the north-east. A big storm was heading straight for us. Ah shit, I thought, just what we need.

41

THE STORM had struck the lagoon just as Annie suffered another panic attack. Now she lay back on the bed and screwed her eyes closed. She felt ill. The boat was rocking in the heavy gusts. She put one hand on her damp forehead and pressed it hard; her brain felt like the maelstrom outside, as it raced to make sense of her thoughts and feelings. Earlier that day she had definitely been feeling better, on a scale of one to ten, maybe a six.

She knew the physical signs of her ordeal had almost disappeared. But looking hard at herself in the mirror, she could see new, deep lines around the corners of her eyes and a tightness around her jaw. I've aged, she thought; I suppose violence will do that to you. The tears started again, coursing down her reddened cheeks.

The crazy thing was that, a few hours earlier, she had thought she had turned a corner. Until they had opened that damned box. It had been like opening old wounds with a jagged knife. They had both been eager to find out what treasures it contained. What secrets and mysteries had the stocky man with the gold tooth been concealing?

As the rain started to sheet against the windows, Jonno had wrenched off the first padlock with the aid of a steel bar. They were sitting in the saloon, their excitement as tangible as the sultry, swampy air. The first case was sitting on a towel draped over the table. She noticed how Jonno was covered in sweat, his singlet showing dark, wet patches as he strained to twist the lock off. They had looked at each other as it finally flew off and bounced twice on the wood floor before startling Wagga awake from a nap in the corner. Then Jonno put the steel bar down on the seat and lifted up the lid.

Annie had stood up to get a better look and together they had peered down at the contents. 'Oh my God,' she said. 'That's my stuff!' She picked up a diamond ring, then a gold watch, and looked at them as if she could not believe what she was seeing.

'This is my watch! And my engagement ring. Martin gave it to me when he proposed.' Her words were interspersed with great gulps of air.

'And this is my grandma's necklace, the only valuable thing she possessed. She gave it to me just before she died.' She sat back down heavily and bent over, holding the jewellery close to her chest, sobbing hysterically, her thin body racked with emotion. It simply had not occurred to her that her own valuables would be in among the pirate trove.

Lying on the bed listening to the heavy rain batter the cabin skylights, Annie thought that her heart might burst. The full force of the feelings she had been bottling up since her ordeal flooded out like toxic waste: horror, terror, guilt, fear, remorse, revulsion. Martin. Dani. Gary. She had had a hint of it earlier in the day standing at the girl's gravesite, that 'corner of a foreign field', as Rupert Brooke described it. What a terrible ending to a short, hopeful life. It could so easily have been me, she thought.

Her feverish thoughts turned to Martin. It still seemed totally unreal that he was gone. She knew she had not properly grieved for him yet. Too wrapped up in your other problems, she lamented. How had it all turned so ugly so quickly? One minute they were relaxing on the *Lady Vesper*, the next moment their whole world was turned upside down. She would always remember the shock, the sheer paralysing terror she felt. Now, she was overwhelmed by guilt for surviving when the others hadn't, guilt for not grieving more for her husband, and guilt for having felt no sorrow over Gary's murder.

She thought about the night she had agreed to marry Martin. Typically, he had taken her to a posh restaurant and, after the dessert and before the coffees arrived, he had got down on one knee in front of all the other diners and, in his deep, loud voice, told her he loved her and wanted her to be his wife. Everyone clapped. She had been mortified.

Martin was nothing like Pascal. Like comparing cheddar and camembert, she often thought. She had met him a couple of months after the tragedy, still feeling bereft. Lonely, heart-broken, unsure about how to continue with life without him; she was anchorless, adrift on a sea of pain. Martin later described his first impression of her as a 'stray kitten'.

He was older. A lot older. On the face of it, a can-do, take-charge person who swept into her life and assumed control of it. He cajoled her, bullied her, and wooed her in his rather charming, old-fashioned way. Only later, when the numbness eased and the fog of grief lifted slightly, did she see him for what he really was: selfish, weak and controlling. Okay, she thought sometimes, he's not really an unkind man – he might have misplaced motives but he does care for me in his own way.

Her brother Jamie had introduced them – he and Martin both worked at the same bank. Martin, a bachelor, had pursued her relentlessly, turning up on her doorstep regularly with flowers, chocolates and/or a takeaway and a bottle of wine. Her numbed resistance was gradually worn down and, eventually, after only three months, he proposed. Once. Twice. Three times. In the end, she had sighed and dully accepted. Easier in the end to say yes than no, she decided.

I wasn't really ready, she admitted to herself now. It was too soon after Pascal. But she had felt all this pressure, the nodding expectations of the other smiling diners, the subtle but constant prodding from her parents, who thought he was a good catch. Put on the spot, hugely flustered, she'd said a faltering 'yes'. And that was that. Things seemed to move so fast thereafter and, before long, she was married to this man whom she didn't really know. Then he had basically taken charge of her life. How silly she had been. He wasn't so bad really, but she had known before long that she didn't really love him. Maybe if they had had a baby together it would have turned out okay, she thought. Or maybe not. Drying her tears, she closed her eyes and said a little prayer for him.

Opening the pirate's case had like been like opening Pandora's Box. It had brought the harsh reality of her situation back in spades: she was now a widow, her life in tatters and stranded on an unknown island with a stranger, albeit one who had saved her life, if not her sanity. Her thoughts turned to Jonno. She felt calmer.

He had been incredible. He was kind and considerate, sensitive even. He obviously had his own demons, the drug thing, for example. But he seemed to have that under control. I owe him so much, she thought. And I like his easy way, his vulnerability. She sighed. What was she doing? She couldn't contemplate being with a man right now. *Any* man. Perhaps I never will, she thought with a sinking heart.

When I get out of this, *if* I get out of this, I'll get help, professional help. I don't think I can do this on my own. But right now I just want to go home.

42

BANGBANG AND his band of pirates attacked the *Caspian Cossack* just as the oil tanker's crew was sitting down to a festive lunch in the ship's canteen. The rainbow mix of twenty-four foreign nationals – including Russians, Scandinavians, Filipinos and Indians – were taken completely by surprise. Elsewhere on the ship, two officers manned the bridge, including the captain, a burly, bearded Swede called Kristoffer Fredriksson, while another officer was in the engine room.

The Liberia-registered tanker, chartered by a Japanese company, was carrying a cargo of diesel from Oman to the Port of Nagoya on Japan's east coast. BangBang had planned the raid precisely for 12.30 pm, when the eighty-metre ship was cruising at just over twelve knots through the Andaman Sea off the coast of Thailand. He had known the crew would all be concentrated in the canteen at that precise moment because the Chinese syndicate he worked for had a man on board relaying intelligence. He had given them details of the tanker's route, its cargo manifest, crew strength and GPS coordinates. The mole had also revealed that there were no serious weapons on board. Once again, BangBang was grateful for the Triad's efficient methods.

Fortunately, this vessel had been easy to board because it was medium-sized and fully laden with 25,000 tonnes of diesel, meaning that it was low on the water. BangBang had directed some of his men, wielding pistols, machetes and assault rifles, to swarm down to the canteen and take the crew hostage. Others had been sent to disable the ship's communications and navigation systems and take control of the engine room. The pirate leader took the bridge because he knew the captain would be there.

BangBang had decided to lead the hijack operation personally; he didn't want any more screw-ups after the last aborted attack. He had no illusions about what another fuck-up would mean: the Chinese sons of bitches would kill him. So now here he was on the bridge of the *Caspian Cossack* pointing his favourite assault weapon at the fair, curly head of Captain Fredriksson. Another pirate covered the first mate, who was also on the bridge.

BangBang didn't know where the diesel would end up and didn't much care. That's not your concern, he told himself. He was aware that the crime syndicate could get rid of it easily and quickly: either selling it on the regional black market to pre-arranged buyers or distributing it to illegitimate petrol stations selling cheap fuel across South East Asia.

His role was simply to act as an enforcer; he and his men were to take control of the ship, secure the crew and take the vessel to a pre-arranged location where the syndicate would have another vessel ready to siphon off the fuel. BangBang was happy to receive a flat fee for his services plus whatever booty he could hoover up on board – like cash and other valuables from the crew and the ship's safe, plus electronic equipment and anything else that was portable and could be sold down the line. In the past he had been extraordinarily lucky to find drugs, diamonds and even bearer bonds while scavenging vessels. It was a perk of the job.

He looked up at the tall Scandinavian towering above him. Both of them knew that the captain's standing instructions were to comply with the demands of any raiders, to forego resistance and do everything to ensure the safety of his crew. That meant no personal heroics. The first mate, however, was a belligerent Russian who wasn't so pragmatic. He started pushing and shoving BangBang's crewman, who had prodded him with an automatic weapon. Then he shouted something indecipherable in Russian, his face red, eyes bulging. BangBang calmly turned towards the merchant officer and shot him in the stomach.

43

STREWTH! ONE minute Annie and I had been hyped up, desperate to see what was inside the boxes, the next she had disappeared back to the cabin, sobbing her heart out. Another mood swing, I thought, a bit unkindly.

Because, of course, she was entitled to be fragile. I remembered how crazy I was in the middle of going cold turkey. And that was a cakewalk compared to the trauma she had suffered. I decided I'd better leave her to work things out on her own. Besides, I was desperate to check out the rest of the pirate plunder.

And so, after Annie had disappeared, I removed the other two padlocks before examining the contents of the remaining suitcases. What I found blew my mind. One by one, I took out each item and put them on the dining table in the saloon, my excitement growing by the minute. Wagga, although spooked by the thunderstorm, did his best to bugger me about by jumping in the cases as I took stuff out. He obviously thought it was a good game.

When I had finished emptying the contents, I stood back and gazed at the items lined up on the table with a mixture of awe and fear. Mr Pirate Leader will be apoplectic, I thought. No, he'll be *apocalyptic*. He'll want to annihilate whoever has stolen his treasure. And that would be me. I shivered at the thought.

There were uncut diamonds in little velvet bags, small gold bars, a shitload of cash in all sorts of currencies and denominations, bond certificates, jewellery of different types and values.

Just then Annie appeared at the door. She looked better, her eyes a bit red and puffy, her hair tousled, but she managed a half smile. 'Sorry about earlier. I just had a little moment but I'm okay now. Bit of a panic attack. I must look a total fright, I don't suppose you've got some makeup stashed away somewhere?'

Her attempt at a joke was a good sign she was feeling better but then her eyes and mouth both opened wide when she spotted what was on the table, her hand flying to her chest.

'Fucking hell.' It was the first time I had heard her swear properly. It sounded strange, like hearing the Queen fart. I hoped it did not signal another change of mood.

Annie hurried over to the table and picked up various items one by one, touching the gold and running the precious stones through her fingers. She held up the certificates. 'I know what these are,' she said. 'Bearer bonds. Do you know you can cash these easily? No questions asked, I mean. They're almost like cash. Wow, two hundred grand. That is serious money.'

I whistled appreciatively and picked up some sheets of paper. 'And look at these documents. It's hard to make out exactly what they are; some are in Indonesian, some in English, but if they are what I think they are, we might be in serious trouble.'

'Do they tell us who the pirate boss is?'

'No, there's no sign of any ID.' I waved a couple of sheets of paper. 'These are cargo manifests, maps showing proposed shipping routes, destinations and other spreadsheets that I can't make out. But I'd guess that they all relate to the gang's next heist or two.'

Annie's brows furrowed. 'But why does that cause us trouble? They're just pieces of paper. Surely he'll be more pissed off about the money and the gold?'

I shook my head. 'Never mind the other stuff, these are by far the most valuable. Unless I'm very much mistaken, he won't have copies and he won't be able to carry out any attacks without them. Plus, he'll be in serious shit with his own bosses. The bottom line is – we can expect no mercy.'

'Maybe we should just put it all back?'

'That's an option,' I agreed, 'but right now it's too dark to find the cave again and, anyway, the storm looks as if it's here for a while.'

'In the morning then?' she said. 'We take it all back, then leave. If the weather clears.'

'Let's pray that it does.' I suddenly had a very bad feeling. 'Because we need to get the hell out of here.'

44

BANGBANG WAS unmoved by the Swedish captain's furious protests over the shooting of his first officer. Oozing menace, he put the still-warm barrel of his wicked-looking automatic weapon against Fredriksson's head. It was a Sig Sauer MCX with a short 230 mm barrel that he had taken off a mercenary who had been hired to protect another vessel he and his gang had hijacked. It was now his favourite weapon: blue-black and shiny with a killer bite. Just like the deadly Sumatran spitting cobra, he liked to tell his men.

He was wearing a tank top, shorts and his signature Yankees cap. His sloppy outfit contrasted greatly with the tanker captain's crisp all-white uniform of shirt, shorts and long socks. Faded prison tattoos covered BangBang's brawny arms like graffiti on a railway siding. He could smell his own body odour, a rank mix of sweat and cloves.

'You shut up. Do as I say,' he ordered the captain before handing him a scrap of paper with map coordinates scribbled on it. 'We go there. Now.' And with that, he gestured to one of his men to guard the captain and ordered two others to take the bleeding Russian below. They took an arm each and dragged his limp body off the bridge, blood-soaked feet trailing on the deck. BangBang nodded and went out into the fresh air.

His hands cloaking the lighter from the breeze, he lit another *kretek*. No problems, he thought. Everything has gone to plan. Now, unless luck deserts us and a patrol boat appears, we'll hook up with the *Crimson Tide* and the other syndicate vessel and transfer the diesel. The estimates he had been given suggested it would take up to eighteen hours to set up the hoses and syphon the fuel. He just had to keep the crew of the *Caspian Cossack* subdued during that time and stay vigilant for any sign of the authorities. He smiled: the crew part wouldn't be a problem, that's why he had shot the Russian officer, to discourage others from doing anything silly. There was also, he acknowledged, the fact that he enjoyed shooting people. Flicking the Gudang Garam over the rail, he turned and went back to the bridge: he wanted to have a little word with the captain about the ship's safe. He smiled again.

Two and a bit hours later, the *Caspian Cossack* chugged through the cavernous gap between the northern tip of Sumatra and Great Nicobar Island and moored on the threshold of the mighty Indian Ocean. Two vessels awaited: the *Crimson Tide* and a small tanker that had been hijacked eight or nine months before and repurposed to serve the syndicate's needs. An expert team was ready to start the fuel transfer.

BangBang watched as the small tanker moved into place. He knew that if they syphoned even half of the diesel from the *Caspian Cossack* it would fetch around eight million dollars on the black market. And the authorities do nothing, he thought.

The area is too big and those pigs are too corrupt. Backhanders to the navy, the cops and coastguards were just the price of doing business. The Triads take care of all that shit.

It took them about twelve hours to move the fuel from the *Caspian Cossack* to the smaller tanker. BangBang used the time to relax and to help his men scour the cabins and crannies of the big ship looking for spoils. He had already netted fifteen thousand dollars from the safe after a reluctant Captain Fredriksson had opened it, gun to head. The stupid fool had attempted to bargain with him: 'I'll open the safe if you guarantee you won't shoot any more of my men,' he said in accented English. BangBang didn't reply; he simply tipped the big Swede's hat off with the gun barrel. 'Fuck you, open now, or I blow head off,' he said. The captain obliged, any fight remaining in him having now gone.

The tanker's crew were still locked in the canteen, guarded by four of BangBang's armed men. Thanks to the special lunch, they were well fed but highly apprehensive; the Russian officer had been brought down and left on one of the chairs in the canteen, his torso glistening dark red under the neon strips of light. He was still alive but groaning in pain, a warning to the other crew members, just as BangBang had intended. He was tickled to see that one of his men had put a Santa Claus hat on the Russian's head, giving the scene a grotesque twist.

All in all, things were looking up, he mused. His men had been easier to control since they had had their fun with those two western women. The thought of the women on the beach brought his mind back to his plans. He looked at his watch:

another couple of hours and they would finish the transfer; he and his men could set off and be back at their island hideaway by sundown. He was looking forward to running his stubby fingers over the precious stones and metal in his cases. In his mind's eye he pictured the bar in Jakarta he would buy where he could run lucrative sidelines in prostitution and drugs. He reckoned he was more than halfway to putting the necessary capital together; another two years of successful heists like this and he'd be set up. His mind conjured up a penthouse suite in the posh building across the road from the Jembatan Besi slum.

But there was one more decision to make: what to do with the tanker crew? His masters hadn't given him any specific instructions on that score. He had two stark choices: kill them all or let them live. On the one hand, he'd enjoy shooting them or throwing them to the sharks; on the other hand, that would make the authorities double their efforts to find him and his bosses wouldn't like that. No point in wasting bullets then.

'Merry fucking Christmas,' he shouted to Captain Fredriksson as he left the bridge.

45

WAGGA SAT on my lap, his little claws digging into my thigh. He was unsettled by the storm raging outside, his eyes wide as we hunkered down in the saloon. It was textbook – thunder and lightning like a continually exploding box of fireworks, king-size sheets of rain and direction-changing gusts of wind that shook *The Scoop* in its shallow mooring. There was a sharp, nostril-nipping tang of ozone.

Yet tonight Mother Nature seemed angrier. Perhaps it was just that Annie and I were both subdued. This would be our last night on Rehab Island. We felt differently about that. Annie was desperate to leave – she had become increasingly agitated at the thought of the pirates returning. I think she regretted not leaving that afternoon. My own feelings were conflicted. Rehab Island had helped me see off my demons. And there was no doubt that it was a beautiful, heavenly place. But I also understood how Annie felt about it – that, even here in paradise, evil lurked. Sounds like a line from a biblical poem, I thought.

We talked quietly, finalising the plans for our departure in the morning and discussing possible destinations. Anything to avoid talking about the elephant in the room – the possibility of the pirates returning. We decided in the end to scrap our decision to take the treasure back to the cave; we shared a compelling urge to get up and go as early as possible.

Since it was our last night, I'd set up the table in the saloon with a formal layout, including napkins and candles, and the last of the wine. No Christmas decorations unfortunately, but for a laugh I'd placed my Oscar statuette on the table as a glittery centrepiece. It had been stashed in the same hidey-hole as the dope. Annie had picked it up: 'Wow, it's heavier than I thought, bigger too.'

'Yeah, nearly four kilos. I use it to exercise with every morning.'

'No wonder the winners always stagger down the stairs! But seriously, it is quite an achievement.'

I shook my head. 'I didn't really deserve it,' I said. 'My writing partner Chilli Gomez was the real reason we got it. He's a top-class screenwriter with a lot of movie credits under his belt. My contribution was limited. I really only acted as an advisor on the newspaper material. He did all the work.'

I decided to change the subject. 'What do you normally do at Christmas?'

'Oh, we were quite traditional, Martin and I would always go to midnight mass wherever we were, London or Sydney. Actually, I dragged him there kicking and screaming.' She smiled gently at the memory. 'What about you?'

'I was usually asked to work on Christmas Day. Because I was single. To be honest, I would have volunteered anyway.

Family events were always heinous, I avoided them like the plague. By the way, I didn't know you were Catholic.'

'What do you mean? I'm an Anglican.'

'You said you went to midnight mass.'

She laughed. 'No, silly. It's just a sort of family tradition. You Catholics always do Christmas best. All that pomp and ceremony. The wonderful hymns. And I love the smell of incense. It's so atmospheric.'

'Yeah well, I hate incense. It reminds me of fire and brimstone.' I poured the last of the wine into our glasses. 'Merry Christmas, Annie.'

'Merry Christmas.' She toasted me: 'And thank you again for all that you've done.' We clinked glasses.

After our meal, I cleared the plates while Annie relaxed. 'Will anyone be looking for you, like friends or family?' I asked.

'Oh God, yes. They were expecting a call on Christmas Day. Today! We were supposed to be berthed happily in Langkawi about now. If they don't hear anything in another few days, they will be seriously worried.'

'Who's they?'

'My mother and father. And my brother Jamie. He's in London. He works ... worked ... with Martin.'

Annie then told me a little bit about her family and her upbringing in the English countryside. It sounded idyllic to me, given my dysfunctional childhood; her father was a solicitor, her mum involved in local charity work. 'They were not happy about me going to work in London after university. Particularly as I was with someone.'

'Someone?'

'A boy I met at uni. Pascal. We were . . . well, we were in love. Ironically he wanted to be a writer . . . like you.' She paused and seemed to gaze into the distance.

'What happened?' I prompted. Annie looked sad. 'He died. Motorcycle accident. I, um, was devastated. In little pieces. Then, well, Martin came along soon after and the next thing I knew, we were married.' She shook her head as if to clear it.

'Enough of me . . . What about *you*, Jonno? Won't there be anyone asking questions about you? Family? Wife or girlfriend?'

'No one.' I let it hang there for a moment. 'Sounds pathetic, doesn't it? I guess I inherited a Garbo gene from my parents, my mum in particular. The fact is, I'm a bit of a loner . . . The priests used to say that I moved to the tick of my own clock, whatever that means.

'The only person who gives a toss about where I am is my agent and that's just because she's got a vested interest. Otherwise, I'm afraid my family won't worry much about me. They never have. And I haven't really kept up with many friends, apart from Cody, of course, but as I told you, I blew that big time.'

'You seem a little bitter. Down on yourself. But you've been so successful, why are you so unhappy?'

I thought about it, decided to be honest: 'Someone, I don't know who, once said: "Success is nothing without someone you love to share it with". I happen to agree with that.'

'What about Percy?'

'Well, sure, he was happy for me. He thought I had a gift. But it's not the same as having someone to experience it together, to share the ups and downs that success brings. And, believe me, there are as many downs as ups when you hit it big.'

'So what happens when we get back to civilisation? Will you go back to LA? To your old life?'

'All that sex and drugs and rock and roll?' I laughed. But then I saw that she was serious. She was looking at me with her head cocked, her lovely green eyes looking carefully into mine. I made an effort to focus. I gazed back at her, equally serious.

'No. Those days are well and truly over. I reckon it's time I took Percy's advice and settled down, perhaps with a nice woman, maybe even kids. I am certainly going to get this next book finished.'

'So you reckon you've kicked the drug thing?'

'Yes, I have. I've had an almighty scare and there's nothing that could ever entice me to use again.'

'Don't you miss it? Isn't it supposed to be hard to get clean?'

'For a while the cold turkey thing was tough. There were moments out there in the Indian Ocean when I didn't care whether I lived or died. And, yes, I miss the intense feeling of euphoria I used to get. But I've found other, less dangerous things to take its place and satisfy my wild cravings.' And before she could quiz me on that, I said softly: 'What about you? How do you think you will cope in the time ahead?'

Annie closed her eyes and paused before responding. 'With difficulty, I expect. Physically I don't feel too bad. But mentally? That's a different story. I'm definitely going to need professional help when I get back.'

'Like a shrink of some sort?' I asked.

'Yes, some sort of therapist or counsellor. I have terrible nightmares about the pirate guy with the horrible face and gold tooth.' She grimaced. 'But the more immediate worry I have is what will happen with the authorities? You know, the police and immigration? What will they make of what happened to me, to the others? I mean, what if they don't believe me? I don't have my passport or any other identification. There are no witnesses to what happened. What if they charge me with something or put me in some sort of horrible prison? It could take months to sort things out.'

'Don't worry. The first thing we'll do is contact the embassy. They'll know what to do. They're used to handling these sorts of problems.'

'Even piracy and murder?'

'Yes, absolutely. Happens all the time. And remember, I'm a witness to how those bastards treated you. No one, and I repeat no one, is going to make life more difficult for you. Over my dead body.'

'Let's hope it doesn't come to that.' She smiled, recovering her composure. 'I don't think I've really processed what happened to me yet. And being on this island with you has simply delayed the inevitable.'

'Which is?' I asked.

'I could be in for rather a bad time. At some point, I'm going to have to confront what happened to me on that bloody beach.'

'You're strong. You can do it.'

'And then there's Martin's murder ... I haven't really been able to mourn him yet. There are all kinds of ramifications to sort out in my head. I'll have to face the authorities and the media. It's going to bring back all the horror. I know it will.'

'Will you go back to work?' I asked gently.

'I can't think that far ahead. Probably not for a while. There will be so much to do when I get back.' She shook her head and changed the subject: 'What will you do with the treasure?' We had taken to calling it that in the absence of a better word.

'I think that's a joint decision, don't you? You have as much right to it as I do. My instinct says we should give most of it to the Indonesian authorities – but not all of it. Corruption is bad here and some of the more liquid elements will simply go missing.'

'Are you suggesting we keep the cash?'

'Yes, and maybe the diamonds. Finders keepers and all that. I don't know about you but I could use some money when we get back. At least until I sort out my new book.'

'What about the bonds?'

'Well, if they are as easily disposed of as you suggest, how about we keep them too?'

'Oh, I don't know, Jonno, I'll have to think about it. Can we talk about it tomorrow? That wine has gone to my head. I'm going to bed. We have a big day ahead of us.' With that, she stood up, came over, put her arms around me and kissed my cheek. Her body was soft and warm and musky against mine. 'Thank you for a lovely evening, Jonno, it was just what I needed,' she whispered in my ear.

Maybe it was the wine but for a moment I almost believed there was a God.

46

THE RAGING storm continued throughout the night and into the early part of the morning. Neither of us got much sleep; I could hear Annie next door thrashing around and occasionally moaning.

By the time the gale finally thrashed itself out around noon, Annie was fit to be tied. I didn't blame her. We had missed the opportunity to leave at first light. The elephant in the room had been trumpeting all morning and we both felt a deep sense of foreboding. I did my best to reassure her: 'Look, there's no way the pirates will have been able to sail in this weather. I'll go sort out the boat and then we'll get going. Won't be long.'

Famous last words. When I went up top, I discovered the tender had gone. There was just the frayed end of the rope I had used to tie it to a guardrail. Its small anchor had obviously not been strong enough to hold it either. Shit. Shit. Shit. Without the dinghy, there was no way we could get *The Scoop* through the channel and into the ocean. Leaving a distraught

Annie to clear the debris from the decks, I got Cody's old kayak out and went in search of it.

The sun returned in full force as I paddled around the glittering lagoon. The light sea breeze carried the normal earthy jungle aroma: a potpourri of rotting vegetation and decaying matter with spicy overtones. Sinister, portentous. After an hour of looking around the edges of the lagoon, heart in my mouth, I guided the kayak into the narrow passage to the ocean. If the bloody thing has come through here, I thought to myself grimly, and floated out into the open sea, then we are well and truly fucked. We won't be able to leave. And then what?

And then I saw the little rubber dinghy dead ahead, trapped in the area where the rocky crag jutted out and created the dreaded dogleg. It was about fifty metres short of the ocean entrance. Thank God, I murmured. But when I reached it and looked beyond to the open sea, my heart nearly stopped. A familiar dark, ominous shape was dead centre on the horizon, seemingly motionless although I knew it was probably moving towards us. Bloody hell!

I clambered clumsily from the kayak to the tender, getting wet in the process. Fingers shaking, I tried the engine. Nothing. Tried again. Nothing. Shit, must be waterlogged or something. Nothing for it but to get back into the kayak and tow the dinghy back.

When I arrived at *The Scoop*, Annie took one look at my grim face and burst into tears. 'Oh my God, Jonno. It's them, isn't it? You've seen them?' She squatted down on her haunches, putting both hands together as if in prayer, her fingertips brushing her mouth.

'Oh my God, oh my God.' Her body began to shake uncontrollably.

'I told you we should have left yesterday!' she screamed, her face ugly. 'Oh my God, Jonno, we're dead!'

I took her in my arms, her tears mixing with the salt water already dribbling down my bare chest.

'Now hold on, I don't know for sure that it's them. It could be anyone,' I said soothingly. 'And whoever it is might not even be coming here. They could be going anywhere. Let's not get too worked up until I go and check.'

'It's them, I know it,' she said in a tremulous voice, white-faced, tears still cascading down her cheeks.

Ten minutes later, I had scaled the rocky headland cliff between the lagoon and Big Bay and was sitting, legs astride my familiar tree – the one I had hugged all night during Annie's ordeal on the beach. I stared out to sea with the binoculars. The water was shining like mercury, heavy and slow. I could see that the smudge on the horizon was closer and the clear shape of a large trawler was emerging. It was definitely headed towards us. I had asked Annie to finish getting the boat ready but moments later I felt her presence behind me, a little out of breath from the climb. 'Is it them? Are they here?' she asked in a small voice. I turned to look at her; her face was still white and her eyes were full of dread. 'Is it them?' she repeated hoarsely.

I put my hands on hers. 'Afraid so. It looks like the same ship. I'm so sorry, Annie.'

'But I don't understand. How could they have got here in the storm?'

'Simple. It was headed our way. They just tucked in behind it and followed it here.'

For several anxious minutes we sat side by side on the cliff-top watching in horror. I was conscious of her body shaking as the nesting birds soared and screeched above the tree line; suddenly she leaned over and put her head on my shoulder and her arms around my waist. 'Oh Jonno, I've never been so scared. I can't bear the thought of being taken by those animals again. We need to leave. Now! Can't we just take off?' Her eyes were frantic.

I shared her fear. We both knew that when the stocky man discovered his stash had been looted, all hell would break loose. He would have his men scour the island for clues as to who took it and, sooner or later, they'd make their way round to the lagoon. If they found us, we would both suffer terrible deaths.

'Annie, even if I can get the little outboard to work, they would see us when we got to the open sea. They wouldn't know who we were but chances are they'd come after us anyway.' I checked my watch. 'Look, it's nearly 4 pm. Only a couple of hours to sunset. By the time they get to the reef it will be getting dark. That makes it unlikely the pirate boss will go to the cave tonight. And that means they won't be looking for us. So we have time to come up with a Plan B.' I tried to sound more confident than I was.

'Can't we find a hiding place up the mountain?' she asked.

'Sure, but they would more than likely find us.'

'Maybe we could just leave the treasure on the boat. They might be satisfied with that.'

'Not a chance. These guys would enjoy the sport of hunting us down. The boss guy does not strike me as someone who would turn the other cheek.'

Being selfish, I also did not want the bastards to get their filthy hands on my lovely boat. Right now it was the only thing I owned in the world. The fact was, we'd have to wait for the right moment to escape. As her silent tears wet my T-shirt, I sat there scheming, buttocks numb, bastard mozzies feasting on my flesh, yet I was also totally alive to her touch, her heartbeat. I could have stayed like that forever but finally I whispered, 'Okay, I've got an idea. Here's what we'll do.'

PART THREE

Love is not running away or giving up,
it is standing and fighting for every moment.
M.F. Moonzajer

47

FROM INSIDE the dingy gloom of the *Crimson Tide*'s wheel-house, BangBang scoured the small island's coastline with his new toy: a pair of Canon binoculars with image stabiliser that he had 'liberated' from the bridge of the *Caspian Cossack*.

He was exhausted but exhilarated from his labours. After the diesel had been syphoned off, he and his crew had headed straight for their island hideaway, tagging behind a south-easterly storm that was targeting the Mentawai Islands. His powerful glasses picked out the familiar wide bay in the looming dusk. They would be there soon. Too late to go to the cave today, he thought ruefully; pity, he had been looking forward to touching his treasures and depositing his latest spoils. He loved thinking of the individual value of each of his precious items and then adding all the figures up, running the numbers in his head, faster and faster, before arriving at a total sum; it was like a deeply satisfying climax.

Buoyed by the success of the tanker heist, he was also keen to pore over the blueprints for the next jobs.

'That's funny,' he suddenly said, his reverie cut short. He was looking at the far south side of the beach; there was no sign of the two western whores he had buried there. He looked again. The tide was halfway out but even with the high-powered glasses he couldn't see anything on the sand. The wildlife must have got to them, he thought. They certainly didn't dig themselves out! He grinned. As far as he knew there had been no outcry, no serious investigation into the disappearance of the four whites and their boat. Doesn't matter anyway, he thought. There's nothing to tie me to their deaths.

He decided he would stay on board the *Crimson Tide* that night and allow the crew to celebrate ashore. They deserve it, he thought, they did a good job back there. I just hope they do the same in a few days time when we hit the next ship. Otherwise, I'll have to make an example of another crew member.

He started shouting orders to the men to prepare the vessel for mooring. They had almost reached the outer edge of the reef and safe anchorage for the night.

48

BRIEFLY BACK on board *The Scoop* to get something to eat and drink, I took the opportunity to double-check that we had enough provisions for the voyage ahead. I estimated it would take us four or five days, depending on the wind and assuming there were no other problems. Then I made sure the dinghy's outboard was dried out and ready to fire before returning to my lookout post on the cliff-top.

There, with a heavy heart, I continued to watch the pirate vessel loom larger in the water until the sun finally went down. By then, the sounds of life on board drifted towards me on the fresh evening breeze high on the headland. I heard the coughs of what I assumed to be the skiff engines kicking in. Before long, in the light from a crescent moon, I could just make out vague shapes moving around on the sand before a large fire erupted, illuminating the men's shadowy figures. At least they don't appear to have any more hostages, I thought with relief. That would have complicated things somewhat.

I had asked Annie to stay on *The Scoop*. She had not wanted to leave my side but I'd insisted. I didn't want her climbing back down the rock face in the dark on her own while I embarked on my dangerous mission. But sitting here now, I could still feel the exquisite warmth of her arms around me. God help her, I thought, who could possibly even guess at the fear she was experiencing now, given what these bastards had done to her? She had told me earlier that she would rather jump off the cliff than be taken prisoner again. And I believed her.

Soon I could smell hints of roasted flesh in the night air – goat or lamb. It made my mouth water. Hopefully they'll start drinking as well. I crossed my fingers; the sooner they bed down for the night the better. In the end, it was just before midnight when the last of the revellers went to sleep. Like before, the pirates didn't bother posting a sentry, which suited me well. The prospect of what I had to do filled me with trepidation but my determination to save Annie from more brutality helped stiffen my spine.

I stood up, my joints creaking noisily. I had to stretch my legs several times before life returned to them. I went to the lagoon side of the cliff and shone my torch towards the sloop, turning it on and off several times. This was the signal to Annie that I was ready to move and she should be ready to cast off *The Scoop*'s mooring ropes as soon as I returned. A couple of flashes back at me showed that the message had been received and understood.

I had never considered myself to be an action man and what I was about to do smacked of James Bond or the SAS. But I could not think of any other way that would help us make our escape. Murmuring 'Once more into the breach', I went over the top of the headland and, as carefully as I could in the darkness, made my way down to the beach on the Big Bay side. Despite trying to be as quiet as possible, it felt like the noise I was making would have woken the recently departed, but fortunately there were no signs of stirring from the pirate camp about four hundred metres along the sand.

The sea was warm and velvet black in the pale moonlight as I slipped into the water at the foot of the cliff and started swimming slowly towards the other end. I was breathing heavily, more from fear than exertion: if even *one* of the pirates got up to take a piss at the water's edge, I'd be spotted and the game would be up. I'd be killed and Annie ... well, that didn't even bear thinking about. The glowing embers of the pirates' dying fire acted as a guide and eventually I reached the first of my two targets: a pirate skiff.

I trod water for a moment, listening and looking for any signs of life from the pirate camp. Not so much as a snore or a fart, I thought with relief. Then, holding onto the skiff's stern cleat, I fished my small gutting knife out of my pocket and started sawing at the fuel line. It quickly split and there was the pungent smell of petrol. Then I reached over and cut the rope to the small sheet anchor and the little boat started to drift in the slight swell. I gave it an extra shove in the direction of the reef. It bobbed away in the quiet slip-slop of the surf. Again, I waited and watched for any movement from the beach. Feeling quite proud of myself, I swam to the second skiff and gave it the same treatment. I watched both boats drift off into the darkness towards the reef.

The swim back to the dark, towering headland seemed to take twice as long and when I reached the bottom of the cliff where the white lacy tops of the surf caressed the beach, I was a quivering, shivering wreck. I crouched there for a few moments until I got my breath back. Then I managed to scramble back up the way I'd come earlier and before long I was flashing my torch down at *The Scoop* to signal Annie. When I finally made it back, she was so relieved to see me. 'Oh, thank God you're okay,' she whispered as she hugged me. The joy on her face made my spirits soar.

'No worries,' I said. 'It was a piece of cake.' I was feeling just a teeny bit heroic. 'Those murdering scumbags were all dead to the world. But now comes the tricky part.'

49

'TRICKY? THAT'S putting it bloody mildly, I thought to myself. We have to get *The Scoop* out to the open water through a difficult, narrow passage – in the dark – without raising the alarm. More like bloody Mission Impossible. For a start, I was going to have to start up the dinghy's outboard so we could tow the bigger boat through the narrow channel. The pirate camp was some way away and their main vessel even further out but the wind can play funny tricks and carry sound great distances, particularly when there's water around. I quickly attached the tender to the Berenger's bow with a rope and shimmied down into the dinghy. We had already pulled up *The Scoop*'s anchor and untied the rear rope, which had been tethered to a tree. Earlier, I had asked Annie to tie fenders to either side of the sloop to protect it from the rocky sides of the passage. I gave her two thumbs up and said: 'Okay, let's get going.'

By now the moonlight was stronger. I could see outlines without using a torch. My nervous fingers fumbled and it took two turns before the tender cranked into life. Shit, the noise from the little outboard sounded like a Boeing 747 in the night air. I engaged the gear and, ever so gingerly, took up the slack on the rope tethered to the sloop. It had already started to drift to the starboard side. There was a heart-stopping moment when I thought the bigger boat was going to refuse to fall in behind the dinghy but, after a small bit of resistance, we started moving. Annie was at the saloon helm station, her hands tightly gripping the wheel, trying her best to keep *The Scoop* straight behind me as we crossed the flat surface of the lagoon. So far, so good. Then, just before the V-shaped bow of the tender nudged through the entrance to the passageway, I heard the gut-wrenching sound of distant gunfire. The pirates had woken up! They must have heard the outboard. God knows what they were shooting at in the darkness. Probably just up in the air, I figured. Maybe they thought they were under attack.

I thought quickly: they can't know for sure where the engine noise is coming from. They can only guess. Without their skiffs, it will take them some time to figure it out and then they'll have to come overland to find us. Stomach clenched, I knew we needed to hurry up but I also knew I couldn't risk it: the small tender's tug-like abilities were already stretched pulling the sloop's twenty tonnes. As it was, *The Scoop* took a bit of a bashing as we pinballed our way through the dogleg in the rocky cleft between the two headlands but, hey, I comforted myself, that was what boat insurance was for. I turned and waved confidently (although I didn't feel it) to Annie, whose pale, frightened face I could just make out through the window, illuminated by a torch in the saloon. I had no idea whether she could see me or not. Then, after what seemed to be two lifetimes, we came around the rocky outcrop and the moon illuminated the dark open sea ahead. My heart leapt. *Yahoo!* I screamed in my head, we're going to make it!

Just then, something whizzed by my right ear and, a nano-second later, the noise of a gunshot followed. Fuck me, they've already found us! As the tender broached the mouth of the channel, the incoming swell turned the bow up and sideways and it flipped over, the rope tether snapping. I was thrown backwards into the sea, my head narrowly escaping being minced by the thrashing outboard propeller as the upturned dinghy bobbed away. The much heavier Berenger, however, kept coming, its momentum carrying it inexorably through the bumpy water. I had to flatten myself against the cliff-face to avoid being squashed like a bug. As *The Scoop* came past I grabbed a stern fender and managed to swing my leg up onto the transom. I heard more gunshots but it was dark and the pirates were firing blind. I realised that they were atop the headland and firing downwards, the pale decking and white sails presenting a target in the moonlight. As I clambered aboard *The Scoop* I had a momentary frisson of fear that Annie might have been hit. I prayed she was all right; I also fleetingly worried that my precious boat would be riddled with holes like Swiss cheese, but then I crouched and ran into the saloon.

Annie appeared unscathed but terror-stricken, her face tight and white but, God bless her, still gripping the wheel as if her life depended on it. As it did, of course. Shouting to her to take cover, I grabbed the wheel. By now the powerless sloop was running out of steam about forty metres out of the mouth of the channel and the swell was beginning to force our bow slowly but stubbornly back towards the northern headland. As the gunmen continued to strafe the deck, *The Scoop* was just moments from crashing onto the rocks at the base of the craggy cliff. I looked at Annie and shook my head. I tried hard but wasn't able to keep the look of despair off my face. That's it, I said to myself. Without power, we are totally screwed.

50

AS THE swell nudged *The Scoop* closer and closer towards the rocks, Annie and I were both paralysed with fear, looking at each other with horror and resignation. I think she understood that without the motor we could not drive forward – or back – and thus escape being forced onto the rocks. Her face was a picture of childlike vulnerability and I was suddenly seized by a new determination: we were not going to fucking die like this! I shouted to her to take hold of the wheel and then I ran out of the saloon and picked my way carefully down the walkway to the foredeck as the boat pitched in the heaving swell.

The bullets from above were still coming fast and furious. As I reached the mainsail, I felt a sudden burning sensation just below my neck, on the left shoulder. I must have been hit. But then more adrenaline kicked in and I forgot about it. Without hydraulics, I had to winch up the mainsail manually; within seconds it was jerking up slowly until the wind caught and the canvas braced with a crisp snapping sound; then I moved to the jib sail and did the same. I moved to the window and gesticulated for Annie to turn the wheel to starboard. She did so and *The Scoop* seemed to give a shrug and come to life; I gave a mental cheer as the boat started to ease away from the cliff. With a shout of triumph, I put two thumbs up to Annie but then saw her ducking in the gloom as a bullet smashed through the ceiling. I made my way quickly back to the saloon and took hold of the helm. 'We might just bloody make it,' I shouted happily.

I spoke too soon. I heard Annie scream a warning and I felt rather than saw a shadow behind me. Turning, I saw a dark figure lunge towards me with a machete. A pirate must have jumped into the water from the cliff-top and managed to scramble on board.

I ducked and the wet blade hit the wheel with a loud clang. I dived towards the saloon table and picked up the only weapon I could find – my gold-plated Oscar. I swung it around like a Federer forehand volley and whacked the pirate on the side of his head. As he went down, I saw another menacing figure enter the saloon. Annie screamed again. He turned the barrel of an automatic rifle towards me. Just then *The Scoop* lurched violently as the wind ballooned the mainsail. The pirate staggered, one arm reaching out to steady himself and I saw my chance. I moved towards him and brought the heavy statuette down on the top of his head with a satisfying crack. He too went down instantly. I hit him again for good measure.

The boat continued to yaw so I dropped my makeshift weapon and grabbed the helm. I turned it to bring her round to starboard and watched anxiously as the stern just cleared the submerged rocks at the foot of the cliff. Moments later she righted herself and then *The Scoop* was gliding away from the headlands like a thoroughbred horse. More bullets pinged and plinked against the transom; now that the light-coloured sails were fully unfurled we were an easier target for the snipers above. I shouted to Annie to keep her head down as more bullets zipped through the saloon ceiling. But then, suddenly, miraculously, we were in open water with nothing in front of us. Soon we were out of range and there was only the sound of the wind and my heart beating like a bass drum. We had bloody done it!

51

ANNIE AND I looked at each other in the gloom and grinned like maniacs.

She put her hand on my shoulder and squeezed it. 'Ouch,' I said, 'that hurt!' When she took her hand away we both saw it was wet. She held her hand up to her face to see better.

'Jonno, you're bleeding!' she cried. 'Oh my God, were you shot?'

I had totally forgotten about being hit. 'Not now, we can't stop, we have to get out of here *now*,' I said, teeth gritted.

'I'll get something to put on it.'

Annie got hold of a torch from somewhere and lurched unsteadily down to the galley while I continued to steer us out of danger. She had to step gingerly over the prone body of one of the pirates I had felled. I could hear her rummaging around in the drawers. 'Where do you keep the first-aid kit?' she shouted up to me. 'Are you badly hurt?'

My T-shirt was soaked in blood, I could even smell it as I held the wheel tightly. Christ, please don't let it be a bullet wound, I prayed. There wasn't much pain but that could just be adrenaline.

The compass showed we were heading north-west; in the distance on the starboard side I could see a bunch of strong lights, some static, some moving. I figured that was the main pirate ship. They wouldn't know exactly what was going on but they would have been roused by the clamour on the beach and headland. I wondered what the pirate boss was thinking right now. He must be totally confused, perhaps starting to feel a little worried. Good!

Annie came back with the first-aid box; she shone a torch on my chest as I continued to grip the helm. 'I can see something,' she said. She moved the torch closer: 'Okay, thank goodness . . . it's not a bullet. There's a bit of wood or something sticking out.'

I looked down and saw a triangular-shaped shard, about four centimetres long, poking out of my T-shirt. It looked like a teak arrowhead as it glistened dully in the torchlight. That's my blood, I thought, feeling a bit faint. Hah, so much for Action Man! And at that moment the wound began to hurt. A lot. I winced at the sudden pain.

'Now listen,' Annie said, 'this might hurt a bit.'

'Ow!' I shouted as she tugged at the shard.

'Don't be such a baby. Here, you'll have to take your T-shirt off so I can clean the wound.'

'Can't it wait until we're completely clear? I'm a bit worried that the pirate ship will come after us. Without power, we're vulnerable; it could overhaul us quite quickly.'

'It won't take a moment. The splinter hasn't gone in very deep. I'll just disinfect it and put a temporary dressing on and we can do it properly later. Here, hold the torch and shine it there.' She tapped my chest and I winced again. 'Oops, sorry,' she said with a giggle.

'With all those bullets spraying around,' she said, 'you were lucky to get away with just a splinter. I thought we were going to be ripped to shreds at one point. I was so scared. The noise, the guns and then when I saw you thrown from the dinghy in the channel I thought you might have been killed. It was like a miracle when you suddenly appeared from the back.'

'The stern. It's called the stern.' I grinned at her.

'Whatever. Then when the shooting started, I thought we would both be killed. And then when the boat started moving towards the rocks . . .' Annie was beginning to jabber a bit, her nerves obviously still jangling after all the drama. 'Even worse was when those two brutes appeared from nowhere. You were incredible. How you managed to stop them, I'll never know.'

'Sheer instinct,' I said modestly. 'But it's not all over yet. I don't want to alarm you but we still have a tough trip ahead.'

'You mean like the weather, the sea conditions?'

'No, the pirates. I don't think we've seen the last of them yet.'

Apart from the stinging pain of the antiseptic, I was rather enjoying Annie's attentions. She was bent over my naked upper torso and her proximity was intoxicating. The smell of her hair under my nose was making me feel giddy . . . or maybe it was the pain from the wound. Either way, when she stood up and said it was all patched up I felt a pang of disappointment.

We could not stop grinning at each other. I think we were both feeling heady, the adrenaline washing through our veins. We had escaped, at least for now, and *The Scoop* seemed to be enjoying being unleashed on the ocean again. I worried about the damage to her from the bullets but the beautiful boat seemed quite unaffected as she sliced through the dark sea. Once again I blessed the day I bought her.

Just as I began to relax and let the adrenaline seep away, I remembered the two pirates I had bashed.

52

THE FAMILIAR clatter of distant gunfire instantly woke BangBang. Normally he loved the sounds of guns popping but now, perplexed, he stood up in the *Crimson Tide*'s wheelhouse, where he had a cot. Were they being attacked? Had a patrol boat found them? What the fuck was going on? He grabbed his binoculars and put them to his eyes but he still couldn't see much in the warm, dark night. He could make out a slight glow on the beach and a hint of some activity but that was all. There was no sign of another vessel, big or small. A few minutes later, he caught a few flashes to the right. They were much higher up. The headland. He shouted to Mamat, the helmsman, who had arrived looking sleepy and confused, to put the ship's small inflatable in the water.

Ten minutes later, he was pacing up and down on the beach angrily demanding to be told what had happened by the lone crewmember remaining there. Nervously, the man explained that one of the others had been having a piss when he had heard the sound of an engine and raised the alarm. Initially they hadn't been able to tell where it was coming from. Some had fired shots at the tree line, thinking they were under attack from the forest. Others ran to the end of the beach and started scaling the cliff. Shortly after, the man had heard more gunshots. He explained that he had remained to guard the camp.

In his mounting frustration, BangBang lashed out with his pistol and knocked the man over. Then he noticed there was no sign of the skiff. 'Where the fuck are our boats?' he yelled, kicking the man as he lay on the ground. He rubbed his mottled chin; this is all fucked up, he thought. A sudden chill gripped his chest: did this have something to do with the cave, with his treasures? Not possible, surely? How would any fucking thief even find it?

Nevertheless he had a horrible feeling and, despite the dark, he started walking across the beach determined to check the cave. Just then one of the other crew members appeared out of the gloom. Gasping and wheezing, he told BangBang what had happened, how they had scaled the cliff and seen an expensive-looking yacht in some difficulty manoeuvring near the rocks. Whoever was steering it had managed to get it under control before heading out to sea. The crew had fired on it but it was dark and the man didn't know if they had hit anybody. Two of the others had jumped into the water to go after the yacht but there had been no sign of them since.

'Wait, you say boat had sail? No engine? Then what you hear earlier?' The man told him they had found a small dinghy with the foreign name *The Scoop Jon B* upturned in the surf. BangBang spat on the sand, turned and stomped off into the jungle, his powerful torch jerkily illuminating the way ahead.

53

I STEELED myself to check out the two pirates while Annie held the wheel. Even in the dim light, it was clear that one of them was dead and the other in a terrible way. I didn't feel bad. These bastards had tried to kill us, had probably been part of the original group who killed Annie's husband and then abused her and Dani on the beach. They did not deserve my sympathy.

'What will we do with them?' Annie asked. Now that the immediate crisis was over and the adrenaline had gone, her earlier mood had also evaporated. She looked pale and tense once more. The sight of dead and bashed bodies can have that effect, I thought wryly.

I thought for a moment. Ideally, we could just chuck them both overboard but I wasn't sure Annie would agree as one of the scumbags was still alive. But there was no way I was going to keep a dead body on board. In the end, Annie reluctantly helped me carry the corpse to the stern, where we eased it into the ocean. Needless to say, there were no prayers said for the ratbag. Without thinking I chucked the machete and gun after him. As soon as I'd done it, I realised how stupid it was not to have kept the weapons. And later I had reason to wish that I had not been so hasty.

The injured guy was moaning but still unconscious. His head was a mess of blood and other sticky stuff – I did not dare imagine what. We tied his hands and feet and laid him in the lazarette – the storage locker where the dinghy and kayak had been stored.

Walking back into the saloon, I stooped down and picked up the Oscar. An unusual weapon, but effective. I rinsed the blood and goo off it in the galley.

Back at the wheel, I pondered what to do now. Annie and I had discussed where the best place to go might be – somewhere within reasonable reach where the authorities would take us seriously and where there were British and Australian embassies in case we needed support. We had narrowed it down to Singapore, Phuket or Jakarta. Singapore would probably give us the best hearing but it was the furthest away. Phuket had seemed a reasonable choice but it would mean crossing the north end of the Malacca Strait. I was not keen to do that without power. So we had decided on Jakarta. If my previous estimate of the location of Rehab Island was right, it was the closest and probably the easiest destination. But now that the pirates were aware of our presence, and once their leader found his treasure gone, they would come after us with an almighty vengeance. I turned to Annie, who was sitting on the saloon sofa, her elbows on the table, staring straight ahead. She seemed listless. Her energy levels must have tanked after the rush of adrenaline from the last couple of hours' drama seeped away.

'Look Annie, I know you don't want to hear this but we're not out of the woods yet. Far from it. The pirates will scent blood. And they might well work out that we have no power. Once they get their act together, they could easily overhaul us in no time.'

Annie turned her head slowly and looked at me. 'So what are we going to do?' It sounded as if she did not really care. I picked up a maritime chart and put it in front of her.

'Look – these are the Mentawai Islands here.' I pointed the torch at the chart and put my finger on the shiny surface. 'It's where I reckon Rehab Island is. Their ship is moored maybe a couple of kilometres to the north of us. I reckon we should turn *The Scoop* around, sail past it and let them think we are heading north up the coast. It will look as if we are trying for Aceh or Phuket. Then we double back and go south. It will be dark for a few hours yet. We might be able to fool them.'

'You mean . . . head towards them? Are you crazy?'

'It's a risk, I know, but I figure we have a bit of time before they come after us. That stocky guy is guaranteed to check out the cave and then have a look at our lagoon. They don't have the skiffs so it will take them a while to get everybody back to the ship. We could be past it before they even get off the beach.'

'And then what?'

'Then, once we're out of sight, we do a long looping turn and head back south-east along here.' I moved my fingernail along the Sumatran coastline.

Annie looked at me with dull eyes and shrugged. 'Whatever.'

Her apathy was beginning to worry me. I knew she must be tired, as I was. Neither of us had had any sleep.

'We should be fine as long as this freshening wind holds. We have to reach the turning point before the sun comes up and they'll be able to spot us with binoculars. I realise it all sounds a little iffy but I'm certain it's the best chance we've got. What do you think?'

Annie thought for a moment. 'Okay, but what if they guess that it's a bluff and come south also?'

'Then we're stuffed,' I told her bluntly. 'Even if we have good wind, they have power and we don't. Unless there's a miracle, they'll catch up with us sooner rather than later. Let's hope they keep heading north after we've made our turn.'

54

BANGBANG SAT down shakily on a ledge by the rock pool and put his huge head in his grimy hands. Acid sweat squeezed through his fingers like hot tears. He had never shed a tear before, not even when his uncle had done those shameful things to him. But right now he felt like weeping his heart out. The cave was empty; everything had been taken, nothing remained apart from the stinking bats. His worst fucking nightmare. He moaned quietly in distress: his carefully accumulated treasures were gone, and with them his long-nurtured dreams and ambitions.

How could this have possibly happened? What miserable, poisonous motherfuckers could have done such a terrible thing? It was inconceivable that someone could have found his cave. Who were they and why had they done this to him? More to the point, where have the ratshit sons of bitches gone? His tortured mind turned to the careful plans he had made to ensure his future was comfortable and profitable; his dream to swap the squalid slum for a Shangri-la had turned to shit.

In one terrible moment, the golden life he had planned for, worked hard for, robbed and killed for, had been ripped away from him.

I'm a dead man now, he thought. He banged his forehead with clenched knuckles in despair. His crime bosses would not care about his personal losses but they would be unforgiving about the theft of the blueprints detailing the imminent high-sea heists. The risk of going ahead would be too great: the thief could hand the documents over to the police, who would then undoubtedly stage an ambush. So the syndicate would cut its losses and abort the robberies. That would make them as mad as a cut cobra – and twice as dangerous. Fuck, fuck, fuck! What can I do?

BangBang took a few moments to recover his senses. He knew there was only one way to save his skin: he had to hunt down the thieving mongrels who had robbed him of his treasures and get them back. Then I will take my own sweet time in making the dogs suffer for what they have done, he resolved. The thought cheered him a little. He stood up, infused with renewed energy and a thirst for revenge. There was no time to lose. He crashed his way back through the jungle, not caring if he left a trail that could be seen from the moon. No fucking point trying to keep it a secret now anyway, he thought grimly.

55

'WE'VE MADE good headway,' I assured Annie as we left the pirate ship far behind us and ploughed our way west, deeper into the Indian Ocean. It had been a hair-raising time as we'd swept by the big trawler but there had been little activity on board. At first I was worried – we actually needed someone to clock us. But then I saw a man silhouetted by lamplight watching us from the door of the pilothouse. Perfect. We sailed on for another few kilometres before starting our long, lazy turn south. I checked my watch. Dawn was less than an hour away. 'Now we need to put some distance between us and them.'

'Do you think they'll suss it out eventually?' Annie's brow was furrowed.

'If that stocky guy has any brains, he'll eventually realise that we're not actually heading north and he'll double back. Pray that this north-easterly wind keeps up and we can maintain this pace.'

I sounded confident but I too was starting to feel apprehensive. My mood was not improved by the fact that the holes in the headsail from the pirates' bullets were starting to rip in the wind. If the rips started to seriously run, we could be in deep shit.

'How long do you think it will take us?' asked Annie. She was feeding Wagga in the galley below the saloon helm station.

'To do what?'

'To get to Jakarta, of course.'

'I told you . . . four to five days. Tomorrow we'll tuck in to the mainland coastline and then follow it all the way down to the Sunda Strait. Then it's an easy passage through to the Java Sea and, hey presto, we're home and dry.'

'You make it sound easy.'

'Well, normally it would be fairly straightforward but those damned pirates will be on our tail so we can't be complacent.'

'God, Jonno. I hope they don't find us.'

There was an uneasy silence for a few minutes while we both thought about the danger looming behind us. To lighten the mood, I said, 'Hey, if my old ancestor Captain Bligh could sail nearly seven thousand kilometres in a seven-metre open boat with nineteen men, we can do this.'

'You're related to *that* Bligh, the *Bounty* chap?'

'Probably not. But he *was* Governor of New South Wales for a while so he could have spawned an Aussie Bligh bloodline that includes yours truly.'

'I've seen the statue of him at The Rocks in Sydney. You do look a bit like him. The same cruel expression.'

'Very funny. So, what are you looking forward to most, when we get back?'

Annie pursed her lips and appeared to consider the question seriously. She stopped working in the kitchen and came up next to me, her lovely face pensive. I noticed for the first time the faintest sprinkle of freckles across the bridge of her nose.

'Oh obvious things, I guess. Girly stuff like hot baths and manicures, lipstick and moisturising cream. What else? My special muesli in the morning and a cold pinot gris in the evening! My guilty secrets: *Sex and the City* and *Coronation Street*. And, of course, my clothes: especially clean underwear.'

'Yes, it'll be a relief to get my shirts back.'

'Ha ha. But most of all, I think I'll just enjoy getting back to some sort of normality. The last few weeks have been ... well, you can imagine. Not just the ... the beach, gruesome though that was. The *Lady Vesper*. Martin, Dani.' Her voice trailed off.

'But in all of this darkness, there's been some light. You, for example. Saving me. Looking after me. Whatever happens, I will never, ever forget my knight in shining armour.' With that, she slipped one arm under mine and snuggled in to my side as I gripped the wheel. I tried not to purr like Wagga who, not to be outshone, had jumped onto my lap.

'Sometimes it's like I was watching a film about someone who looked like me; someone familiar, but not actually me.' She paused for a moment, then she looked at me with those great green eyes: 'And what about you? What are you looking forward to?'

'Aw, just blokey stuff: watching sport, going to the pub, eating meat. First chance I get, I'll have a big, juicy steak. And fries. The biggest treat, however, will be having some decent company for a change.'

'Oh, that's cruel. Really cruel. Just like your ancestor Captain bloody Bligh.'

56

BACK ON the beach, BangBang saw that his men had retrieved one of the skiffs. It had been found at the other end of the bay, washed up close to the headland. They were repairing the fuel line, which had been deliberately cut. There was no sign of the other skiff. Anxious to get going, he ordered the men to board the remaining skiff and the inflatable. It was a tight squeeze but, before long, the two small craft bumped across the reef to the *Crimson Tide*.

One of the pirates told BangBang that they had discovered some evidence of recent human activity including a makeshift barbecue at a small lagoon on the other side of the cliff. No signs of an actual camp, but that would make sense because the boat would have sufficed for shelter.

'You sure there no engine?' he asked one of the crew again.

'Yes, boss. The man was struggling to put up sail. If boat had engine, he use it. I think he use small boat to tow big one.'

'How many people were there?'

'Too dark to see. I think maybe someone else inside.'

He quizzed the man further but got little more information from him other than that the man was probably a westerner and that the boat looked big and new. When they reached the *Crimson Tide*, Mamat told him that he had seen the yacht go past just a hundred metres away on the port side, heading north. BangBang looked at the map. Two possibilities, he calculated. Either the dogs keep going north or they turn and go south. They can't go west, there's nothing out there but the vast open ocean. And the mainland to the east is just jungle. He smiled grimly for the first time since he had woken to gunfire earlier that morning. Without power, his quarry could not hope to escape the big-engined *Crimson Tide*, despite a few hours head start. Maybe things would turn out okay after all. He made his decision. Lighting a cigarette, he tapped Mamat on the shoulder and pointed north.

57

NOW THAT they were committed to a course of action, Annie felt better. In fact, she was beginning to feel surprisingly energised by the confident thrust of the sloop as it cut cleanly through the low waves. *Maybe it's because I'm on my way home – wherever that is now,* she mused.

As she prepared a makeshift lunch for the two of them, she thought back to her earlier sailing experience on the *Lady Vesper*. It had been a nightmare, even before the pirates had attacked. When that squall had hit them she had almost been as sick as Dani. Of course, the pirate threat still hovered over her like a menacing cloud. But being at sea felt more positive now, more purposeful. Perhaps it was because of Jonno; perhaps it was the smooth performance of *The Scoop*. *Instead of a white horse, my gentle knight has this beautiful boat and he's carrying me off to a new life.* She smiled. *What tosh! I sound like a Mills and Boon tragic.* But as the faraway sky began to lighten, heralding the new day, she *did* feel different, less consumed by recent events, more optimistic that she could take hold of the future with both hands. Surviving the morning's dangerous escape had only served to heighten that feeling.

But does that future include this big, complicated, lovely man, Annie asked herself. And anyway, why would he want me after everything that's happened? I'm damaged goods after all, she told herself again. But, in her heart, she knew he cared for her, and not just out of pity — she saw the way he looked at her and how he responded when she touched him. And, anyway, he had had his own issues to contend with, hadn't he?

Yet the thought of being with a man in that way still seemed alien, unimaginable, after what happened. She shivered. It would be easy to hate all men after that, but she knew that would be stupid, unreasonable. They're not all bad. She thought of her father, who had had such a positive influence on her life; Jamie, her little brother, whose warm, bright personality always delighted her. And Pascal. Her eyes suddenly glistened. He had been such a lovely boy. And now here was Jonno. How could she possibly hate him? She owed him so much. Whatever happens when we get back, I want him to be in my life in some way, she decided.

After lunch, pleading exhaustion, Annie went for a nap while Jonno held *The Scoop* on its southern course. As she closed her eyes, her mind drifted back to her first amour, Pascal. She pictured him — the handsome hippy — in their flat around the corner from Belsize Park tube station. They had been so happy there. The place belonged to an art dealer friend of his French papa, Julien Marchand, who was a celebrity chef with restaurants in both Paris and London.

Later, when she met the charming Julien for the first time, he had kissed her extravagantly three times on her cheeks – right, left, right – before standing back to admire her. '*Elle est superbe*, Pascal! Mademoiselle, you look just like my friend Sophie Marceau,' he said to her. Later, Annie had Googled the French actress and was thrilled by the comparison. She had never considered herself a 'looker' but Pascal told her she was beautiful so often that she had almost come to believe it.

She had been so naïve about so many things when she left her sheltered home life for uni; Pascal had opened her eyes to many new, sophisticated ideas and places; to books on philosophy and eastern religions; to foreign travel. Her mind drifted to the time he had taken her to France to visit his father's historic hometown, Perigueux in the northern Dordogne. They travelled on his 'bloody bastard motorbike', touring the south-west of France, sampling the local food and wines and the rich culture of the Bergerac and Bordeaux regions.

Waking up in a sweat less than two hours later, one dream-like scene was stuck in Annie's mind. She and Pascal were having dinner in Julien's upscale restaurant in Chelsea. But when she looked across the table, it was not Pascal sitting there. It was Jonno.

58

I WAS just letting the anchor down by hand when I heard noises from the rear of the boat. Muffled shouts and dull thumps. Shit, must be the injured pirate, I thought; when I had checked earlier he had still been unconscious.

The Scoop was bobbing in the lee of a small island, one of the most southerly, I was sure, of the Mentawais. It was too dangerous to sail in the dark and so we had sought shelter for the night. The island screened us from any traffic (including the pirates) on the ocean side. We were facing the dark mainland, there did not seem to be any sizeable towns on that stretch of coast, and no distant lights either. Tomorrow there would be mostly open water as we headed south parallel with the mainland.

I finished dropping the anchor and made my way to the stern. I flinched as I noticed the scars that *The Scoop* wore as a badge of honour from our battle with the pirates. As well as the rips in the sheets, the decking looked like a dartboard ... it was pitted with angry marks everywhere; the curved windscreen was starred in several places and chunks of fibreglass had been gouged out; and one of the two helm consoles in the cockpit had been shot to pieces. The next time I go on a sailing adventure, I thought, I'll buy a decommissioned navy corvette.

Reaching the transom, I opened the lazarette. The stench nearly blew me overboard. I almost gagged. His wounds must be infected. I had done my best to clean the head injury that old Oscar had inflicted on him but he urgently needed more professional attention. The trussed-up pirate looked up at me with pain-filled eyes. He seemed small and pathetic ... a far cry from the murderous marauder I remembered. His dark skin was mottled and unhealthy looking. I reckoned he was Thai or Malay. His mouth opened, showing a mix of black, brown and yellow teeth. He was trying to talk, his eyes bright, burning holes but I had no idea what he was saying.

Probably wants some water, I reckoned. I went inside to get some. Annie asked what was going on and I told her to stay inside. It would not be a good idea for her to confront one of the men responsible for her ordeal. I knelt down, one hand over my nose, and cut the rope around his hands so he could hold the flask of water. He drank greedily and I turned around to look at the open sea, checking in the dying light for any sign that the pirate's colleagues had caught up with us. As I turned back to him, I felt, rather than saw a dark blur come towards me and the next moment something smashed into my head and I keeled over.

When I came to, Annie was kneeling over me, her face a mask of concern. She was holding a damp cloth to my head where the pirate had bashed me. With Cody's kayak paddle, I saw. It was lying a metre away on the transom.

'Are you okay?' Annie said. 'I was so worried that he might have killed you. You might have concussion.' She held up three fingers and asked me how many there were.

'Stop it, I'll be fine. Where is that bastard? Where's he gone? Did he threaten you in any way?' I sat up, holding my head in both hands.

'No, no. I was in the saloon as you said. I heard a commotion and I came running out. I saw him go over the back there.'

'The stern. I told you, it's called the bloody stern.'

She laughed. 'It didn't take you long to get your sweet dis-position back, Mr Grumpypants. Anyway, he's gone. I presume he's going to try to swim to the shore.'

Good luck with that, I thought to myself. The state he's in, he'll be lucky not to end up as a shark's supper.

'Ah well, saves us the problem of having to put up with him until we get to Jakarta,' I said. 'He was beginning to stink the place out.'

The sky was adorned with sparkling stars, like a black velvet dress studded with rhinestones. A half-moon cast its radiance on the gently rippling sea. The only sound came from the bucking of the boat against the anchor chain, thanks to a strong current. We were sitting on the foredeck, gazing up at the heavenly vista, marvelling at its dark majesty and chatting quietly about our time on Rehab Island.

So far so good, I thought. There had been no sign of pursuers and the weather had been kind to us. Enough wind to keep us moving steadily at around twelve knots, the sloop's sails still holding fast despite their increasingly ragged appearance. It had been extremely hot in the afternoon and, but for the strong breeze, would have been stickily oppressive. Some rain had come in just before dusk, a desultory discharge from charcoal-smeared clouds that felt like being mugged by a bucket of warm soapy water. I realised I didn't smell too good. Not as bad as that pirate, but I should have had a swim, I thought. But I had been too tired and my head hurt. Luckily I was upwind of Annie.

'You know, despite the lack of steak and live sport, I'll miss Rehab Island,' I said. 'It was much better than one of those Betty Ford places with the Twelve Steps and bloody people in white coats asking you how you feel all the time. I don't know how Percy put up with all that AA shit.'

'I know I'm going to have to talk to a white coat when we get back,' Annie responded.

'After everything that's happened, you seem incredibly sane.'

'Thanks, but I know it's the lull before the storm.' She squeezed my arm: 'You won't want to be around me when I finally confront my own demons. I'm going to have to focus all of my attention on what's ahead of me and it's going to be ugly.'

'Nonsense, you won't get rid of me that easily.'

Our luck didn't hold; as we headed south the next morning, the wind dropped, the sails sagged and my hopes sank faster than an Admiralty anchor. We were virtually stalled, a slight swell our only form of propulsion. I had already been fretting because of the enforced overnight stoppage; I knew the pirate ship would keep on coming, day and night. Frustrated, we sat in the cockpit hardly talking. Even Wagga looked pissed off as he pawed a piece of rope without much enthusiasm. At last, a few hours later, the wind freshened and our spirits soared with it. Annie gave me a thumbs up as I increased sail and suddenly we were back on track, running alongside the smudgy grey–green coastline like a white gazelle. We were sailing on a full reach – sixty degrees off the wind, a perfect tack.

For two whole days, we had much of the same weather – feast or famine, wind-wise. Hours of doldrums punctuated by strong bursts of favourable winds that swept us steadily south. Finally, through binoculars, I saw the outline of an island on the starboard side that I believed, according to the charts, to be called Enggano. I may have passed it several weeks ago on the ocean side on my way north but I was probably too screwed up to notice at the time.

If so, it meant that we were about halfway home. By my estimate, it was about another two hundred kilometres to the Sunda Strait and then a quick hop and a skip to Jakarta. I shouted from the cockpit wheel station to Annie in the saloon: 'Good news! See that island over there? That says we are nearly home and dry. All being well, we'll reach Jakarta in another two days, three at most.'

I spoke too soon. Just a few hours later, as I was looking back at the distant Enggano through the glasses, I noticed a tiny blemish on the horizon to the far north-west of the island. Fuck, that looks like a ship, I thought, my guts clenching.

59

BANGBANG WOKE with a start at the wheelhouse chart table, unconsciously wiping a snail trail of drool from his jawline with the back of his hand. He realised Mamat had been nudging him.

'What is it? What's happened?' he demanded. He had hardly slept in the last couple of days, grabbing naps when he could, looking anxiously out to sea most of the time, drinking thick, dark Java coffee and smoking.

Mamat said nothing, instead he handed BangBang the binoculars and pointed forward through the pilothouse window.

The slight speck on the ocean would have been impossible to see but for the high-precision quality of the Canons. 'You think it's them?' BangBang wiped his jaw again and quickly calculated. If it *is* those fuck dogs, we can probably catch them later today, tomorrow morning at the latest. Most likely they'll try to find anchorage before dusk and that's when we can get on top of them.

Mamat shrugged. 'Only few hours of light left,' he said. 'Probably they head towards coast soon and we not able to

237

find their shelter. But tomorrow!' And with that, the old Malay chopped his right hand down hard on the top of the large wooden wheel and grinned to reveal a few brown-stained teeth like rotting hulks in a marine graveyard.

BangBang lit yet another spicy Gudang Garam and shook off the feelings of cold dread that had gripped his guts since leaving that damned island. The *Crimson Tide* had charged north for a few hours before he reluctantly decided that their quarry must have doubled back after all. It was no surprise but it had further enraged him. He had remained in the pilothouse ever since, shouting 'faster' constantly to Mamat, knowing full well they were already running at top speed, the turbocharged diesel engine sounding like a chainsaw chewing up a redwood. 'But now I've got you, you bastard monkeys,' he whispered as he looked through the binoculars, 'and I'm going to make you pay. Whoever the fuck you are. I look forward to meeting you … and killing you.'

In a sudden wave of uncharacteristic excitement, BangBang clapped the old man on the back and shouted again, 'Faster, faster!' just as he used to do when he sat on the back of Yuda's motor scooter as they trawled the streets of Jakarta looking for tourist prey.

60

I DREADED telling Annie what I'd seen, decided to wait until the smudgy shape became a bit clearer. In case it was nothing. Could be anything, I told myself: a rainstorm, a pleasure cruiser, maybe even a cargo ship, although I knew most merchant vessels would use the Malacca Strait. But after an hour or so, Annie eventually noticed me constantly looking sternwards with the binoculars and said calmly: 'What is it? What do you keep looking at?'

I swallowed hard. 'There's something back there. I can't make it out yet.'

'But it could be them?'

'Could be anyone,' I said. But we both knew the chances were it was the pirates. Her face fell but there were no tears this time. 'So what do we do now?'

'All we can do is head for the mainland and hope like hell we reach it before whoever it is can catch up. Then we can find a safe spot to anchor, hopefully hidden enough to stop them finding us in the dark.'

Annie nodded. 'But then? What happens in the morning, if they spot us?'

'We could either swim to the shore and hide in the jungle or make another run for it in *The Scoop*.'

'Neither sounds a great option. What do *you* think we should do?'

'We don't even know for certain that it's the pirates. So I think we find a good place to anchor for the night and then weigh up our odds in the morning.'

That night, we huddled together in the saloon, Wagga included. A lone candle provided some ghostly light. We had skipped dinner. Neither of us was hungry.

We were moored in a cove on the coastline. I had taken the risk of possibly foundering the sloop on a reef or sandbar by tucking in close to the shore. Then I'd taken a further risk by waiting until after dusk before turning in to the cove to prevent the pirates, if that's who was in the vessel we had seen a long way behind, from knowing where we had gone. My last sight of the dim shape had been inconclusive but I was pretty certain that it was a large vessel of some sort. Meanwhile, there wasn't much of a moon so I was sure we couldn't easily be seen where we had anchored.

There wasn't the same banter of the previous evening, when we had our tails up and escape looked likely. Instead, we talked more seriously. Annie asked me how I got into journalism.

'I got expelled,' I said.

'Oh my God! From school? What happened?'

'St Jude's was run by Jesuits ... the SAS of the Catholic Church. No sense of humour. One time a condom was found dangling from the outstretched hand of a statue of the Virgin Mary in the assembly hall. Someone dobbed me in.'

'That's gross,' Annie said, her nose wrinkling. I had forgotten she was a bit religious.

'In my defence, it was not a used one.'

'Oh well, that's all right then,' she said with heavy sarcasm. 'But how did that lead you to newspapers?'

'My father knew someone at the local paper – the *Sans Souci Sentinel*. English had been the only thing I was good at. It turned out to be a good fit. I spent four years there – flower shows, council meetings, the odd bit of petty crime, you know the sort of thing.'

'Then what?'

'Then I met Percy Mimms. He was my boss at the *Sunday World* in Sydney. I told you about him, remember?'

'Yes, of course. Martin used to read the *Sunday World*. Bit of a scandal sheet, isn't it?'

'Yeah, but also a highly professional operation. Percy had been a top guy in Fleet Street and he turned me into a gun tabloid reporter. I owe my career to him and a lot else besides. Later he set me up in London and tipped me off to the scoop that led to the book and the film. I remember him once warning me: "Watch out son, it's jugular journalism over there. They'd sell their granny for a wee showbiz exclusive."' I said it in an exaggerated Scottish accent.

'Ah yes. The book. Haven't had a chance to read it yet. So it's about a story you did at the *Tribune*? I used to read that at the office. So what was it about ... this famous scoop of yours?'

'Well,' I said, 'are you sitting comfortably ...?'

I told her about how Percy had tipped me off about a politician that he had tried and failed to nail some years earlier when he had worked in London. The member for Letcham in the Cotswolds, James St John Carmichael, and his wife Josephine were an odious couple, media tarts who had slimed and sleazed their way into the public consciousness via C-List appearances on TV and radio talk shows and comedy panel progs like *Have I Got News For You*. 'They claimed to be committed Christians, just like you,' I smiled at Annie. 'They were the very stuff Sunday tabloids are made of. One of Percy's sources had told him that the couple had been regularly attending swingers' parties in the suburbs. He had made cautious inquiries but soon found himself on the wrong end of a tersely-worded Exocet from the couple's lawyers. His editor took fright and told Percy to back off.'

I went on to tell her that, by the time I started at the Trib some years later, the 'Letch from Letcham' as he later became known by the tabloids, had become Junior Minister for Defence Procurement in the government. His promotion had not deterred the couple from their relentless pursuit of celebrity or, as it turned out, their swinging lifestyle.

'"Maybe it's time you took another look at yon wee shites," Percy had suggested. So I did. For the next seven weeks I worked the story, researching them at night and spending my days off on their trail. Bit by bit I established beyond legal doubt that Josey and her charmless husband were indeed enthusiastic swingers; incredibly, their swinger names were "Josephine" and "Boney-part".'

'You have got to be kidding!' Annie's eyes went wide at that.

I told her that some of the parties involved drugs, underage girls and rent boys. So far, it was just another standard redtop tabloid story that might make a spread in the Sunday edition. But what turned it into a major scoop that brought the government down was this: 'Boney-part' had persuaded two Cabinet ministers, including the Education Secretary, to join their sordid little soirées. One of the rent boys had provided us with photos of both pollies in flagrante delicto with his fourteen-year-old friends.

'Ugh. I am beginning to think all men are irredeemable bastards,' Annie said. I found it hard to disagree with her.

'So,' I concluded, 'to lose one minister to a sex scandal might be construed as careless, to lose three was disastrous. My scoop hammered the final nails into the coffin of a government already reeling from an economic crisis and global terrorism. Not a very pretty story but it had huge consequences.'

'Wow. I vaguely remember it. I think I was still at uni. And the book obviously followed.'

'*Hard News* was more about my investigation into the scandal and the roadblocks that were put up to try to prevent me from getting to the truth. The film, on the other hand, focused on the sleazy couple, how their arrogance and hubris brought them down.'

'And it brought you fame and fortune. And, of course, *The Scoop Jon B*.'

It brought me a lot more than that, I thought. It brought Charlie. It brought shame and self-disgust. But then, it also brought me you.

'So you can see what an influence Percy had on my life.'

'Sounds like an amazing character.'

'I only wish you could have known him.'

Annie smiled, a genuine, heart-warming smile that lit up her face and seared my soul. 'He would be proud of the way you have sorted yourself out. And he'd be thrilled by what you did for me on Rehab Island.'

Wagga was the only one who slept soundly that night. Annie and I sprawled uncomfortably on the saloon settee, our arms around each other for mutual comfort, occasionally dozing off for a few moments before waking up again with a start. I kept thinking over and over how wonderful it was that she trusted me enough to be this close, particularly after what she had said earlier about men.

On board the *Crimson Tide*, BangBang was feeling a mix of triumph and frustration. He had watched hungrily as the smaller craft had headed for the coast, its sails reflecting the dying rays of the setting sun; he'd watched it and watched it until the high-powered glasses cut into his cheekbones and the gloom finally wrapped the sleek sailboat in its dark, invisible embrace. He was sure in his bones that the yacht was the one they were hunting.

Their chances of running down the mongrels had faded with the light. But victory was within his grasp. He could taste it. Tomorrow he would get his precious possessions back and those dogs would pay for their impudence with their lives. More importantly, his own life would no longer be in danger because the syndicate would never know how close to disaster he had come. He would threaten each of his men with extreme violence if they ever told anyone what had happened back at the island.

At last, he put the binoculars down and rubbed his reddened

eyes. 'Okay, I get some sleep now,' he'd told the replacement helmsman. 'Wake me at dawn. Not a moment later, or I toss you to the fucking sharks.'

Now all we have to do is stay put for the night and wait for them to appear again in the morning, he mused as he headed for bed. His mouth twisted into a cruel smile as the blood-soaked images of what he'd do to the thieves ran through his mind again and again.

61

I WAS still wrapped in Annie's unconscious embrace when dawn picked out the rugged cliffs of the small cove we had sheltered in overnight in a wan, yellow light.

Already missing the warmth of her arms, I made my way quietly up to the cockpit without waking her. I figured she needed as much rest as possible. The coming day could be the most frightening and challenging yet. It might even be our last. Like me, she would have to be at her sharpest.

In that first pale light I looked at the maps: the coastal area was sparsely populated with few towns of any size. Certainly, the terrain looked unwelcome with lots of mangrove swamps and thick vegetation. Looks dangerous, I thought. I'd rather take our chances at sea. So, anxious to get going, I nudged Annie gently awake and told her that I believed we should continue sailing south. 'We'll hug the coastline and, worst case, if we see any sign of the pirates, we can still make a dash for the shore and take our chances in the jungle.'

'Won't they come after us there?'

'If we leave the loot on *The Scoop*, the bastards might settle for that.' In fact I was sure they would be hell-bent on hunting us down and killing us but I wanted to sound reassuring. 'So, basically, I think that's our best bet.'

Annie smiled nervously. 'I don't like the odds much. But you're right, we have to take the gamble.' I could see that she was terrified but she hid it well.

'Okay, let's get this show underway,' I said, more heartily than I felt.

We made a good start. Emerging from the cove's cocoon there was no sign of life anywhere, apart from a few seabirds. We immediately caught a brisk tide. Then *The Scoop* was flying along in fifteen knots or more of wind. I smiled at Annie. We were in the cockpit, me standing at the surviving steering helm, Annie sitting at the other one that had been destroyed earlier. She looked a little tired and tense but she smiled bravely back. 'This is good, isn't it, Jonno? We're making great headway and there's not a sign of a buccaneer or an old seadog to be seen. Apart from you that is!'

'Cheeky. Less of the old, if you please. Fingers crossed, if this keeps up we'll be having that steak in downtown Jakarta tomorrow.'

'I'll settle for a nice bath and crisp white sheets.'

Our positive mood lasted less than two hours. Just as we thought we were home and dry, a familiar, sinister shape came into view off to the west. Ah shit. Despite the distance, we both knew it was the pirate ship. It sat on the ocean surface like a giant spider in its web waiting patiently for its juicy prey.

The vessel was still four or five kilometres away; it would take them a little time to cut us off if our wind held strong. I quickly calculated: probably an hour if we were lucky. Hugging herself, Annie gave me a look of quiet terror tinged with resignation. I think she knew all along that they'd be there. 'Are you okay?' I cupped my hands and shouted to Annie in the whistling wind, as I tried to coax another knot out of the sails.

'I'm scared shitless, to be honest. What do we do now?'

'Plan B. I'll get real close to the coast and we'll look for a spot where we can land *The Scoop*. Ideally a bay with no reef. If necessary we'll just beach the boat and make a run for it. It will probably ruin her but that's not important now. If you like, we'll leave all the treasure on board and hope they settle for that and leave us be.'

'Will we have enough time to get away?'

'They won't be able to bring their ship in close so it will take them some time to get the skiffs sorted and come after us, assuming they found the skiffs. By then, we should be able to find somewhere to hide in the jungle. After that, who knows?' I tried to keep the despair out of my voice.

What followed felt like the longest period of time I'd ever experienced. It couldn't have been more than fifty minutes but it felt like an eternity as I watched the pirate ship charge towards us at a right angle.

Spotting a landing place on the shore had been difficult; the continuing coastline was jagged, with rugged cliffs and rocky inlets. I looked back: I did not need the binoculars to tell me that the pirate vessel was within spitting distance.

'We're just going to have to risk the next inlet,' I said. Annie nodded and I started to turn *The Scoop* towards the mainland.

Just then Annie stood up and shouted 'What's that in front?' She pointed dead ahead but nearly fell over as I brought the sloop steeply around. I looked. Jesus H Christ on a bike, I must be bloody dreaming. 'Give me the binoculars!'

A couple of kilometres ahead, there were dozens – no, hundreds – of shapes on the water. 'Hallelujah!' I shouted, glee rocketing through my body. I turned the wheel again to take us back on a southern trajectory.

'What is it?' Annie sounded anxious.

'It's a fucking fishing fleet! You beauty!'

Annie looked as if she didn't know if this news was good or bad, and she gesticulated dementedly to starboard where the pirates were bearing down on us. It seemed as if they would ram *The Scoop* before we could reach the fishing boats. It was going to be close.

62

THE FLEET seemed to line the entire southern horizon; at a quick count, there must be upwards of two hundred large and small craft plus log platforms with coloured flags that trailed their nets on a lumpy sea. Cody and I had seen a similar fleet fishing for skipjack tuna on the trip from Bali to Jakarta. And then I saw another alien shape amid the dark fishing boats. It was much bigger and lighter in colour. With one hand, I trained the glasses on the alien craft, my other hand firmly on the helm.

'It's a navy ship,' I cried.

'Jonno, they're nearly on us!' Annie's scream riveted my attention. I looked back to starboard and saw the pirate vessel up close for the first time as it bore down on us like a demon from hell. A majestic, foaming bow wave swept several metres upwards and outwards. Random details imprinted themselves on my mind: the peeling orange paint, the towering prow, the long, fluted timbers of the hull that flared back to the low-slung stern ... the stocky figure standing squarely on the looming foredeck with a broad smile on his ugly face and a huge weapon in his hands. Jesus!

I quickly corrected *The Scoop*'s course so we were heading straight to the fishermen. Then I heard gunfire. 'Get down!' I shouted to Annie. When I turned again, it was like a scene from a Tarantino movie: as the big vessel loomed towards us, the grinning bastard was braced in the prow, feet planted on the deck like a sumo wrestler and an automatic weapon kicking in his hands as he sprayed bullets in our direction. Most went over our heads. The vicious *ratatatat* was audible even above the shrieking wind, the ship's grinding engine and Annie's screams. Holding the helm with one hand, I half pushed, half pulled her roughly to the deck with the other and shielded her from the gunfire. Then I felt a sharp, hot tug on my shoulder. Ah shit, not again.

In the noise and confusion, I heard Annie shout something. Hazarding another look back, I saw a skiff had separated from the mother vessel and was closing in on us. Fuck, fuck. What the hell can we do? There were no weapons on board. I cursed myself for having thrown the dead pirate's gun in the sea. Then, remembering a stunt from some old Bond movie, I bent down and fumbled open the small door on the steering binnacle, my hand slippery from the blood running down from my shoulder wound. I took out a red and yellow cylindrical canister.

'Annie, quick, take the wheel,' I shouted. Then, bracing myself against the guardrail, I held the tube up like an Olympic torch. The skiff was just ten metres away. I caught a momentary glimpse of four rough-looking men before I pointed the distress flare at them and pulled the toggle cord. I said a prayer to St Jude, the patron saint of lost causes. Instantly, the flare ignited, emitting dense clouds of vivid orange and grey smoke. It shot towards the skiff. Bullseye! All four men immediately jumped overboard as the small wooden craft caught fire and then fishtailed off to our port side in the direction of the mainland. A few moments later, it suddenly exploded in a mass of flames. The flare must have burnt through the fuel line.

Annie flinched at the explosion but still held on grimly to the helm. I retrieved another flare, pointed it towards the sky and pulled. More clouds of orange and grey as the shining beacon painted the sky above. Surely the navy patrol boat must have already seen the smoke and flames from the skiff explosion? Bullets were still strafing *The Scoop* and I took the helm again as we continued to fly towards the fishing fleet. It lifted my spirits to see them growing more and more distinct. Maybe we'll make it? I dared to hope.

But then, risking another look back, I saw that the pirate ship – sinister against the sun's glare – was just moments away from ramming us. Fuck, fuck, fuck. We had been so close to reaching safety. I took Annie's hand and kissed it as we crouched in the cockpit. This is it, I thought. This is the end. The bad guys have won and we are about to die.

63

SUDDENLY, UNEXPECTEDLY, the gunfire ceased. Stunned by the abrupt silence, I stood up. The pirate vessel, by now only metres away, was curving away in a steep, starboard arc towards the great open maw of the Indian Ocean. The wash from their turn violently rocked *The Scoop* and I had to grab Annie to stop her falling over. What the hell? Then I looked ahead and saw that the navy vessel had left the flock of fishermen and its sharp grey bow was now pointing firmly towards us.

Suddenly there was a huge flash from the cruiser and I saw a rocket take off. I instinctively ducked. But it was not aimed at us and, a moment later, there was a bang and the top corner of the pirates' wheelhouse disintegrated in a shower of tiny splinters. The shabby vessel seemed to stagger at the impact before resuming its westbound course. I raised my fist and pumped the air. Yesss! Then I winced – it was my wounded arm. I quickly put it back down again.

I winched up the sails to slow the sloop down in the heaving swell. While we waited for the patrol boat to arrive, Annie and

I jumped up and down like Irish dancers, jigging and stomping as we watched the pirate ship disappear into the great blue beyond. Moments later, the navy cruiser swooshed up alongside us, its frothy wake roughly buffeting *The Scoop*. We went to the stern rail, my arm around Annie's narrow shoulders, both of us grinning at each other like maniacs. The forty-metre patrol boat, the *KRI Viper*, finally settled in a commotion of foam, bubbles and rippling waves. I noticed the grey superstructure was bristling with weapons and comms equipment. The noise was deafening as its klaxons blared and indecipherable orders boomed from its loudspeakers. I threw them a line and we put a couple of fenders down between the two boats. For the first time in weeks we were safe.

'Jonno, you're bleeding again!' In all the drama, Annie had only just noticed that I was wounded. Before I could tell her that I had actually been shot this time, an officer dressed in a dark grey uniform with black epaulettes and a black beret came on board with three ratings. He was unsmiling but not hostile. Two of the sailors immediately moved past us and headed to the saloon. I pointed to the fast disappearing stern of the pirate ship and said, 'Look, pirates.' The short, slim naval officer continued looking at me and put one hand up, looking stern. 'ID. Passport!' He held out his other hand. The third rating stood impassively, an automatic rifle held flat across his chest.

'But they're bloody *pirates*,' I said, louder.

'You give passport,' he repeated.

Sighing, I gave Annie's arm a squeeze and went below to get my stuff from the main cabin. There I found the two ratings searching drawers and lockers. Shit, I thought, I hope they don't find the cash. Feeling slightly unsettled, I returned to the cockpit where Annie was trying to explain that she didn't have ID. The man didn't seem to understand. 'Passport,' he kept saying, his hand still outstretched, fingers snapping.

I handed my passport to him just as the two ratings below shouted something. The officer gave us an angry look and gestured for us to go below with him. There the two seamen stood to attention, the pirate leader's three cases open on the table in front of them. One reached over and picked up a solid-looking package and said something harshly in Indonesian. It looked suspiciously like dope of some sort, covered with a yellow plastic wrapped in duct tape. There were several other similar bricks stacked on the table. Suddenly the atmosphere sunk to sub zero and a pistol appeared in the officer's hand.

'What the bloody hell? Where did that come from?' I looked at Annie but her face registered the same shock I felt. Then I saw it – the three cases all had false bottoms. The pirate must have hidden the drugs there.

'No, wait, I can—' I blustered but the officer silently pointed the pistol at me and motioned for me to sit down beside a white-faced Annie. 'Jeez, talk about from frying pan to fire,' I whispered as we both put our hands in the air. In my wounded condition, that was rather a painful thing to do.

64

'*NGENTOT! EEK! Jancuk!*' BangBang screamed out a bitter spray of curses and hit the wheelhouse door savagely with the parang clutched in his fist. 'I don't fucking believe it! A few minutes more and we have the bastards.' He hit the door a second time. '*Ngentot! Fuck!*'

Part of the pilothouse roof was missing where the rocket had struck and Mamat had been killed but the *Crimson Tide* was still operational. BangBang knew he was lucky that he had been on the foredeck when the rocket hit. He now had the helm.

Where the fuck did that naval boat come from? I must have been too busy running down the mongrels to see it, he thought. He had dimly registered the fishermen in the distance but they were of no consequence. The patrol boat was another matter; its speed and firepower were vastly superior to the *Crimson Tide*'s.

That morning when he made out the blurry shape of the boat against the darker coastline, he'd given Mamat a thumbs-up and shouted, 'Go, go, go!' Grinning, Mamat had steered the pirate ship forty-five degrees to port and increased its speed to the max. As the *Crimson Tide* had carved out a path towards the yacht, leaving a wake of foaming sea, BangBang had lit a cigarette with one hand, the other holding the binoculars to his face. Got you, he breathed, as the sailboat came into sharper focus and he was able to make out the features of both the mysterious blond *anjing* dog and the white *jablay* bitch that he now recognised through the powerful Canon glasses. Her? Amazing. How was she still alive? And now they were together. That would make his revenge even sweeter.

He had smiled. 'Here I am, I'm coming to get you. No one help you now.' He could taste it. Victory. Vengeance. He would get it all back. His precious possessions, his future. And he would have his revenge on this *bangsat* that had the temerity to steal from him.

All that had been less than an hour ago. Then, he had been ecstatic. Relieved. Triumphant. Fuck, they had been *that* close to running them down. The man and the woman were cowering in the cockpit awaiting the inevitable. He replayed the horrible scene again in his mind: the skiff blowing up and then, at the very last moment, his arms braced against the console as they readied to ram the fragile yacht, the heavily armed patrol boat had appeared as if by magic. Horrified, BangBang had urgently signalled the helmsman to cut away from the yacht as the naval craft charged towards them. The rocket had been a nasty surprise but thankfully the navy had not fired more.

And now *he* was the one on the run, heading west into the Indian Ocean, putting as much distance from the gunship as possible, hoping it would not pursue them. His wealth stolen, his hopes and dreams turned to ashes. More importantly, his life was fucked. The syndicate would be pitiless.

'You are dead man walking,' he whispered to himself.

PART FOUR

I never knew until that moment how bad it could hurt
to lose something you never really had.
The Wonder Years

65

THE POLICE van's windows were blanked out and we couldn't see anything of the city as we sped through the chaos of Jakarta's central district. But we could certainly hear it and smell it: the honks and hoots, the sirens and shouts, the screeching tyres and the acrid aromas from a zillion food stalls. The stink of diesel and drains added to the raw, ripe pungency of eleven million human beings living on top of each other. The van was travelling as fast as any vehicle could in that choked, constipated metropolis; in its barely lit confines I could feel Annie shaking gently. I put both my hands on hers to comfort her, both pairs of handcuffs clinking together as I told her yet again not to worry, we'd sort things out.

Earlier, on board the patrol boat, we had been left alone, handcuffed and humiliated, in a small, windowless room. There was a bench down one side with a long cushion on it; a table and two chairs were the only other items of furniture. Occasionally someone would come in and look at us without saying anything, including an older guy adorned with gold braid and an

authoritative air about him who I took to be the ship's command-
ing officer. He had kindly allowed Annie to go to the toilet and
clean herself up; I noticed she had some of my blood on her face.
Meanwhile one of his men took a squiz at my wound. It looked
worse than it was. The bullet had torn a chunk of flesh from my
right shoulder but had not caused major damage. It was painful
but not life threatening. After the rating had cleaned, stitched and
dressed the wound, he gave us some water but no food. A pity –
after all the excitement, I was hungry.

The navy blokes had all been decent enough but had kept their
distance, clearly suspecting us of being drug smugglers. Presumably they thought our skirmish with the pirates had simply been
a case of thieves falling out. A drug deal gone wrong. I could
still hear Cody spitting out the potentially lethal consequences
for drug smugglers. Jeez, I thought, just my luck to be innocent
of this when I was no longer even using the bloody stuff. And
I cursed the fact that Annie was now facing a new threat.

I hoped the navy wouldn't find the other spoils. The
diamonds were well hidden in a pipe in the bowels of the
engine room; it would be a miracle if they were found. Meanwhile, I'd hidden the bearer bonds in plain sight among a pile
of charts tidied away in a cockpit locker. Somehow I didn't
think the Indonesian forensics people would be as rigorous as
the slick professionals you see on television shows.

I had left the pirate leader's cash in the same place that
Cody had found my coke stash. There was about twenty-five
thousand in US dollars plus a load of other notes in foreign
currencies. If they found that, so be it, I could easily claim I
needed it for travel purposes. But the dope was the real issue.
How could we prove that we had nothing to do with it?

Annie was still dressed just in my shirt. It was torn, dirty and decorated with dried splotches of my blood. I had tried to assure her that everything would be okay, that we would be able to explain everything. That at least we were still alive and the pirates had gone for good. But she just sat there sunk in depression, her eyes dull, the looming prospect of what she faced in Jakarta weighing heavily on her. Once I thought I heard her humming a tune; it sounded like a hymn that had been sung at my aunt's funeral a long time ago.

'What if they don't believe me?' she suddenly said. 'I don't have any ID, three people close to me are dead and I have zero proof that any of it happened the way that I say it did. The pirates are long gone and, unless we can persuade the authorities that the drugs belonged to them, we are both going to be in the shit. Especially me.'

'They'll believe us. It's too incredible a story for it not to be true. Besides, why would we have attracted their attention with the distress flare if we had anything to hide?'

'Because we would be dead if we hadn't,' she said bitterly. I wanted to put an arm around her but couldn't because of the handcuffs. So we lapsed into a sombre silence as the big patrol boat took us speedily towards our fate. Once she turned to me and said: 'Jonno, once this is all over – if it is ever over – will we see each other again?'

'You bet. I'll take you to Sans Souci. We'll have lunch at Omeros on the Beach and watch the sailboats on Botany Bay. I might even take you out for a spin.'

'Not sure I ever want to set foot in a boat again.' Then she had lapsed back into silence.

The navy guys handed us over to the cops at Tanjung Priok, the main Indonesian naval base fronting Jakarta Bay; ironically only a couple of kilometres along the harbour road from the Pantai Mutiara marina where I had berthed *The Scoop* just a few weeks and several lifetimes before. My poor boat, I thought. Between the storm and the pirates, *The Scoop* had taken a real battering. I hoped the Indonesian authorities would not tear her apart looking for more contraband. Once this is all over, I'll make sure she gets a full makeover, I resolved. I suddenly remembered Wagga was still on the boat. Fingers crossed he's found a good hiding place, I thought.

After an hour's staccato mix of speeding and braking through the clogged streets, the van stopped and I heard a barrier being raised. We started up again but just a few seconds later, we came to a full stop and the engine died.

'Here we go.' I gave Annie's hands a final caress. 'Chin up, whatever happens, it's still better than being caught by the pirates again.' I saw a brief glimpse of a pale smile when the overhead light came on as the rear doors opened. And then they pulled her out and she was gone.

66

INSIDE THE building, I was put in a cramped, windowless cell reeking of disinfectant that failed to mask the underlying odours of piss, vomit and faeces. Abandon hope, all ye who enter here, I thought. There were seven other men sardined in the small space – about five metres square. They stared at me with ill-disguised malice. Great, just what I bloody need right now.

But my main concern was still Annie: I hope the bastards are treating you okay, I thought. After about an hour I was given some food, not the steak I had been lusting after in my dreams but more of the same fare I'd existed on for weeks at the island: rice and microscopic bits of fish. Not having eaten for I don't know how long, I scooped it up with my dirty fingers and devoured it before any of my cellmates could help themselves.

Then I was taken to be strip-searched, fingerprinted and photographed. As I gazed into the camera, I was suddenly conscious that I hadn't washed in a while. My hair was shaggy and raspy blond stubble covered two thirds of my face. I was still dressed in just a singlet, shorts and thongs. My appearance must have offended my jailers because I was given a fetching thin cotton jumpsuit to wear. It was a faded orange, several sizes too small and my arms and legs stuck out comically. The garment's tight crotch gave me a serious wedgie as I walked.

I kept trying to tell my captors that I was an innocent party, a decent Australian and please, please could I speak to a lawyer. Not surprisingly, the officers hardly looked at me as they went about their business. They uttered nothing other than simple grunts as they gestured for me to bend over, roll my digits in ink, and smile for the camera. I'm joking about the last one, but it all seemed banal, like a scene from *Midsomer Murders*. Then I was given a perfunctory medical; as they took samples of my blood and urine I was ridiculously proud that they wouldn't find a single trace of dope in my system. The doctor tore off the dressing and examined my gunshot wound. He grunted with appreciation at the naval rating's handiwork before cleaning and dressing it again.

Finally I was put, still handcuffed, in an interview room with a scuffed, stained Formica table and four chairs that looked like they had come from the staff canteen. As a reporter, I had seen many similar rooms in police stations over the years. The room felt as though all the oxygen had been sucked from its bland, shabby, utilitarian interior. A uniformed policeman stood in one corner, arms folded across his barrel chest. They had taken my watch so I could only guess at the time: must be a bit after midnight, I decided. I wondered how Annie was getting on; presumably she was being subjected to the same process.

Several minutes passed before the door opened and two men came in. One wore the same style of uniform as the other policemen, although he had more insignia on his chest and shoulders. His hair was cut short and his dark face was flat and expressionless. The other man was a completely different fish. He was wearing a short-sleeved shirt of some abstract floral design that hung over his black trousers. He had a small, wispy goatee beard; his hair was spiky and his thin face was small and pointed. Strangely, he was smiling, a gleam of mischief in his black eyes. Despite myself, I warmed to him. Of the two, he must be the good cop, I decided. They both sat down opposite me.

The more casually dressed policeman opened the batting. 'Mr Bligh, Jonathan Bligh,' he started. 'Hah. I am Senior Police Inspector Haka Waseso of Badan Reserse Kriminal department of National Police. We police Narcotics and Organise Crime.' I didn't think it politic to point out his unfortunate slip of the tongue. He didn't introduce his colleague. Instead I watched him as he picked up my passport and waggled it at me.

'You famous man. Big writer. Why you do this thing with drugs, hah?'

I said resolutely: 'I have nothing to do with drugs. There's been a mistake. We were attacked by pirates. I am an Australian citizen and I demand to see someone from the Australian embassy. And a lawyer,' I added for good measure. It sounded a bit feeble, even to my ears, and the cop looked suitably unimpressed.

'Where am I anyway?' I asked.

'Mabes Polri – Indonesian National Police headquarters. Now, you tell us who you deal with and maybe go better for you, hah?'

'I told you, I know nothing of the drugs. They belonged to pirates. They were hidden in false bottoms in the cases. We had no idea the bloody stuff was there.'

'Hah. Why you take cases?'

'Because they assaulted Annie – the lady you arrested with me – on the island. That was where they took her and her friend after they murdered her husband. We wanted to punish them for what they did. We were going to hand the cases over to you guys when we reached safety.'

And so it went on for hours. The same questions, the same answers. I tried to tell them everything that had happened – the storm, my time on Rehab Island (omitting the bit about cold turkey, of course), the pirates arriving, their two captives and a sketchy account of the ordeal the two women had endured. I explained how we had escaped from the cut-throats and how they had nearly caught us again before the navy came to our rescue. And no, I did not know who they were exactly. Only that they were murderers and thieves. I told my interrogators to check out the blueprints in the case. They surely proved what I had been saying about them being pirates.

Eventually, I kept losing the thread of the questioning and began to blabber, telling them I hadn't slept for two days and I had the right to make a phone call. My inquisitor was clearly of the opinion that I had no rights whatsoever and he persisted in asking the same bloody questions until my head finally slumped on my chest in weariness and I simply refused to say another word.

Some time later – I had no idea how long – I was taken back to my cell. The other men were asleep on the filthy concrete floor, most curled up in the fetal position, snoring, coughing or grunting in their sleep. There were no mats, far less beds. The prisoners used their arms as pillows. The only available scrap of space was in the corner next to the malodorous bucket that acted as our toilet. I sat there, pinching my nose and trying not to think about what might happen if any of the others woke up. Before long, the guards came to take me back for yet another grilling. This time I refused to answer any questions; instead I kept asking to see Annie. After several more hours of stalemate, there was a knock on the door. The uniformed cop opened it and had a conversation with whoever was there. He came back and whispered something in the ear of Waseso or 'Inspector Hah' as I'd come to think of him.

'You have visitor, hah?' he said reluctantly. 'We talk more, later, Mr Bligh.' And with that he went out, taking his silent colleague with him.

67

ABOUT TWENTY minutes later, the door opened and a
tall, thin, sandy-haired man with heavy black specs entered,
a document case under one arm. Similar in age to me, he
was wearing a white, short-sleeved shirt, blue tie and khaki-
coloured trousers. He smiled in a friendly fashion and held out
his hand.

'Mr Bligh? G'day, my name is Richard Hennessy,' he volunteered. It was great to hear an Aussie accent. I couldn't shake his
hand properly because of the cuffs but I stuck both my thumbs
in the air.

'Call me Jonno,' I said.

'I'm from the Australian Embassy and I'm here to assist you,
sir – Jonno – in any way I can.' Turns out he was a fan of my
book, but he quickly turned serious, pointing out that I was
in some bother: 'Drugs, well, that's a touchy subject in this
part of the world. You should be prepared for some unpleas-
antness ahead.' That's a bloody understatement, I thought, but
just nodded. He asked me about 'Danielle Johnston' – Dani,

I realised – who was also an Aussie citizen. I told him she was dead but I wasn't able to provide much more detail, he'd have to ask Annie. I had not even known her second name.

'What about Annie? Is she okay?' I asked quickly.

'One of my consular counterparts from the British Embassy is here to assist Mrs Greenwood. I'm afraid I don't know anything more about her situation.'

It was strange to hear Annie called by her married name. It sounded so alien. Hennessy went on to ask me how I was being treated. 'Like shit,' I told him.

He explained the ways he could help me and then continued, 'Normally it would be several days before we even heard about your internment at national police HQ. But the authorities here are anxious that a celebrity such as yourself is seen to be treated appropriately.'

'Does that mean I can get out on bail?'

'That will probably require a lawyer to sort out. They may charge you and Mrs Greenwood with drug smuggling offences. There could be very heavy penalties involved. And I think they will milk the publicity that your celebrity status will engender to the full.'

'Look, for what it's worth, we haven't done anything illegal,' I lied glibly. And I gave him the same edited version of the story I had already provided to 'Inspector Hah'. Hennessy looked amazed.

'Good lord, that's incredible. Sounds like you two have been through the mill.'

'Too bloody right! On top of that I have had hardly any sleep since they brought me here and I'm actually getting a bit pissed off,' I said. 'We are the victims here. The police should

271

be hunting for those pirate bastards. So can you please find me the best bloody lawyer in Jakarta? I'd like to get things moving as soon as possible. And I'd like him or her to represent Annie also.'

Hennessy pursed his thin lips and pushed his specs up the bridge of his nose. 'I'm not sure it would be in either of your interests to have the same lawyer. Given the seriousness of your respective positions.'

'Very well, mate, find me *two* bloody lawyers then.'

68

TIME STOOD still. With no watch and no windows in either my cell or the interview room I had little idea of whether it was day or night, far less what actual time it was. Any hopes that I entertained of a slick lawyer rolling up with some clever legal device to have me and Annie set free gradually evaporated. Meanwhile, I alternated between fending off the hostile blokes in the fetid cell and the equally hostile blokes grilling me in the interview room.

My cellmates were growing bolder. I knew they were talking about me. They continually appraised me with hard, calculating eyes. They want to either bash or bugger me, I thought with despair. Probably both. One of the men, who the others seemed to defer to, looked similar to the one I had killed on *The Scoop* – big and ugly with horrible facial scars and a monobrow like a giant hairy caterpillar. Unlike me, the other men in the cell were wearing just shorts and T-shirts. Bare, dirty feet. Unshaven, they stank of sweat and piss and shit. But then, I suddenly thought, you don't smell so good yourself. I couldn't recall the last time I'd washed.

Later, it must have been night-time, the man with the facial scars got up and picked his way through the other bodies on the floor over to my tight little corner. In the dim light, his skin had the colour and consistency of biltong. Unable to stretch my legs out, I sat with my knees up, arms clasped around my legs. Scarface grinned malevolently at me and proceeded to urinate in the bucket, his dick in his left hand. But then he turned slightly and the trickle splashed my bare feet and calves. What the bloody hell? I jumped up ready to hit the bastard when he grinned again and showed me his right hand. In it was a short, cruel-looking blade. Despite being a few inches taller than him, I backed up against the wall, hands out, palms up. He pointed the shiv at my stomach and made a vertical ripping motion.

'Okay, mate. Take it easy.' Jeez, this was getting a bit bloody scary.

'Dollah?' he said. 'You have dollah? Sigret?'

I shook my head. 'No. No dollars.' And I put two fingers to my mouth and waggled them to indicate I did not smoke.

'*Ngehek!*' Scarface shouted and thrust the flat side of the blade against my shoulder wound. Shit! Fuck! I screamed, and shrank further against the wall.

Just then, there was a rap on the cell bars and I saw a guard with a short stick standing with his back against the electric light. He looked at my attacker and slowly shook his head. The thug palmed the blade and turned away from me. I sat back down in my corner, the dressing on my wound wet with fresh blood. I knew I had to do something or the cell walls would soon be redecorated . . . with my guts.

★

Hennessy returned late the next morning. He had a smile on his face. 'Good news,' he said immediately. 'It seems the police found fingerprints on the pirate cases that match those of an ex-prisoner. A very dangerous man apparently. It gives your story a lot more credence. Plus, the blueprints were indeed detailed plans for future hijack operations. Inspector Waseso is very happy.'

That was good news indeed but I had other, more pressing problems. I told Hennessy about the difficulties I was facing in my cell. Hennessy nodded. 'I'll talk to the senior guy here and try to get you moved.' He scribbled something in a small notebook. 'Is there anything else I can do to help?'

'Do you smoke?'

'Excuse me?'

I explained that some cigarettes might keep my cellmates from gutting me in the meantime.

'Sorry, I gave up years ago. Why don't I give you some cash and perhaps that will put them off for the moment. Hopefully we can get you out of here soon.'

I took all the cash he had in his wallet – 500,000 rupiah, or about fifty Australian dollars. Hardly a fortune given my life was at stake but it would have to do for now. He asked me to sign a receipt. Bloody bureaucrats!

'One more thing,' I said. 'Can you get a message to Annie from me?'

'Possibly. Apparently she is not doing so well but the British Embassy has sent one of their best people – Stuart Wooldridge – to help her. I know him well, he'll do his utmost to look after her. I could ask him to pass something on, if you like.'

'Ask him to tell her that ... that I'm thinking of her. And that I'm looking forward to our lunch at Omeros on the Beach.'

Hennessy gave me a quizzical look but made another note.

'Wooldridge will probably want to talk to you as well.'

'No worries.' I had a lot to tell this Wooldridge character about Annie's trials and tribulations. As Hennessy got up to leave, I had a sudden thought.

'Anything else going on out in the real world? I have not been near a paper or the internet for weeks.'

He gave a little cough.

'I am afraid that *you* are the big story right now. Your erstwhile colleagues are already onto the story. About you. And Mrs Greenwood. In fact, there's a bit of media frenzy going on.' He coughed again. 'You know the sort of thing – *Oscar-winner in drugs bust*. Twitter and Facebook are already full of it.'

I groaned. Bloody journalists.

'Look,' said Hennessy, 'there's an upside. It reinforces your celebrity status and puts more pressure on the police to sort things out quickly.'

I was not entirely convinced by that argument but thanked him anyway and went nervously back to my stinking cell, my hand gripping the banknotes in my pocket.

69

NOT LONG after Hennessy's visit, I reached the end of my tether. My cellmates had been giving me the evil eye all afternoon. Their leader had been unimpressed by my fifty-dollar contribution to his personal charity. At lunchtime, he stole the meagre meal that the guards had brought me. Later, as I squatted in my miserable corner, Scarface and his mates joked and laughed among themselves, pointing in my direction constantly and making stabbing gestures. Then the bastards took turns to come over to the bucket and try to piss over me, while their compadres laughed. I kept trying to shift a few inches away but my friend with the knife would wave it in my direction. Don't move. Eventually, exhaustion took over and I must have fallen asleep. I dreamt that I was sitting on the beach at Rehab Island with my toes in the shallows; when I woke up, the bucket was overflowing and I was sitting in a putrid puddle.

Filthy, exhausted, hungry and scared, I was trying desperately to think of a way to wrest the knife from my tormentor-in-chief, when 'Inspector Hah' arrived. His nose wrinkled when he saw my sordid state, but he smiled brightly.

'You go now, Mr Bligh, hah?' he said abruptly. 'We no believe you drug runner. You free, hah?' And with that he stood to one side of the cell door and gestured for me to leave, a smile on his face. Though mystified, and a little afraid it was some sort of trick, I didn't need any second bidding. Without even a backward look at my former cellmates, I got up and followed Inspector Hah through various corridors and up in a lift until we finally reached what I assumed was his office.

'What about Annie? I mean, Mrs Greenwood?'

'Hah! She go too.'

Thank God! My spirits soared even higher.

They gave me back my watch but not my passport. They gave me my clothes but didn't let me have a shower. I was told not to leave town and to be available for more questioning in the next few days, yada yada yada. Waseso shook my hand and handed me over to a cop in uniform. Hennessy appeared.

'What day is it?' I asked him.

'It is New Year's Eve,' he said with a smile.

Part of me had a million questions. I wanted to know what had prompted this sudden turn of events. What had persuaded the authorities that we were not, after all, major international drug dealers and all-round bad guys? But the bigger part of me was desperate to see Annie, have a steak and a shower – in that order – so I let it be.

But while we were standing in a yard outside the police HQ, waiting for Annie to appear, Hennessy revealed that the fingerprints on the three cases and their contents belonged to

278

a scumbag called Bambam Budiman, a gangster who had done time for violence and robbery.

'He's also known as "BangBang" ... for reasons that will already be apparent to you,' he added.

I assumed this was the stocky guy who had been the pirate leader. After the fingerprints had been identified, the police had received a grainy mugshot from the prison authorities. Their own intelligence linked him to the maritime mafia and they were now treating him as the prime suspect in the deaths of Annie's husband and friends. The clincher came, however, when a group of American surfers had reported spotting a sunken boat off the island of Sembilan. It was the *Lady Vesper*.

'You will be pleased to hear that the Indonesian police now believe the testimony provided by you and Annie,' Hennessy added. 'That is why they decided to let you go – at least for the time being.' Then he looked at me with obvious distaste and sniffed. 'Now sir, I suggest you might want to have a shower and a change of clothes as soon as possible.'

70

ANNIE FINALLY arrived through a side entrance. We stood together under a concrete portico. It had been more than forty-eight hours since we'd last seen each other. Annie smiled wearily. She smelled a lot nicer than I did. We hugged and, despite the hardship of the last couple of days, I felt ready to take on the world again.

A police media person had come out with her. He warned us that a posse of my fellow hacks, photographers and TV people were lying in wait at the main door to the building. Sure enough, as we walked through the barrier, escorted by Hennessy and the balding British official, Stuart Wooldridge, a baying pack of reporters and cameramen ran around the corner and pounced on us.

Annie recoiled in alarm as TV camera lights ignited and still cameras flashed in the swampy gloom of an overhead wall light. She was wearing a thin cotton dress provided by Wooldridge, at very little taxpayer expense by the look of it. She appeared wan and weary but I still thought she looked terrific. Wooldridge must have brought her some toiletries: it was the first time I'd seen her with a hint of lipstick.

'Can't we just make a run for it?' she asked.

Tempting as it was, I said, 'No, it would be better to get it over with now. Otherwise they'll hound us all night. I know how to handle them. We'll give 'em a couple of soundbites and they'll be happy as a pig in poo.'

I recognised a few of the reporters and snappers, mainly ex-pat stringers for Aussie and British papers, but I didn't know any of the local pack, particularly the TV people. They half surrounded us in a rough semi-circle, already firing questions from different directions.

Although bone tired and smelling like a dead possum, I took a hold of Annie's arm and fronted up to the cameras. I put my other hand up to signal silence and told them I'd be making a brief statement but that we would not be taking any questions for the moment. 'We'll hold another press conference tomorrow,' I said, 'when we've both had a chance to rest and clean up.'

The police had already produced a press release with a brief outline of what had happened but the hacks lapped up my first-person summary of the sensational saga: how Annie had been attacked and kidnapped by pirates, her husband and friends brutally murdered and their boat sunk. I skipped any details of the terrifying ordeal both women had suffered on the island but told them how Annie and I had escaped by the skin of our teeth in *The Scoop* while dodging pirate bullets. It sounded sensational, even to me. When I finished, they started shouting more questions, mostly directed at Annie. I held up my hand again and said: 'That's it. See you tomorrow, guys.'

Then I took Annie's hand and we started to move away. But the pack was still looking for more blood, it seemed. A woman thrust a radio mic in my face: 'Is it true that Mrs Greenwood was sexually assaulted by her abductors?' Disgusted, I pushed her away and we started walking faster. I could see that Annie was shocked by the intrusion and seemed as if she was about to faint. I held onto her more firmly and shouted to Hennessy: 'Where's the car?' He shepherded us towards a corner where two dark, medium-sized sedans waited, exhausts fuming nearly as much as I was. Another question sailed over my shoulder: 'Did you have drugs on board your boat, Jonno?'

Ah shit. Journalists, don't you just love them?

71

HENNESSY, GOD bless him, had booked two adjoining rooms for us at the Ritz Carlton in the south of the city. It was about fifteen minutes drive away, close to both embassies. I asked him if he knew what had happened to *The Scoop*.

'As far as I know, your boat was towed in to the port yesterday. The police will still be going over it with a magnifying glass, no doubt. I'll check it out tomorrow morning and let you know.'

I asked him to also check if there was a cat on board. If so, could he have it fed? He looked a little surprised at the request but took a note.

Not surprisingly, Annie and I were both feeling dead on our feet, totally flat after all the recent drama. Nevertheless I was keen to know every detail of how she had been treated in detention and what she had told the police. But when we got up to our floor she said she wanted to call her parents and then go straight to bed.

We stood at my door: 'Is it really all over, Jonno?' she said.

'I dunno. Maybe it's the beginning of the end, or the middle of the beginning or the end of the middle. I'm too damned tired to think straight.'

She stood on tiptoes and kissed me on the cheek. 'Thank God we're out of that prison shithole. Mind you, I don't know which was worse, the jail or the journalists. Good night, Jonno. See you in the morning.'

I watched as she went to the door next to mine, swiped her card and entered the room without a backward glance.

Once inside my room, I picked up the phone and immediately ordered a 300 gram Wagyu ribeye and a shitload of fries to be sent up. I switched on the television and a picture of Annie and I immediately appeared; I quickly turned the sound off and went for a long, luxurious shower. I smeared myself with every soap and lotion I could find. After drying myself, I felt cold for the first time in a long time because of the aircon and put on one of the hotel's fluffy white dressing-gowns complete with gold monogram. I thought about going down to the business centre to check my emails. Nah, there's only grief there, I thought, and retrieved a cold Bintang from the minibar instead. I downed it in one and burped happily. Bliss.

There was a knock on the door; must be my steak, I thought. But when I opened it, there was a much better surprise. Annie was standing there in a similar white dressing-gown. 'Snap,' I said.

'Happy New Year, Jonno,' she said, holding up a half bottle of champagne. 'Can I come in?'

Annie looked about ten years younger. My heart tightened when I thought back to the first time I'd seen her – on the beach, buried up to her neck in the sand. Then she had looked less than human. Now there was no trace of cuts and bruises. Her skin glowed; her thick, glossy russet hair, still a little damp from her bath, was brushed straight back off her forehead. She had put on a minimum of makeup. As she brushed by me into the room, there was a sweet waft of expensive soap and shampoo. I must smell like that too, I mused; a bit nicer than the eau de shit I was wearing earlier.

I poured drinks: champagne for her, another beer for me. We sat on a comfy sofa sipping and talking about our time in prison. She had been treated a little better than me. No cavity searches and no dodgy cell mates like I'd had. A nurse had given her a cursory medical examination. 'At least they didn't find anything seriously wrong with me,' she said. Then she asked about *The Scoop* and I told her I'd track it down the following day, although I didn't think they'd give her back to me for a while after that.

'They are treating it like a crime scene,' I explained.

'Oh my God, Jonno, I've just remembered, what about Wagga? Do you think he's all right?'

She smiled when I told her that I had commissioned the full majesty of the Australian Embassy to look into that very matter.

'So, did you reach your parents?'

'Oh yes, thank God. My mum was beside herself. They'd rung the marina people in Langkawi, were shocked that we hadn't turned up. When she heard my voice she couldn't stop crying.'

'What did you tell them?'

'Pretty much what you told the media earlier. Obviously they were devastated to hear about Martin. They simply could not believe it.'

'Did you tell them about, you know . . .'

'What happened on the island? No way! I couldn't. It would have been too much. I'm not sure I'll ever be able to tell them. My mother would . . .'

A knock on the door interrupted her; my steak dinner had arrived. We shared it, although I ate most of the fries. After my healthy diet on Rehab Island, my tastebuds were in overdrive. Even Annie seemed to savour every morsel. Eventually I noticed that the New Year countdown clock on the muted television said 11.59 pm. We stood and toasted each other 'Happy New Year' and then we kissed. At first, it was rather chaste but then we both seemed to like it. Before long we lay down on the bed beside each other. Her finger traced the outline of the dressing on my wound. We were both nervous: me because I'd dreamed of the moment for so long, and she, well, I guess because of what the pirates had done to her.

She looked deeply into my eyes and took my hand. 'Jonno, I am not sure what, if . . .' I put one finger against her lips and shushed her before turning and putting out the lights.

We lay in the darkness in a soft, sweet, tender embrace, hardly touching. After some time, it could have been hours, we started gently kissing again, tongue tips touching, teasing. Whispered words and feather-like caresses. It felt more spiritual than sexual. Mystical, magical rather than physical. A dream world of desire. Our bodies scarcely moving. No sweaty pyrotechnics, no gymnastics, no wild, abandoned coupling. Just a slow, languid fusion of minds and souls and skin. Like two shadows merging on a sunlit terrace, our spirits soaring in unison. Then the slow, exquisite release. Charlie be damned, this was the closest I'd ever come to experiencing sheer ecstasy in my whole life.

72

I WOKE up late the next morning. The alarm clock said 10.37 am. There was no sign of Annie apart from a dent in the pillow and the ghost of her scent. I stretched in pleasure and yawned extravagantly, feeling rested and complete. I smiled; I missed her already. After another lengthy shower, I wandered down the corridor to her room, past the tray with the microscopic remains of last night's steak smearing the plate. A maid's service trolley was parked outside Annie's room; the door was open and I stuck my head in. The tiny maid, who was carrying a couple of wet towels, looked startled at the sight of the half-naked blond giant in a fluffy gown that was miles too small for him.

There was no sign of Annie. 'Where is the lady?' I asked. The maid frowned and shook her head uncomprehendingly. A funny feeling gripped my stomach. I padded back to my room for my clothes. They still stank. Bloody Hennessy should have provided me with some new stuff, I thought bitterly.

At the reception desk, a polite man told me in perfect English that Annie had checked out two hours earlier. 'I think she went with a gentleman from the British embassy,' he said. 'Would you happen to be Mr Bligh?' I nodded. He handed me an envelope. I opened it eagerly, expecting details of where I could meet up with her. Inside was a letter, handwritten on Ritz Carlton letterhead:

My darling Jonno,

Please, please don't think too badly of me. I just feel compelled to go away and sort myself out. Don't blame yourself. In fact, I want to thank you for last night. You made me feel almost like a whole woman again. And when you told me you loved me, well, it speared my heart. I've not stopped crying since. But it has made me afraid that I might never be capable of loving you back in the way that you deserve. I need some time to get better.

For a time there on the island I didn't think love was a feeling I'd ever experience again. Now you've given me hope and the determination to deal with what's ahead. Forgive me for leaving you like this but I must confront these issues on my own. I've burdened you enough these past few weeks.

For now, take good care of yourself. And give my love to Wagga. I'll be in touch when I feel able. One day, we will have that lunch at Omeros on the Beach! Thank you for being my friend and for your care and compassion. You saved my life in more ways than you will ever know.

Love,

Annie xx

PS: Good luck with your new book, can't wait to read it.

Ah shit, another 'Dear Jonno' letter. First Percy, now this. What the fuck is it about me that the people I love most send me these bloody letters after they've gone? Jesus Christ, Annie. Please don't do this to me. Not now.

Devastated, I slumped in a chair in the hotel foyer, my newfound happiness having disappeared like a puff of smoke against a grey sky.

73

THE FIRST attempt to kill him had come much sooner than BangBang had expected. Just two days after the *Crimson Tide* had tried to run down that mongrel dog's sailboat, one of his own men had come at him from behind with a sharp-edged parang. The man, a raw-boned Cambodian, had been sent recently by the Chinese syndicate to replace the crew member BangBang had murdered following the previous aborted raid.

The moron had made the mistake of attacking with the sun behind him. His instincts already heightened, BangBang had seen his would-be assassin's shadow growing on the foredeck, complete with upstretched arm. He turned, dropped his *kretek*, and threw up an arm to block the killer blow. The machete cut deeply into his forearm but he was able to get his other hand around the killer's scrawny neck and squeeze his windpipe while wrestling him to the deck. BangBang leaned over the man, his rank sweat dripping onto the man's bony chest.

'*Bajingan!* Bastard, why do this?' He released his grip slightly so the man could talk. Hoarsely, spit dribbling out of one corner of his mouth, the crewman told him a paid informer inside the national police had told the syndicate of BangBang's involvement in the murder of the westerners and, more importantly, of the loss of the blueprints. The police were planning to use the information to ambush the pirates and catch them in the act. The syndicate bosses had promptly aborted the raids and demanded BangBang's head. *Jancuk!* Shit! Fuck! He had been stupid. The police were corrupt dogs. He should have realised the Chinese would have had their claws deep into them. BangBang looked at the scarred brown face below him, already turning a deep, mahogany red as his powerful, stubby fingers squeezed the life out of the assassin. Blood from his own wound mingled with the man's foamy spittle as he died, his sly eyes rolling up to show yellowy whites.

Now, just a few days later, BangBang was slumming it again: he had fled his bosses' murderous wrath and was back in the teeming, steaming Jembatan Besi slum. Out on the high seas, he had almost forgotten the stench, the squalor, the sheer mass of heaving humanity that shared the shantytown's dark alleys and stinking hovels. He wrinkled his nose at the putrid stink of fish drying in the sun, the rotting food, and swarms of flies and mosquitoes and horseflies. He saw rats as big as cats scampering through huge puddles of milky green water. He could barely breathe as he passed the canals of piss and shit that pooled in the unmade roads. He watched junkies, beggars and conmen rubbing shoulders with social workers and even western tourists who had been brought to the slum by enterprising tour operators. They were taken in bright orange Bajaj vehicles to the cramped, sweltering soybean cake and tofu factories where people were lucky to earn a dollar a day.

It's like a big fucking anthill, he decided as he strolled around dressed in shorts, sandals and a Chicago Bulls tank top, his ham-hock arms glistening in the heat. There were masses of street vendors, scavengers and illegal squatters sleeping on benches and in crevices. Then there were the *gerobaks* – mobile shops on wheels – and the throaty motorbikes and scooters, which were the only vehicles able to navigate the choked corridors and canyons. He passed *odong odong*, the colourful children's amuse-ment rides, and minstrels or buskers – *pengamen* – walking the streets playing music, singing songs and begging for money. There were prostitutes everywhere, of course. He spat in disgust. Most of them were mothers, he knew. Selling their skinny bodies for fifty or sixty cents a fuck just to feed their bastard kids. And the kids were everywhere he looked. Wearing fake football tops, superhero costumes or Disney T-shirts. Playing, fighting, laughing, spitting, cursing, never once stopping to draw breath.

Often he passed blackened shanties, probably the result of faulty electrical wiring hitched up illegally. This place is the deepest, darkest part of the city, he thought. A noxious sludge of rubble, raw sewage and other human detritus. Perfect for my needs!

The irony of hiding out so close to the National Police headquarters hadn't escaped him. It was only about ten kilo-metres away on the city's inner ring road. He knew the cops were plotting to find him and put him on a fast track to the firing squad but the sole photograph of him they had given to the media was many years old and grainy. No one in the slum would recognise him; they had no idea of who he was or what he had done. If they did, he knew they'd shop him in a heartbeat. Not to the police, unless there was a significant reward, but to the Chinese mafia, who would undoubtedly pay a year's wages or more for any snippet of information that would lead them to him.

But here he felt safe. He had bribed the Pak RW, a sort of headman for the district, to find him a house in the teeming anthill that was Jembatan Besi. As a safety measure he had also threatened to kill the man's entire family, including grandchildren, if he was tempted to sell him out. Compared to most of the slum-dwellers, BangBang was now living in comparative luxury. He had a small but adequate living area plus a tiny kitchen and bathroom. The floors were roughly tiled and a threadbare rug and thin mattress completed the furnishings. Elsewhere in the slum, two poverty-stricken families might be crammed into the same sapce. It would suffice as a bolthole for him until he worked out what he was going to do next.

But first he was going to kill the mongrel who had caused him all this grief, the man who had shattered his dreams. Jonno Bligh. He had discovered the dog's name while looking at a day-old copy of *Kompas* newspaper in a café. The *bangsat* writer was all over the front page – Hollywood, Oscars, his battle with pirates. BangBang could not read very well and none of it made much sense to him. But that was okay. Because all that mattered was that the newspaper photograph showed the same yellow-haired man he had seen on the yacht a few days before. And, best of all – he almost hugged himself with glee – the dirty, thieving bastard was pictured outside a swanky hotel right here in Jakarta. Just a few kilometres from where I am standing! BangBang had thought. And now that I know where he is, I will go kill him.

74

I WAS lounging about listlessly in my hotel room when Hennessy sent me a text: *Police finished with your boat.* Some good news at last.

In between more grill sessions with 'Inspector Hah', I arranged for *The Scoop* to be taken to a boat repair yard on the Jalan Martadinata. She looked a little forlorn when I went to see her the following day. She had been through so much. The scars of the pirate attack were clearly visible including a mosaic of bullet holes in the deck and sails. Nosy police had also made a mess inside; searching for more contraband, I assumed. Lockers and drawers were hanging open and the saloon looked like a winter wonderland with liberal quantities of white fingerprint powder sprinkled everywhere. I didn't think they'd found any of the loot, otherwise they would have grilled me about it. Mind you, the bent bastards could just have nicked it, I thought. But it was all there – the diamonds, cash and bond certificates. That was a relief.

Even more relief came when a rather woebegone Wagga

popped his head out of a vanity cabinet in the main stateroom toilet where he had obviously been holed up. I am not ashamed to say that it made my heart sing to see the little fella. He looked a bit thin and bedraggled as he clung to me and meowed plaintively, his tiny claws digging into my shirt and scratching my chest.

'Ouch! You must be starving, you little bugger,' I said and headed for the galley. Thankfully there were still some tins of cat food left and Wagga began purring as he eagerly tucked into it. Bloody Hennessy, I thought. Typical civil servant . . . did not follow through as I asked.

An hour later I left the boat with a carrier bag containing the treasure, some clothes and other bits and pieces. The superintendent of the yard introduced me to an experienced Indonesian skipper who was looking for work. I took to Supriadi ('call me Super') Prakoso immediately. He suited his name: he had a megawatt smile and looked both cheerful and competent. Super told me, in excellent English, that he had been to Sydney many times. After going through his references, I immediately hired him along with his mate to bring *The Scoop* back to Sydney once the repair work was finished. In addition to his fee, I told him I'd pay a $5000 bonus if he brought Wagga back safely with him. Super whistled when he saw *The Scoop*. I don't know whether it was because of the damage or the fact that she still looked so beautiful. Probably both.

Once I had shown him around and filled him in on the repairs required, we shook hands and I took off across the yard with the carrier bag under my arm. When I got to the end of the pier, I felt – rather than saw – a figure move close to me and put a hand on my shoulder. My wounded shoulder. The hand squeezed down hard and forced me to my knees. The pain was excruciating. I felt the stitches burst. I let go of the carrier bag. Shocked, dazed, I squinted up into the sun, my eyes screwed up in agony. Then I felt something hard and metallic against my face. I could smell oil and burnt gunpowder. A gun. The stocky figure shifted slightly and I saw a face through blurry eyes. Ah shit, I thought. Hooded yellow eyes, pitted skin and a gold tooth. Him! The man I had seen on the prow of the pirate ship shooting at us. The man who still haunted Annie's dreams. Then the gun drew back before whipping forward and hitting me on the temple. I fell forward onto the hard ground, my cheek grazing the concrete. I heard the man say something guttural and then laugh before cocking the hammer.

75

THE NEXT sequence of events passed in a slow-mo blur. One moment the pirate boss was holding the gun to my cheek and about to shoot me, the next he was gone – *pfft*, in a flash. As if a giant hand had come out of nowhere and swatted him away.

When I sat up, dazed and confused, I saw both the pirate's gun and my carrier bag lying on the ground. My new friend Super was looking over the edge of the dock, peering into the oil-glazed water.

'Saw you were in a bit of bother,' he said, 'so I ran over and tackled him; I hit him hard and he tumbled into the water.'

'Mate, I'm really grateful. You saved my life. I owe you one. Can you see him?' I asked anxiously.

'Nope. No sign of him. Did you know him?'

'Sort of. It's a long story.'

Super helped me stand up. 'You're bleeding,' he said. I looked down and saw that my shirt was bloody where the bullet wound had reopened. Christ, I had just bought the damned thing.

'I'll live. Look, mate, thanks again. That took some balls. I won't forget it.'

By then, a few of the local workers had come over, including the dock manager, who was on the phone to the police. They were all looking into the water, pointing and shaking their heads. Super and I joined them but there was no trace of the pirate boss, nothing to tell us whether he was alive or dead. I fervently hoped the evil bastard had drowned.

The police and an ambulance arrived and my wound was treated at a nearby medical centre. I was waiting for the doctor to sign me out, when I received a visitor.

'Mr Bligh. You in wars again, hah?'

He was intrigued to learn my assailant was his prime murder suspect. Inspector Hah immediately made a call to his colleagues, presumably ordering his men to look for a body in the water.

'So Budiman back in Jakarta. Interesting. We will find previous haunts in city and look there.'

'You think he is still alive?'

'I hope for you sake not. He does not like you very much. If not drowned he will again try to kill you.'

And, on that happy note, he left.

Over the new few days I tried looking for Annie everywhere. I had even asked Haka Waseso where she was when he visited me in hospital. Of course he knew but would not tell me. Bastard. I told him he should be giving me a frigging medal for handing him the drugs and the pirate blueprints on a plate but he still wouldn't tell me. Then I had several goes at Hennessy, who I suspected also knew damn well where she was, but his lips remained resolutely sealed. The guy at the British embassy, Wooldridge, wouldn't even take my calls. In desperation, I'd even tried calling a few hotels asking for a 'Mrs Greenwood'. The answer was always the same: 'Sorry, sir, no one staying here with that name.'

Jesus, where the bloody hell are you, Annie?

At least my appearance had improved: I was respectably dressed in a newly purchased blue Oxford button-down, chinos, a brown leather-weave belt and desert boots, having consigned the remnants of my island attire to the bin. The stubble had gone but my hair still had a whiff of Boris Johnson about it. Suitably dressed, I felt more confident when, as promised, I fronted the media again on the front steps of the hotel. They were pissed off that Annie was not there, but then so was I. There was nothing really new to tell them so, after I denied having anything to do with any drug smuggling and posed for a few pictures, I retreated to the hotel bar.

Annie had made me swear on the hotel bible that I would call my parents to tell them I was safe. She said the story was bound to be all over the Aussie papers so they would be worried. I wasn't so sure about that but I called them anyway. To my surprise, my mother became quite tearful and I had to promise her I would visit them as soon as I got back.

Next I called my agent, Drusilla Gottlieb. And, once I had stopped the flow of foul expletives that rained down on me, I explained why the promised book wasn't ready yet. I told her everything: the drugs, my breakdown and Rehab Island. And I told her about Annie and our escape. And how I had loved and lost her. I explained that I had put the original story I'd been developing to one side and was now working on a different one – an epic love story set against the background of modern-day piracy in South East Asia.

After a short pause, she said: 'You know what, darling? I fucking love it! Tom Hanks' new movie is about Somalian pirates so your story will be very topical. And it has all the ingredients: pirates and plunder plus violence and sex. Just make sure there's plenty of steamy sex in it all right?' Dru was even happier when I said I could finish it in just four months if I got my head down. We agreed to meet in Sydney as soon as I was allowed to leave Indonesia.

Over lunch the following day, Hennessy told me unofficially that 'Mrs G' had been staying in a different hotel in the city, but after being issued with a temporary passport, she had gone back to Oz that same morning. He said the cops had warned her that she might have to return in due course to 'help them with their inquiries'. They had said the same thing to me, of course. But Hennessy reckoned the case wouldn't go anywhere until the police found Budiman so it was unlikely I would have to come back anytime soon. He was shocked when I told him of my violent encounter with the pirate. 'Bloody hell,' he said, 'you do live an exciting life.'

'Mate, I am looking forward to a quieter one as soon as they give me my bloody passport back.'

Finally, after two more days, I was told I could leave if I wanted. Did I want to? You bet I did! I picked up my passport, paid one last visit to the dock to finalise *The Scoop*'s trip home with Super and say goodbye to Wagga before heading for the airport.

76

ANNIE HAD chosen St Andrew's Cathedral, a gothic pile next to the Sydney Town Hall, for Martin's memorial service. It was mid-January and Sydney was sweltering in the summer heat. It had been over a week since she had left Jakarta. She had chosen St Andrew's partly because she thought its proximity to Martin's old office would help encourage his former colleagues to attend. Besides, Martin would have appreciated the grand gesture: a cathedral, no less.

A few people had already arrived, mostly men in dark business suits, as she sat down in the front pew looking up at the great east window with its magnificent stained-glass panels. Rays of blue, red, purple and yellow light spilled across the marble tiled floor of the chancel. She gazed around at the comforting solidness of the nave, the soaring sandstone arches, and the carved, ribboned pillars that rose majestically to the blue and vermilion roof above. She breathed in through her nostrils – a glorious smell that reminded her of Sunday church outings with her family back home. I feel more at peace here than I have in a while, she thought.

Martin's boss, Ian Fitzgibbon, sat down beside her. He was younger and smaller than expected. He has a boyish face, she thought. Neat, clean hands. He was clearly uncomfortable. No wonder, Annie thought bitterly. What *do* you say to a woman whose husband has been brutally murdered by pirates and thrown into the sea in South East Asia? 'Sorry for your loss' doesn't really cut it, does it? Nevertheless, she was grateful not to be sitting alone and turned to exchange a few pleasantries with him.

Moments later, the minister appeared on the steps of the chancel and he nodded to her as he turned to face the sparse congregation. Touching briefly on the tragic circumstances of Martin Greenwood's passing, he uttered a few platitudes about the Englishman having been born and brought up as a Christian. A man of faith, he said, who had now gone to his reward. Then the minister nodded to Annie and announced that Martin's 'devoted wife' would like to say a few words.

She stood up and walked to the chancel, where a large framed photograph of Martin sat on a wooden easel. She turned back nervously to face the audience. The natural gloom of the long, narrow nave was lifted slightly by the glass-coloured rays of the late morning. About half-a-dozen rows on either side of the main aisle were filled, mainly by suited men with some serious-looking women dotted here and there. Just Martin's banking colleagues and a few other mutual friends. Not nearly enough people to fill the cathedral. Most people looked as if they wanted to be somewhere else. Making money, she supposed. They'd probably been dragooned by Fitzgibbon to show up and wave the flag. However, Annie was pleased to see that Stuart Wooldridge from the embassy in Jakarta had turned up. He had been a tower of strength to her back there.

With a clenched stomach and constricted throat, she looked down at her notes to begin her eulogy when she heard the sound of heavy, leather-soled footsteps from the back of the nave. She looked up and saw a familiar tall, blond figure. Her heart lurched. It was Jonno, looking lean and tanned, his blond thatch combed into a semblance of neatness. He was wearing a tailored charcoal suit, crisp white shirt and dark tie and looked impossibly handsome.

A mosaic of images of him flashed in her mind: on the island, on *The Scoop*, at the police station. Above all, in the hotel room. His brilliant smile, his brown shoulders, his strength. But here in front of her was not the large, shaggy surfer dude in board shorts she remembered in tortured dreams. Instead, there was a sheen, a smoothness about him that she had not seen before as he took a seat towards the back of the congregation.

Momentarily thrown off balance, she coughed into her fist before reading out her carefully penned lines about the man to whom she had been married, all the time thinking about the man in the back pew. Just seeing him had made her blush. She still could not believe that she could have been with a man in that way so soon after her ordeal. Yet, and she could not explain why, it had felt right, almost a relief, to be in the arms of a man who she knew respected her, loved her unconditionally and had demonstrated more than once that he would even die for her. But I am so messed up, she thought, I can't work out how I really feel about him.

After the service I hung about outside the cathedral while Annie thanked the minister and arranged to meet some of Martin's colleagues for a drink at the Belvedere Hotel around the corner. When she finally appeared, I was standing in the shade of a nearby jacaranda tree in the Town Hall Square. I gave her a careful hug, thinking she looked exquisite in her simple black dress and high heels. She accepted my embrace but I noticed she didn't hug me back. Tension tightened her pallid face.

'Jonno. I didn't expect you. How did you even know the service was on?'

'Hennessy. I've kept in touch with him, and his British counterpart must have told him.'

'Well, thanks for coming, but it wasn't necessary. You didn't know Martin.'

'I didn't come for him. I came here to show my support for you. I've missed you, Annie. I've really missed you. How are you?'

'Well, you know, it hasn't been easy. But thank God it's almost all over. I've said I'll meet up with Dani's folks but after that I'm going home.'

'Home? As in England?'

'Yes. I need to see my family. As you can imagine, they have been going out of their minds with worry. Besides, you and I both know that I need professional help. I am still having nightmares, flashbacks to the, you know, the beach. Panic attacks. I wake up crying. My mother knows of a good psycho-therapist I can see back there.'

'But surely I can help—'

'No, Jonno, you can't!'

We were both surprised by the force of her reaction.

Annie let out a long breath. 'The only feelings I have right now are anger and fear. And a sense of helplessness. I hate it. And you know what the real problem is?'

I shook my head.

She came closer, put her hands on my shoulders and sighed. '*You* are the problem, Jonno, you remind me of what happened – the whole sorry, sordid nightmare on that island. I'm sorry, it's not your fault but I just can't be around you right now. That's why I need to go home.'

Thin tears suddenly appeared on her face. Her glistening green eyes briefly locked onto mine and then she was walking briskly away along George Street.

77

COUNTRY SONGS do not do it justice. Back in Nashville, Wes Dreyfus might disagree with that but now I knew what heartbreak really meant. It meant feeling like shit most of the time. Just like when I heard Percy had died: sick, numb, empty. Ironically, I had followed Percy's advice and found a good lassie ... then she walked out on me. It broke my heart that I might never see her again. In Wes's world it would be enough to drive a man to drink or drugs, I thought wryly. But I had been down that road once and there was not a skerrick of doubt in my mind that I would never be tempted again.

I had taken a three-month rental lease on a great place in the Finger Wharf building in Woolloomooloo, less than two kilometres from Sydney's CBD. It was also relatively close to the Rose Bay marina, where I planned to berth *The Scoop* when Super brought her back. The apartment building also had a row of fantastic ground-floor restaurants. I did not plan to have any time for cooking.

Looking out of the wall-to-wall bedroom window I could

see the hulking grey slabs of the warships parked next door in the naval yard. They reminded me of the patrol boat that had rescued Annie and I from the pirates.

I met up with my agent the day after I got back from Jakarta. Drusilla Gottlieb was fifty-two, tiny, Jewish and voluptuous – a force of nature. She was wearing her standard Dru uniform – a sharp black pantsuit and bright red, 'fuck me' stilettos that matched the colour of her hair dye. At first she feigned outrage that I had avoided her calls and failed to deliver the book I had promised. But when I apologised for my bad behaviour, she gave me a hug, her arms barely making it all the way around my stomach, her head resting on my lower chest. Then she looked up at me intently with her shrewd grey eyes.

'Well, you certainly look good, Jonno. Swashbuckling obviously agrees with you. But, mon petit, do I detect a certain *tristesse*? Anything to do with that gorgeous lady I saw you with in the papers? The one you allegedly saved from the clutches of those naughty pirates?'

I laughed. Dru took very few things seriously apart from books and money. 'Sadly, Annie – that's her name – has to go back to the UK for now. But you'll be glad to hear that that's a blessing in disguise: I'll be able to work harder and faster without the distraction.'

'I like the sound of that. And this pirate book – when did you say you can produce it?'

'How does a hundred days sound?' I waited for her shocked reaction. That was an incredibly short time for a substantial piece of fiction.

'Are you fucking serious? The publishers will be ecstatic. But how is that possible? I don't want you churning out some piece of shit just to please those bastards.'

I smiled as I remembered something Annie had said: 'You tabloid guys are good at writing fiction, aren't you?' I assured Dru it was doable: the material was, of course, still fresh in my mind and I was working on the book night and day.

Once she had gone, barking down her iPhone at some poor secretary and already plotting how to finesse potential film rights and negotiate another screenplay, I got back to work.

78

THE WAITING room was just as Annie had imagined it: floral watercolours, beige carpet, two or three wooden chairs with fabric seats and a pine coffee table with new magazines. The psychologist was not what she had imagined, however. She was tall, in her forties, long straight black hair tied back in a youthful ponytail, stylishly dressed in a silk top and loose pants, gold sandals on her feet, her face striking, with flinty cheekbones and clever eyes. Her voice had a soft Irish lilt to it.

'Hello, you must be Annie Greenwood. I'm Dr Madeleine McCabe. It's a pleasure to meet you. You can call me Maddy.' She smiled gently and clasped both Annie's hands in her own. 'Please come into my room.'

Unlike the waiting room, Dr McCabe's consulting room exuded taste and warmth, with subtle striped wallpaper and comfortable armchairs in a deep red and gold fabric. Subdued lighting, rich red silk rugs and a vase of fresh roses provided a soft, welcoming touch. Annie was surprised not to see a chaise longue or some other couch in the room. Dr McCabe, as if reading her mind, asked her to sit on one of the plush armchairs while she took another. 'I like to look people in the eye when we are talking,' she said.

'Now Mrs Greenwood – can I call you Annie? I want to tell you from the outset that anything we discuss today or at any time during treatment is completely confidential.'

Annie nodded that she understood. Her mother had recommended Dr McCabe. Earlier, in a couple of emotionally charged chats at the kitchen table, fuelled by gallons of pinot gris, Annie had opened up to her mum about the whole story, although she had stopped short of mentioning the rape.

The flight home had been a nightmare. The memorial service and, more particularly, that last meeting with Jonno had drained her energy and sapped her spirit. On the plane she had come crashing down. A series of flashbacks flickered through her bruised brain as if on a film loop, silent tears running continuously down her cheeks.

Finally, exhaustion had kicked in and she'd managed a short, tortured sleep on the second leg before arriving at Heathrow. There she had walked like a zombie through the gauntlet of immigration, baggage carousels and Customs. Then, finally, she'd collapsed, weeping, into her parents' arms.

Now, sitting opposite Dr McCabe, Annie was nervous about a stranger probing her mind, rummaging around in her subconscious like a thief in her panty drawer.

Sitting back in the armchair, eyes closed, hands clenched in her lap, her ankles tightly crossed, Annie began at the beginning: November, Singapore.

Ninety minutes seemed to go by in a heartbeat. Outside the window, the street lamp penetrated the cold, brittle darkness of a British winter evening as Annie disgorged the whole story, every heart-wringing, gut-wrenching syllable forced out like an exorcist expelling a foul demon. Often she wept, her voice faltering as she came to particularly grisly details of the story, including the sexual assault.

Her voice dropped to a whisper: 'I feel incredible guilt that Dani got the worst of it. Maybe I could have done more to help her. She was in such pain, her screams . . .'

Annie's eyes opened and she felt as if she had come from a faraway place. She took a drink of water, her throat sore from the hot, hard words that had poured out of her.

'Well, God bless you, Annie, you certainly have had a rough time of it,' Dr McCabe said, her soft Irish accent emphasising her deep-felt sympathy. 'And you say you have not spoken about the fact you were raped until now? What a terrible burden to carry.'

Annie nodded. 'Actually, the man I mentioned, Jonno, I'm sure he knows what happened but we never really talked about it properly. My decision.'

'It was good that he was able to provide comfort after what you endured. Perhaps we can talk more about your relationship with him the next time we meet. One question before we finish: have you seen a doctor?'

Annie's face showed her puzzlement. 'You're a doctor.'

'Yes, but I deal with the mind and there might be physical issues associated with the attack. Injury to tissue or internal organs, for example. Or an STD. It is usual in these circumstances for the victim to undergo a full medical examination.

I see from your face that you have not. Annie, I strongly urge you to see someone. As soon as possible.'

To her relief, Annie found her twice-weekly sessions with Dr McCabe hugely beneficial. She could tell that Dr Maddy was deeply touched by her suffering and clearly admired the courage she showed in facing up to it.

The psychologist's voice was gloriously soft and mellifluous but she could be equally hard, pushing and prodding Annie to confront her issues and deal with them. She reinforced Annie's firm belief that she deserved no blame or shame. Nothing she had done had contributed to what happened to her. It had been a tragic case of wrong place, wrong time both for her and the other victims. Nevertheless she felt guilt. Guilt that she had survived while the others had not; guilt about Dani, and guilt about her lack of love for Martin.

Dr McCabe had quickly established that Annie was suffering a combination of post-traumatic stress disorder and rape trauma syndrome.

'But I thought the trauma thing was more to do with soldiers in battle and shell shock, that kind of thing?' said Annie.

'*Anyone* exposed to a traumatic event, such as a car crash, street violence, sexual assault, warfare, or even something like the loss of a loved one, can experience it. You qualify on several counts. And you have had many of the usual symptoms, including flashbacks, nightmares, anxiety and depression.

'You have also spoken about feeling numb and lacking feelings or emotions. The anger you are now beginning to feel is actually a good thing as long as we can find ways to channel it more positively.'

I'm not angry, Annie thought ... I'm fucking *outraged!* Those brutal men humiliated me. Treated me worse than they would a dog. They've changed me, changed me irrevocably as a person, as a woman. I hate them. Especially that evil bastard – 'BangBang' they called him in the newspaper. His image haunts my mind. His gold tooth, that horribly scarred face, his sing-song voice. The heinous smell of his cigarettes. He was responsible for it all: the abduction and the abuse. He left me for dead. And then he hunted us down ... me and Jonno. I've never been an advocate for capital punishment but I'd happily make an exception for that scumbag.

'Now we have to confront what has happened,' Dr McCabe continued, 'and learn to accept the trauma as part of your past. At the same time, deal with your relationship with Martin and now your feelings for this man Jonno.

'It will take time. How fast or how slow will be down to you. You might find that medication helps the process. Have you been to see the doctor I referred you to?'

Annie felt bad. 'Not yet. I will soon. But no medication, thanks.' At the mention of drugs, she had thought instantly of Jonno and her heart beat a little faster.

Since she had left Australia, he had emailed her every day, telling her how his book was progressing and that he loved her and hoped to see her again. She looked up because the doctor was still talking.

'You should have a general check-up, Annie.'

'Sorry. Yes, fine, I'll go soon. Promise.'

79

THE GP'S practice was close to the Gloucester city centre. When Annie arrived there three days later for her appointment, it was a cold, wet Friday. She didn't relish the prospect of having to provide another full account of her ordeal but now that her mind was beginning to heal, thanks to Maddy McCabe's help, she knew she also had to consider her physical state. She hadn't been eating properly and, at her mother's suggestion, she had gone along to self-defence classes for women at the local community centre. She felt good about the exercise and the empowerment it gave her. Yet she seemed to be putting on weight and her body seemed different somehow. Probably just the lingering effects of the trauma, she thought.

The doctor turned out to be an Indian woman called Munita Joshi. She was a plump-faced woman in her mid-thirties with a slightly formal manner who listened carefully to Annie's summary of the tragic events before, during and after her ordeal. She leaned forward over the desk and said: 'Mrs Greenwood, I am really sorry for your loss and for the

trauma you have suffered but I think it is now very important that we do some urgent tests to ensure that no physical
problems have resulted.'

Annie told her that she actually had been briefly examined by
medical staff at the Indonesian jail, but submitted to Dr Joshi's
prodding and poking. After nearly an hour, the doctor smiled
and told her that she had not been able to find any obvious
damage to body tissue, organs or bones. 'There were also no
obvious signs of infection or disease but we'll have to wait for a
day or two until the test results come back before we can give
you a clean bill of health.'

Feeling relieved, Annie went back to Stroud and bought
some lunch in the area just off the High Street quaintly named
The Shambles. Sounds just like me, she thought wryly – a
right bloody shambles! The next day, she was in her bedroom
reading Jonno's book for the third time when the house phone
rang. Her mother answered and shouted up to Annie that it
was the surgery. She heard a click as a receptionist transferred
her to Dr Joshi.

The Indian doctor had some shocking news. 'Mrs Greenwood, I must tell you that you are pregnant.'

80

IT WAS a rat that shopped him and a rat that saved him, BangBang thought later when he had caught his breath. He was asleep on the floor on his thin mattress when the SWAT team from the Brimob Polri, Police Mobile Brigade, kicked down the door to his hovel. A moment earlier a rodent, probably startled by the cops outside, had run over his slumbering body. He awoke instantly, his right hand instinctively reaching for his parang despite the darkness. Shame about the gun I lost at the pier, he thought.

The flashlight on the first cop's helmet through the door provided an easy target and BangBang hit him reflexively, the sharp blade chopping down on the man's exposed neck. He grabbed the victim's gun. The second cop crouched down behind the cop's prone body, firing single shots from his assault rifle. But BangBang was already gone, scrambling through the small square he had cut out of the rickety wall months before as a precaution against just such a raid. It was second nature to him; as a boy he had been used to planning escape routes to avoid the filthy attentions of his uncle.

As he ran through and out the back of the next-door 'residence' that belonged to a Malaysian meth dealer, his mind raced. How? Who? Why would the cops come? It must have been that dogfuck headman. No one else knew that I was there. He wanted the reward! I'll fucking kill that rat and all his stinking family. But he parked that vengeful thought for later as he raced randomly along the labyrinth of narrow, claustrophobic alleys that crisscrossed the slum like splashes of pigment on an abstract painting. He could still hear gunfire behind him as the cops kept on shooting randomly.

After nearly ten minutes of scampering through the muck and debris underfoot, he stopped briefly to catch his breath, his thick chest heaving. He leaned against a stationary *gerobak*. Fuck those clove smokes, they're killing me, he thought. But better them than the dirty, black-clad cops who tried to kill me a short time ago. He tightened his grip on the pistol. I won't be taken, he vowed. I would rather die than go back to prison. And now I've probably killed a cop. Those bastards will have a hard-on for me now. If they catch me, they'll make my life back in jail an absolute hell before turning a blind eye while the syndicate has me killed. Not that it has been a bowl of cherries in the Jembatan Besi slum, he mused. Three months of shit stink, crap food and lousy water. And the noise. It was bedlam every hour of the day and night. The muezzin called for prayers from the mosque minaret five times a day. Scores of jet planes flew overhead every hour. Then there were the screeching *ojeks* – the motorcycle taxis and scooters. The constant blare of radios and old television sets. And the people: the sheer teeming mass of human flotsam and jetsam who spent their days outside hovels that had no space and no ventilation; their constant talking, shouting, joking, arguing, singing. Enough, BangBang said to himself. Enough of going to the local *warungs* to buy basic food items. Enough of buying clean water for drinking and cooking either from the vendors transporting water in jugs or from the local mosque. I'm done with all of that shit.

It's time I had another go at that *bangsat* bastard Jonno Bligh. The name curdled in his mouth. He had almost had him that time at the dock. He still did not know what had happened. One moment he was exultant – about to blow the white devil's brains out and pick up that bag, no doubt full of *his* earnings – the next somebody had come from nowhere and bundled him into the water.

He'd swallowed a gallon of the scummy water and thought he was going to drown. Somehow he had managed to grab one of the wooden pillars holding up the piers, steady himself and get his breath back. In the confusion that followed, he had made his escape. He still dreamt of his gun on Bligh's upturned face – the confusion and fear he saw there. Yep, time to pay the motherfucker another visit.

81

ANNIE SAT on her bed for a long time. Of course, you idiot! The strangeness of her body in recent weeks. Her period, or lack of it. The extra pounds. Tender breasts. How could she have not realised? How bloody stupid can you be? she asked herself. She lay down and closed her eyes, her mind racing in circles like a little ball bouncing and clattering, searching for a pocket on a roulette wheel. My God! she thought, her hand covering her mouth. 'A baby?' she whispered. Her heart beat faster. She had dreamt of having a child. She smiled and opened her eyes. But then a shadow clouded her mind.

I know it can't be Martin's, she thought. We didn't have sex once while we were on the boat, despite my best intentions. He was too drunk most of the time and too focused on Dani. So then . . . Jonno? The pirates? Dr Joshi had told Annie that because she had undergone such mental and physical trauma, it was difficult to pinpoint the exact moment of conception without further tests. Meanwhile, the time-frame was jumbled up in her head. She could not work it out. But if I'm honest, she thought with dread, it could be either.

Oh please, please God let it be Jonno's, she prayed. The thought of the disgusting pirates was too much to bear. There was a tap on the bedroom door. Her mother.

'Everything all right?'

'Yes, just a slight migraine.' There was no way she wanted her mother to know about the baby. She was not ready to discuss it with her yet. Not by a long chalk. She desperately needed to talk to Maddy.

If Dr McCabe was surprised by the latest dramatic turn of events, she did not show it. Annie sat across from her, her bare feet tucked under her legs on the plush armchair. A Chopin nocturne tinkled in the background. Dr McCabe pushed a box of tissues over the coffee table towards Annie. 'How does your pregnancy make you feel?' she said.

Annie looked up, her eyes puffy. 'I didn't think you were one for clichés.' She smiled grimly.

'Sorry, default position. From what you say, the father of the baby could either be one of your attackers or this man Jonno Bligh. You told me you have always wanted a child, so the question is: would you keep it even if you knew who the father was? I know you're not ready for this yet, but you can get a paternity test while you're pregnant and that might help you in your decision.'

'I keep changing my mind. On one hand I really, really want a baby, but on the other, I'm scared to death. What if I hate it when it comes? I mean, it's not the child's fault, is it? But what if it looks like one of those pirates, will that continually remind me of the terrible things that happened? Will I then blame the baby?'

'I won't lie to you, Annie,' Dr McCabe said. 'Many will advise you to have an abortion. Family, friends, even health care professionals. People will have strong opinions. To many women in particular, the thought of carrying their rapist's baby would be unimaginable. But no one really knows how she will react in these circumstances. Ultimately only you can make the decision on whether to keep it or not.'

'Right now I'm not capable of making any decision. I feel too traumatised. I need more time to sort out my true feelings.'

'Of course, Annie, that's to be expected. On top of everything else that you have suffered, this is another confronting issue. First Martin. What you went through on that island. Now this. You are bound to feel a range of emotions, from fear to confusion and numbness.'

'Whatever happens,' Annie said, 'if I *do* decide to have the baby I will *not* get rid of it afterwards. I'd do everything in my power to give it a healthy and loving upbringing. However hard that will be.' Annie was nodding her head fiercely.

'There, you *are* already making decisions,' Dr McCabe said. 'You are such a strong person. You will make the right choice in the end.'

'I keep thinking – what if it's Jonno's baby? I simply could not bear the idea of getting rid of his child.' A snowy mountain of wet tissues was forming on the coffee table between them.

'Do you think he'll be supportive if it is his? After all, he says he loves you.'

'Yes, I think so. No, I'm totally certain of it. But I could not begin to know how he will feel if, God forbid, it is someone else's.'

82

THE NEW book — working title *Dire Strait* — was nearly finished. I was proud of my productivity. Working night and day, I had averaged 14,000 words a week. I was proud too of the quality. Given that I had lived through the whole nightmare, they were vivid, searing words that exposed the piracy problem in the Malacca Strait. The 'factional' story unfolded through the eyes of a journalist hero (guess who?) and his attractive offsider as we escaped the clutches of evil, bloodthirsty pirates on the high seas.

Unfortunately I had not been able to speak to the real heroine since she had left me behind at the cathedral. But I had managed to get an email address thanks to my new best friend Richard Hennessy, and I had resolved to send her a note every day until I met her again. My emails were short, simple and upbeat. I talked about how my book was going, my continued sobriety and my hope that we would get together some day. She had replied just twice with brief, guarded comments. Once to tell me that she was staying with her parents and was seeing a therapist, the other to urge me to give Wagga a big hug from her.

I had informed her that the kitten – now reaching cathood – had finally arrived in Sydney on board *The Scoop*. Both seemed in good shape, considering. The sloop's engines and electrics were working beautifully and there were no signs of bullet holes in the sails or on the infrastructure. Wagga also seemed free of scars from his experiences. Both looked wonderful, a sight for my sore eyes, reddened from working until late at night.

Super, the skipper who had saved me in Jakarta, had reported no problems with the voyage. The paperwork at both ends had proved to be relatively straightforward, although he had not 'declared' Wagga to the Customs people when arriving here and I felt a little bad about that. But I figured one little kitten did not represent a major biosecurity risk to the nation. I resolved to have him checked over by a vet and given the right shots as soon as I finished my manuscript.

In the meantime, he and I were happily shacked up together again on the boat in the marina at Rose Bay, with views of the Opera House and Harbour Bridge. The first evening back on board, I stood on the transom with a glass of wine and looked fondly over my lovely boat, remembering the incredible experiences she and I had shared. And everywhere I looked on board I saw the ghost of Annie.

It had been a relief to finally leave the apartment after so many weeks of comfortable claustrophobia. Life at the marina was intoxicating – the spacious luxury of *The Scoop*, the fresh air, the sensational sunsets and the seductive sashay of the sloop as she strained against her thick mooring ropes in the soft swell.

Dru was already busy organising interviews with magazines and TV people as well as future book tours. Despite my admirable output to date, she was chasing me to finish the story.

'You know, darling, this book is going to be bigger than fucking Ben Hur! Certainly bigger than *Hard News*. A film deal is guaranteed.'

'Good,' I said. 'But you can forget about me going to LA.'

'Enough already. Look luvvie, you know you'll have to go there to write the screenplay. That will be part of the deal. They'll insist.'

'Forget it, I'll never return to La La Land,' I told her firmly. 'It was nearly the bloody death of me the last time. I'd rather have no deal than go back there again.'

After I ended the phone call to Dru, I rang another number.

Initially Cody was reluctant to come to the marina but I finally persuaded him. He had read the stories about my escapades in Indonesia and I suspect he just wanted to hear all the gory details. Anyway, he came. That was all that mattered. Now we were sitting in the cockpit of *The Scoop* drinking beer together.

'Mate, thanks for coming. It means a lot. I want you to know that I'm totally clean. Have been for some time. I will never use drugs again. Ever.

'I'm sorry. Sorry that I put you at risk. Sorry that I screwed up our friendship. Sorry that I was a complete prick. I realise that it's a big ask but it would mean a great deal if you would forgive me.'

Cody didn't say anything for a few moments while he continued stroking Wagga. There was just the sound of the water slapping against the pontoon pilings and scores of halyards ting-tinging like cowbells on a Swiss hillside. Then he put the cat down, walked over to me and gave me a manly hug.

'So mate,' he said, 'when am I going to meet this mix of Joan of Arc, Mother Teresa and Angelina Jolie? What's her name again? Annie? Why the bloody hell isn't she here?'

83

Hi Jonno,

Thank you for your messages. Sorry I don't respond very often but I do enjoy reading them and finding out what you are up to. My treatment is going quite well, although one or two complications have arisen. Dr Maddy (good name for a shrink!) is wonderful. I'm not sure what I would have done without her.

Anyway, I wanted to tell you that I will be returning to Australia soon. An inquest is being held into Dani's death and I have been summoned. It will be a formality I expect but I hope it will help her family get some closure.

I hope to see you. Will send details nearer the time. In the meantime, take care of yourself (and Wagga!).

Annie x

Annie was aware of a little warm flush on her face as she pressed send. I wonder how I'll feel when I see him, she thought. Once again Annie weighed up the pros and cons of having the baby. Or not. Yes, she would love to have a child, particularly if it were Jonno's, but she still wasn't sure how she would feel if it were clearly the result of the rape. No, she did not think it was in her to hate it, but yes, it was possible that she might feel repelled. After all, didn't she still have nightmares about that monster with the gold tooth and the scarred face – BangBang Budiman? She had been shocked by Jonno's news that the pirate had tracked him down again and tried to kill him. I hope he's dead, she thought with a surge of bitterness.

Maddy had been a great sounding board for her concerns. But she had made it clear that ultimately it was Annie's decision. Annie was also aware that Dr Joshi seemed to assume she would have an abortion. Not in so many words perhaps, but her views were clear nonetheless in the way she talked stiffly about 'the psychological and emotional difficulties ahead'.

'Oh, I don't know,' she exclaimed aloud. 'How can I decide? A child's life is at stake.' But then a little voice whispered in her head: 'But it's your life too, do you want to see it destroyed? Haven't you already suffered enough?'

The next day she went to her local Anglican church – the Holy Trinity in the nearby village of Slad – to pray for guidance. Annie had been baptised there and it had always seemed like a refuge to her. The church was a place of peace and serenity. And that was what she needed right now, she thought, some balm for her tortured soul. And when she left more than an hour later, feeling fortified and resolute, Annie had made her decision.

84

BANGBANG BUDIMAN was holed up in Bali in a budget hotel on the outskirts of Padang Bai on the island's east coast. It was costing him less than eleven dollars a night. It wasn't much, but compared to Jembatan Besi, it was the Ritz. Besides, he would not be here long. He was en route to Sydney.

That morning he had asked the young guy behind the hotel's reception desk to look the mongrel writer up on the internet. BangBang knew little and cared less about the web but he was aware that it had its uses. In less than a minute he was riveted by an image of the smiling blond man on the screen. He felt a black, poisonous rage engulf him. The fact that he could not read the English words and headlines on the page ratcheted it up even higher. Frustrated, he asked the young guy to give him the gist of the story.

Later he sat in a roadside café close to the ferry port, smoking a clove *kretek* and sipping a *kopi tubruk*, a hot sugary coffee. So, he thought, the dog who stole my money and my life is now in Sydney, Australia. The hotel guy had pointed to the picture

of the man on his boat and said it was berthed in a place called
'Rose Bay'.

His pitted face broke into a horrible caricature of a smile.
He noticed that the café owner who had been looking at him
turned away with a shake of his head. BangBang didn't care. He
had a purpose again. He would track down this motherfucker
in his fancy boat who had destroyed his dreams. And make him
pay. Big time.

I'm gonna find you, Mr Dog, he thought with satisfaction.
And I'm gonna get my money. He smiled again, his mind
already picturing how he would make Jonno Bligh suffer.

85

IT WAS nearly dusk and the golden red sun was dropping low on the western horizon as I sat on *The Scoop*'s foredeck with a glass of chilled Cloudy Bay in one hand and Wagga purring happily under the other. I felt tired but mellow. *Dire Strait* was virtually complete, done and dusted in just ninety-four days. It might have taken less than half the time to write that *Hard News* had, but I felt it was twice as good.

I put this new creativity down to my drug-free state and the new lease of life my poor old addled brain had been given.

It wasn't that there hadn't been any distractions. Lurid stories in the local media about my pirate adventure had caught the public imagination and I had been bombarded with offers to appear on TV and give magazine interview, as well as invitations to parties and events galore. I'd even had a text message from the weather girl, whose name I had forgotten, asking if we 'could get together for another evening of stormy passion'. To my shame, I hadn't recognised her name at first. Hammo was a distant memory.

To Dru's disgust, I turned everything down. Despite my

confidence that I would never get hooked on drugs again, there was no point putting myself in temptation's way. So I simply got my head down and worked. And worked.

My entire focus had been on attacking the keyboard, just getting the words down. I had hardly thought of anything else. But now that it was almost over, I realised that, far from acting as a catharsis, the book had stirred up emotions that intensified my feelings of confusion and bitterness. I felt relief that I had kicked the coke into touch and that Annie and I had escaped; I felt deep love for this woman who had briefly and dramatically entered my life before exiting it again; and I felt an utter, seething hatred for the bastards who had harmed her.

I held a particular loathing for their leader, BangBang. Jesus Christ, how I detested that psychopath. The cops had never found his body after he attacked me. Well, mate, if you are alive, I hope you are feeling like a hunted animal and I pray your bosses find you and put you down like the savage beast you are.

I thought again of Annie. What's she doing right now? By my calculation, it must be about breakfast time in the UK. She had emailed me the day before. Was the message a good sign? I wondered. She had rarely responded to my daily missives. But she wouldn't have let me know she was coming back if she didn't intend seeing me, surely? I finished the wine and went below, carrying Wagga with my free arm. It was time to call Dru and give her the good news about the book. She was characteristically upbeat.

'Darling, that's fabulous! You are a fucking star.

'And now that you have some time on your hands, sweetheart, you can do all those interview requests you turned down. Every last one of them!'

'Ah shit, Dru, do I have to?'

86

IT WAS a cold, crisp morning in late May when I stepped back aboard *The Scoop*. Something caught my attention right away – the door to the saloon was open. A bit odd. 'Cody,' I shouted, 'you still here? I thought you were . . .' I stopped. I could smell something burning. Something spicy, cloying, sickly sweet. What the fuck?

I was exhausted after a couple of days at a writers festival in Melbourne. Too much meet and greet, too little sleep. But I was happy: tomorrow I'd see Annie again.

It was early, the city just beginning to cough and splutter into life. My 6 am flight from Melbourne had touched down in Sydney just over an hour later. I was keen to get home, have a decent kip back on *The Scoop* and generally chill out. Cody had planned to stay on board for one more night to look after Wagga and sort out one or two remaining technical glitches, but he should be halfway up the Hawkesbury in a Princess cruiser by now with a fund manager and his latest mistress.

Dropping my bags, I walked through the cockpit and down

into the saloon. There was a man sitting at the table smoking a foul-smelling cigarette. And it wasn't Cody. 'What the fu—' And then I realised who it was. Ah shit, he was alive! I felt a cold dread squeeze my guts like a wet dishrag. But searing anger overcame any fear that I felt. This was the bastard who had caused Annie so much distress and despair. Fists clenching, I said: 'You've got a fucking nerve, you evil bastard. What the hell do you want?'

That seemed to amuse him. A malevolent smile appeared on his scarred, ugly face. He stood up, stubbing the cigarette on the light oak tabletop. Annie had described him well: he was shorter and wider than me but he had an intimidating presence. His head was an odd shape. He was wearing baggy denims, white trainers, a dark brown windbreaker and a stained white cap. Despite his nondescript appearance, an aura of menace surrounded him, something about those lizard eyes. The epitome of evil, I thought.

Then I noticed something else – a wicked-looking knife with a wide blade lying on the table beside him. A machete. His hand curled around it and my guts felt another squeeze. He waggled the weapon, gesturing me to move. I hesitated, pondering my options but then he bulldozed forward and put the blade to my throat. My body jerked back and I was off balance when he grabbed my arm and then manhandled me down the two steps to the small galley kitchen. Now I was trapped. He stood on the top step, giving him a height advantage, his rictus smile appearing once again.

'Mr Dog, now you give my money, other things.' His voice had a curious high pitch to it. It was in shocking contrast to his heavy-set, brutal appearance. I might have laughed if the situation wasn't so serious. I put my palms up and out to face him.

'I don't have your money. It's not here.'

Not the right response. The ferocious blade crisscrossed twice in the air as he thrust it towards me and his ugly face turned a dark red. He falsettoed a few words in what was presumably an Indonesian dialect, saliva spraying his ravaged cheeks. Then he steadied himself.

'You give. Now. Or I cut you.' The knife glinted in tandem with his gold tooth. My synapses were in overdrive. How the bloody hell do I get out of this? I didn't doubt for a moment that he intended to kill me, cash or no cash.

'I have money. But most is in bank.' I found myself speaking in a loud, precise voice, as if he were an idiot, the way the Brits routinely do to foreigners. The truth was that some of his cash, and all of his diamonds, was still here on board the boat. I would have been happy to give him his stuff if I thought he'd be satisfied. But I knew that he would kill me whether I gave him any of his treasure back or not. So I had to find a way to stall him.

Think! Perhaps if I could somehow get him off the boat, take him someplace out in the open where I could regain the advantage, I might still have a chance of getting out of this in one piece. I looked around the galley for something I could use to defend myself but there was only a stainless steel kettle. Not exactly a lethal weapon. The heavy Oscar would have been handy, I thought wryly, but it was now being used as a doorstop in the loo.

'We go bank now?' I said hopefully. The pirate's ugly face darkened again, his eyes narrowing to slits. He raised his right arm, reversing the knife handle, ready to strike downwards and gut me like a fish. It came to me then, sharp and searing: you'll never see Annie again. Well fuck that, I thought savagely and my brain seemed to snap; it was like a box of fireworks suddenly going off inside my skull: popping and fizzing and exploding, shrieking and whistling.

Then my body seemed to move of its own accord: I reached over, grabbed the kettle and threw it at him. It was a pretty feeble tactic but he started to duck. I was just getting ready to go at him when, out of nowhere, I heard a shrill shriek and Budiman suddenly seemed to grow an extra pair of legs and arms. For a moment he looked like a weird parody of the goddess Kali but then hands and fingers were groping for his eyes as the impact catapulted him off the step towards me in the small, narrow galley.

His momentum toppled me back against the door to my cabin and I fell to the floor. The combined weight of him and whoever had jumped on him from behind crashed down on me, crushing the air out of my body. Stunned, my startled eyes briefly flashed on something familiar. *Annie?* What? How? The thoughts came and died in the same moment as I felt a sharp pain in my chest and my forehead collided with the pirate's rocklike skull. Then all the fireworks in my head fizzled out.

87

THE THOUGHT of seeing Jonno again made Annie's heart race a little faster in the cab on her way to Rose Bay. In the serene quiet of the church back home, she had been resolute about her decision regarding the baby but she was still tortured by the potential consequences. She had thought of nothing else on the flight from London to Dubai and then on to Sydney. He was in for a big surprise: she was arriving a day earlier than she had told him; she wanted to reduce the effects of jet lag before her inquest appearance. She giggled ... I can't wait to see the look on his face when I turn up on his doorstep a day early. One thing's for sure: his reaction will tell me immediately if he loves me or not, she thought.

A little doubting voice in her head had kept saying, 'What if he has moved on? Decided that he doesn't love you anymore?' That's silly, she decided, he wouldn't have emailed me every single day for months saying he loved me if he didn't mean it. But the little voice persisted, 'Maybe he was just saying that to make you feel better while you were receiving treatment. Maybe he doesn't want to get tangled up with a basket case.'

Predictably, Maddy had shushed away her fears: 'If he's half the man you think he is, he'll greet you with open arms. If he doesn't, he's not worth a bit of you anyway.'

As she looked out the window of the taxi as it took her to the marina, she imagined what the future might hold. Here in Sydney? With Jonno? What might it be like to be a normal couple?

Ten minutes later they came to a halt on the road above the marina. She paid, clambered out and gazed at an island in the near distance, the pale morning sun sharpening the contrast of its greenery with the blue sea. She breathed in the fresh, briny air. Just then, off to her right, a seaplane rose from the glittering water and soared heavenwards. Lovely. She made her way down to the marina, her eyes searching the scores of boats for a glimpse of *The Scoop* and her heart soaring like the seaplane when she spotted the familiar vessel berthed at a distant pier. Even sitting among a bevy of expensive boats, the sloop stood out. Its sleek grey lines, tall mast and proud persona gave it a lustre all of its own.

There was no sign of anyone when she arrived at the berth. Good, she thought, the element of surprise will be greater. Slipping off her shoes, she stepped on board and made her way quietly through the cockpit to the saloon. She heard voices and stopped. One of them was Jonno's but the other was an eerily familiar singsong tone that electrified every nerve in her body. She shuddered and then peeped through the open door. Inside she could see the back of a squat figure standing at the far end of the saloon looking down into the galley.

Her worst fears came flooding back like a tsunami. Oh my God! It was the pirate boss, Budiman. But where was Jonno? Then she realised he must be trapped below in the galley. Just then she saw the monster's arm come up above his head brandishing a huge knife.

Without a second thought, Annie hitched her kaftan-style dress up to her thighs and ran through the saloon with a shriek that would have put Sharapova to shame. She launched herself at the pirate's back, her limbs wrapping around his torso and her fingernails seeking out his eyes, gouging and digging, the way her self-defence teacher had shown her. She focused her energy: this was the fucking bastard who had made her life hell, who had thrown her to his pirate dogs like a piece of meat. And this animal was threatening the man she now knew she loved with all her heart, the man who had saved her life, who had helped restore her dignity and her faith in humanity. And, just like the day she had rushed to the aid of her pet dog Paddy when he had been attacked, without thinking of the consequences, Annie's thoughts now could only focus on one thing – saving her man.

As she crashed into the stocky figure, her momentum carried them both forward and down the steps, knocking Jonno over like a bowling pin. She was still screaming in anger as all three bodies concertinaed on the floor, their collective breath squeezed out like a bellows. She thought she heard Jonno grunt and then there was a surreal silence.

After a moment, she tried to clamber up but one of her arms was pinioned below the pirate's body and she had to wrench it free. Budiman didn't move. Crouching down, she saw Jonno's eyes were squeezed closed, his creased face a mask of pain.

He had a nasty gash in his forehead. Then she felt something warm trickle over her toes. She looked down. A puddle of thick red blood was seeping out from between the two entwined bodies and pooling on the walnut floor.

EPILOGUE

IT WAS a hot, sunny day and I was busy putting up the Christmas decorations in our new Rose Bay penthouse apartment. Wagga was making a bloody nuisance of himself trying to paw the shiny baubles on the Christmas tree. I heard Annie banging about in the kitchen preparing food for the next day's Christmas dinner. Against my protestations, she had invited my parents. 'You need to kiss and make up,' she had scolded me.

'Bit late for that, isn't it?'

'Never too late. Did you know that your mother has given up alcohol? It's because of Percy. Says she does not want to make the same mistakes with him as she made with you.'

I capitulated. How could you argue with a woman like my wife? A woman who had saved both my life and my soul? Sometimes I just looked at her and marvelled at my good fortune.

Down below, *The Scoop* chafed at anchor in the marina, her hull glinting in the sunshine. The apartment had cost a fortune but the initial success of *Dire Strait* helped pay the mortgage, along with the pirate diamonds that I had quietly converted to cash. I had also wanted to use the bearer bonds but Annie had dug her heels in; muttering something about 'blood money', she insisted on donating the proceeds to a rape survivors charity.

Just then I heard a familiar noise from the outdoor deck. I went to investigate.

The little guy was grizzling in a pram parked in the shaded corner of the wide, expansive deck. I picked him up. He's getting to be a hefty little bugger, I thought. He gurgled happily as I swung him in the air, his face wreathed in smiles, but I felt a sharp pain. BangBang's machete had nicked a kidney and I had lost a lot of blood. It still hurt when I laughed.

At least I don't have to worry about that bastard anymore, I thought. The newspapers said a fellow inmate had cut his throat in a Jakarta jail after he had been extradited back to Indonesia. A contract killing, it was alleged … Triad stuff, according to the media. I bet his mafia bosses were less than happy that he lost those blueprints, I mused. It tickled me that I had a little something to do with that. Rot in hell, you evil bastard, I thought to myself.

I gazed at the baby looking up at me. What a handsome little devil you are, I thought. You've got your mother's lovely lips and her gorgeous big green eyes. And, of course, my blond hair. His little fingers tried to grab the bronze token on a chain around my neck – the priceless gift that Percy Mimms had bequeathed to me.

'Now listen, son,' I said, holding him up to my face, 'when you are a little older I had better teach you how to fight. You might have some trouble at school. Isn't that right, Percy?'

THE
SCOOP

ACKNOWLEDGEMENTS

I OWE a great deal to the thousands of authors I have read, enjoyed and been inspired by throughout my life, from Enid Blyton to Robert Louis Stevenson and John Buchan to John Sandford and Bernard Cornwell.

Grateful thanks also to Adam J. Young and Stefan Eklof for useful background information on modern piracy in South East Asia. And my sanity was maintained thanks to DI.FM's Chillout radio, providing a daily soundtrack to my scribbling.

Two people were crucial to my winning the lottery – otherwise known as landing a book contract: a thousand thanks to Noel Whittaker, and the amazing Jon Attenborough, who is now my agent. A couple of others kept me going with their morale-boosting enthusiasm and encouragement: Ann Rickard, Donald Stewart.

Of course, most of the heavy lifting is done by those great people at Simon & Schuster Australia: Dan Ruffino, Fiona Henderson, Jo Munroe and the hard-working marketing team, with a special nod to my editors Roberta Ivers and Deonie Fiford, who both shaped and nurtured my first novel.

Finally, my undying love and thanks to my wife Patricia, who tirelessly read every word and every line of every draft and gave me honest (sometimes *brutally* honest) feedback. She was such a heavy-hitter that I named a cyclone in the book after her.

Terence J. Quinn

ABOUT THE AUTHOR

TERENCE J. Quinn grew up in Scotland. He had a success-ful international career as a newspaper journalist, editor and publisher in the UK, US, Canada, NZ and Australia. He now lives in Noosa, where he is currently working on his third Jonno Bligh novel. His second in the series – *The Editor* – will be published by Simon & Schuster Australia in 2019.

For more on Terence J. Quinn visit
www.terencejquinn.com.au